The battle between the Dragons of the Eastern District and their bitter rivals, the Twisted Vipers, is reaching a dangerous point. The Anti-Gang Task Force is hard at work trying to bring down the Vipers. Tensions ratchet when Johnny Hwang guns down a prominent inspector on the task force, and Conroy Wong, Wei Tseng's second-in-command is a witness. Now, to keep him safe long enough to locate a second witness and put Hwang behind bars, Conroy is forced into close quarters with Allen Hong, a man who once fought side by side with the Dragons until he turned his back on them by joining the police, betraying them. As sparks fly between them once more, the two men must put aside their differences and work together, because the Twisted Vipers aren't going to let Hwang go down without a fight.

A NineStar Press Publication

Published by NineStar Press
P.O. Box 91792,
Albuquerque, New Mexico, 87199 USA.
www.ninestarpress.com

A Matter of Justice

Printed in the USA
First Edition
February, 2018

Print ISBN: 978-1-948608-15-2

Also available in eBook, ISBN: 978-1-948608-07-7

Warning: This book contains sexually explicit content, which may only be suitable for mature readers, graphic violence, and murder.

A Matter of Justice

Hong Kong Nights, Book Three

J.C. Long

This book is for Laura, Matt, and the community of incredible writer friends I've made on my writing journey so far.

Prologue

INSPECTOR RICHARD YANG was not at all surprised when he received word from Johnny Hwang's people that Johnny wanted to see him. Actually, he wondered what had taken Hwang so long; he'd made the arrests three days ago, and they'd been all over the news and in newspaper headlines.

Hong Kong Police Department Anti-Gang Task Force makes headway with the arrests of three highly influential and well-placed members of the Twisted Viper triad. It was long and wordy, as far as headlines went, but it spared anyone the need to read the damn thing. No one read newspapers nowadays, especially with the Mainland trying to crack down on the press.

Yang debated whether or not he should take Hwang up on the offer, finally deciding that it would be amusing to hear, if nothing else. Just after six in the evening he left the apartment he shared with his wife of forty-one years and made his way to the meeting place Hwang had suggested, a *ye shi* not that far from Aberdeen.

The night market was just beginning to see a lot of visitors when Yang arrived, but there was still parking space available near the market's entrance so he didn't have to walk that far. It wasn't that he couldn't; he was a tough old bastard, even at sixty, and got more than his fair share of exercise as a member of HKPD. He wanted to have a quick getaway available for him in case Hwang decided to pull some shit.

He doubted he would, it being a public place and all, but he'd learned in his years on the force to be very careful with criminals, especially the crafty ones. And Johnny Hwang was about as crafty as they came, at least in Hong Kong. Still, the market was a very public place, and if Hwang were to do something, it would cause a lot of complications, so Yang didn't expect trouble.

Hwang's message said to meet him near a noodle stall called Mrs. Chu's Noodles. Considering how many food stalls went up in the night markets, Yang thought it would be a problem, but almost as soon as he entered, he saw a sign over a large noodle stall that read "Mrs. Chu's."

Mrs. Chu's stall was easily twice the size of the other stalls around hers and had about the same advantage in customers. Behind the stall an older woman with slate-gray hair in a hairnet bustled about, tending to her customers, who were seated along three sides of the square that was her stall.

"Mr. Yang." A young man—thirty-three or -four at the oldest, young by Yang's standards—in a well-tailored suit approached him, giving him a polite and respectful bow of his head. "If you would come with me, Mr. Hwang is waiting for you."

"Well, at least one thing can be said for your boss," Yang said as he followed the man to where Hwang sat in the farthest seat along the right side of the square, where he could be partially concealed by the stall itself. "He's got you *puk gai* trained to at least pretend to be human beings."

If his words irritated his escort, he didn't show it.

Johnny Hwang was almost finished with a bowl of ramen when Yang joined him, a cloth napkin covering the front of his dress shirt. Slurping a long line into his mouth, Hwang gestured toward the chair next to him.

"You've got to try the noodles here." Hwang motioned toward the woman—presumably Mrs. Chu—who immediately moved to dip out a bowl of noodles for him.

Yang shook his head to signal to her he didn't need anything. "I'm not here to sample the fare with you, Hwang. So why don't you tell me why I'm here—not that I don't already know."

A vein throbbed in Hwang's temple at Yang's words, but he otherwise showed no reaction. "Straight to business, then? Yes, of course—I imagine you're quite eager to get back home to your lovely wife."

The observation was not made with any particular tone, but Yang recognized it for what it was: Hwang making it clear he had done his homework on Yang. It also reeked of the potential for a threat. The implication that his wife might get brought into this did not have the effect Hwang most likely desired. It just pissed him off.

Yang could feel the heavy gaze of the Twisted Viper's leader as he observed him, looking for some sort of reaction.

Making sure to keep his words and expression casual, Yang replied, "Something like that, yeah."

"Well, I guess we're both busy men, so I *will* cut right to it, since you insist. Your Anti-Gang Task Force recently arrested three men—"

"You're referring to the three members of your triad that I brought in for possession of illegal weapons and drug trafficking, right? Just so we're clear."

Hwang's lips drew back in the slightest sneer. "I do believe you're purposefully irritating me, Mr. Yang."

"Not at all, Hwang." Yang left out the respectful prefix, ensuring that it was glaringly noticeable in its absence. "Perhaps you're simply not used to people calling you on your bullshit. I'm not one of your underlings, so don't expect me to act like it."

Over his shoulder, Yang could hear the sharp, angry intake of breath from his escort. Hwang, though, just sighed melodramatically. "This would go so much faster if we could just be civil to one another."

"This would go so much faster if you'd just say what you came here to say," Yang replied. "But since you want to just beat around the bush, let me save you the trouble. If you're going to ask me to release your men, the answer is hell no."

Hwang finished the last of his noodles, pushing the bowl away from him and giving his stomach a satisfied pat. "Delicious. Mrs. Chu's noodles are truly the best I've ever had in Hong Kong." He made a motion with his right hand, smooth and simple. Yang's earlier escort stepped over to Mrs. Chu and paid Hwang's fee.

"And no," Hwang went on, crossing his legs as he relaxed back, no doubt to ease the tension on his stomach post eating. "I don't give a fuck about those three—they got caught; they deserve what happens. What I want from you is for you to turn your attention elsewhere. Leave the Twisted Vipers alone. There are plenty of other triads on the island you can take off the streets. It would certainly look better for you to get some victories, wouldn't it?"

"What's wrong, Hwang? Can't handle the heat?"

"I'm not scared of you or your task force, Yang." Hwang sneered, straightening. "However, it is becoming a slight inconvenience as far as my business interests are concerned. Naturally I don't like it when anyone messes with my money. It's a simple request: take the Twisted Vipers out of your sights for a while, clean up the riffraff wannabes on the edge of the island, or the Dragons. Just stop focusing on me and mine."

Yang couldn't help it; he laughed, a deep, rumbling belly laugh that moved through his whole body. "I'm curious, Hwang. Did you really think I was going to say yes to the offer?"

Hwang's face had gone cold when Yang began to laugh. "You should think about this seriously, Mr. Yang. You'll live longer."

"My mother-in-law was Korean. My wife makes kimchi damn near every day. I read somewhere that kimchi is one of the healthiest foods in the world. I like my chances of living longer."

Yang stood, and Hwang did the same. "You have a good night, Hwang. Try not to do anything illegal."

One

CONROY WONG LOOKED at the gathering of young men and women in front of him. They sat at the largest table in Mama Fo's dim sum shop, Conroy at the head. He had often been told he had movie-star good looks, and he vainly agreed with that assessment. He was taller than average in Hong Kong, six foot three, with a broad, muscular frame he showed off with pointedly selected fashion choices—tank tops, tight V-necks. Today he wore a tank top underneath a short-sleeved button-down that was navy-blue with white polka dots.

Among the people he sat with, he noticed quite a few interested gazes from woman and man alike, and more than a few starstruck looks, as well. These he didn't pay any attention to; he was used to them.

Eleven people joined him in the dim sum shop. The restaurant was empty aside from them, closed down to allow for Conroy to handle this business in peace. Mama Fo could always be relied on to help the Dragons.

They'd eaten dinner first, and now that everyone was finished, Conroy stood to address them. "You're all here because you've expressed an interest in joining the Dragons. That's cool—we're always looking for new blood—but before we go any further I want to make one thing clear."

He paused, taking the time to look each of them in the eye. *Man, Wei should be here doing this, not me*, he thought with an inward sigh. He didn't know why he always got stuck taking in the potential grunts.

"You might be sitting here right now, but that doesn't mean you've got what it takes to be a Dragon. Only time will tell if that's the case or not. I want you to ask yourself why it is that you're here. Joining the Dragons isn't a way for you to build your reputation, make a name for yourself. You won't get famous being with us. It isn't a way to get girls or guys—okay, well, it does help," he amended, earning a few chuckles.

While he spoke, he made careful note of who was paying attention and what they were paying attention to. It was pretty easy to see the glory-lust in some of their eyes, and anyone looking for glory like that wasn't welcome among their numbers. Glory hounds usually only accomplished one thing—getting people around them killed.

"It's also not the place to come if you're just looking for violence, either," he added, catching the gaze of a short but brawny guy at the far end of the table. The remark earned the slightest roll of the eyes, and Conroy knew he had him pinned. The guy was looking for trouble. "I like a good fight as much as the next guy, but that's not what the Dragons are about. We're not about fighting and money, guns and drugs. If that's the shit you want, you need to bounce outta the Eastern District and maybe hook up with those *puk gai* in the Twisted Vipers."

At the mention of the Twisted Vipers, the triad that ran the territory neighboring the Eastern District, there were scowls all around, and a few of them actually spat to the side. *Good*; idolization of the enemy wasn't allowed in the Dragons.

The Vipers were the chief rivals of the Dragons, and everyone knew it was only a matter of time before a full-fledged war broke out between the two groups. The approach of the inevitable conflict had Conroy there with these people. Wei wanted to shore up the Dragons' numbers in case everything really did go to shit.

Conroy took off the button-down then, pulling up the tank top and presenting his back, showing the colorful dragon tattoo that curled up his back along the left side, its head coming to rest on his shoulder.

"This is the symbol of the Dragons," he said, making sure that they all got a good look at it. "This represents power, compassion, and a noble heart. Those of us who wear it have dedicated ourselves not only to the Dragons, but the cause as well."

Conroy lowered his shirt and turned back to face them. "What's that cause?"

"The people," a woman, no older than nineteen, answered immediately. She sat to Conroy's right, a seat she'd hurried to take when they arrived. There was a fierce intensity in her eyes when she spoke, a look that reminded Conroy of Wei.

She just might have what it takes.

"That's right. The people. We're protectors of the people, first and foremost. We fought five years ago to make this a safe place for people to live and raise their families, and we aim to ensure that. Now, as time goes on, you'll each be meeting with other members of the Dragons, and eventually those we think have what it takes will meet Wei and it will go from there."

The door from the restaurant opened, and a whipcord-slender figure came in. Conroy didn't need to see his face to know it was Chris Ma; the man's hair was a dead giveaway. He'd recently changed it from copper red to what he called "mermaid blue" and cut it so it fell jagged across his face, reminding Conroy of an emo singer from early 2000s America.

Chris stood with his arms crossed over his chest. He was an inch short of six feet, but his hair always made him look three inches taller. Despite his slenderness, he was damn good in a fight, and no one Conroy had ever met was better with a knife than Chris Ma.

Conroy wrapped up with the potential recruits, sending them on their way after letting them know someone would be in touch. Once they were gone, Chris approached Conroy.

"How were the newbies? Any of them gonna actually get through?"

Conroy shrugged. "A few, I think. We'll need to weed through some of the more bloodthirsty ones, though. I've got my eye on one or two I'm pretty sure would be exactly what we're looking for."

"That's good to hear. So, you up for hitting Indulgence tonight?"

Conroy considered for a moment. Indulgence was a popular bar and karaoke place in the heart of the Eastern District. It was a favorite spot of the Dragons. Conroy loved karaoke and sometimes spent three nights a week there. It helped that Dragons drank and sang at a very deep discount.

"All right," Conroy said. "But I'm driving." Conroy hated allowing anyone else to drive. They always ended up frustrating him. Why let other people do it when he could do it so much better?

Chris chuckled. "I knew you'd say that, so I took a taxi here."

Indulgence wasn't very far from Mama Fo's, and traffic was light. It was the second week of October, and the nights were finally getting chilly. It seemed like summer was finally releasing its oppressive hold on the island. Conroy had no complaints about that—he loved fall, especially since its crisp air signaled the approach of Hong Kong Pride, which would occur the next month.

Chris and Conroy were immediately given a booth and provided several rounds of free drinks to get them started. By their second hour there, they were having a damn good time. They had company join them—a few people drawn by how wildly and into the singing Chris and Conroy got—and more drinks flowed—for Chris, at least; Conroy was driving, so he stopped after the second round.

Around nine, Conroy made his way to the toilet. On his way back to the booth, he noticed a familiar figure sitting at the bar, bent over the remnants of a bottle of Tsingtao beer, a hat on the bar next to him. It was impossible to mistake the distinguished, aging figure of Inspector Richard Yang, especially after his big television appearance for busting three of the top Twisted Vipers. Hwang was probably pissing himself with anger. Conroy couldn't help but grin at the idea.

He walked to the bar, keeping a respectful distance, careful not to startle Inspector Yang. "Sorry to bother you, sir, but I feel like I owe you a beer."

Inspector Yang's eagle-sharp eyes took Conroy in quickly, particularly the part of his dragon tattoo visible since he'd left his button-down in the karaoke booth.

"Dragon, huh? Heard this was a hangout for you. Didn't think the Dragons were too friendly with cop-types, given the history between Superintendent Dang and your boss, Wei Tseng."

"For a man who's causing as much trouble for Johnny Hwang as you are, I'll make an exception."

Yang's smile was as sharp as his gaze. "The enemy of my enemy, huh?"

"I didn't think we were enemies," Conroy said.

Yang pushed away from the bar. "You Dragons operate outside the law, just like the Twisted Vipers. Sure, you're worlds better than them, but the fact remains. As long as people like you and Tseng and Hwang think you're above the law, Hong Kong will never know peace. You have a good night."

Conroy watched Inspector Yang go with a mixture of respect and annoyance. The man had balls of steel, he'd give him that—he had to, to stare down men like Hwang. But to lump the Dragons with the Vipers? The man was nuts. If he hadn't been a figure Conroy respected, that would have earned him a fist to the jaw.

Conroy shook his head. He happened to glance back at the bar before making his way back to the karaoke booth and spotted a hat. It was an old-fashioned bowler hat, the sort people wore in noir movies. He didn't tell many people, but he was a little bit obsessed with the noir genre, had seen just about every film he'd been able to get his hands on.

For a moment Conroy contemplated just leaving it—it would serve Yang right after the shit he'd said—but decided to take it out to him.

Conroy hoped Yang hadn't departed, and he scooped up the hat and hurried through throngs of people making their way to the bar or a karaoke booth. The booths in Indulgence weren't soundproof by any means, and a varied mix of music—from traditional Chinese songs to Japanese and Korean pop music to famous Western songs, like the eternally popular Beatles—sung with varying degrees of skill created a background hum that would stand out to him later, one of the few moments of the evening that did.

As Conroy stepped out into the late evening, Hong Kong created a background hum of its own: traffic, talking, laughing people, street vendors selling their wares. Conroy looked to his left and saw a younger woman, dressed in the uniform of Indulgence. No doubt she was a waitress or hostess there. The tip of a cigarette glowed, and she had her face buried in her phone. Conroy guessed she was on break.

To his right was a taxi stand. Inspector Yang was the only person there. It was still a bit early for people to be leaving the nightclubs, and the taxi drivers were more focused on the plentitude of fares wanting to go there instead of the few people wanting to leave. Yang would probably be waiting a while.

"Inspector," Conroy called. He took three steps when his fourth refused to follow. He looked over to the traffic light, a fluorescent green, and the simple black town car moving in slow motion while the world around pressed play.

The car crawled to a stop and sat quietly. Another breath—in, out—and Johnny Hwang exited the backseat.

Shit.

Conroy didn't know what the hell he was doing there; this was Dragon territory, a place Hwang had no right to so casually enter. Conroy bit back his irritation, the imminent war between gangs on his mind. He couldn't confront Hwang without talking to Wei.

"I didn't think we had anything more to say to each other after our last meeting, Johnny," Yang said, his voice terse, unintimidated.

Balls of steel, man, Conroy thought with grudging admiration. *Balls of steel.*

"Don't worry. I'm not here to talk."

Two

ALLEN HONG DID his best not to check the clock on his phone as he sat at his desk at the Eastern District Precinct of the Hong Kong Police Department. It would only depress him.

Technically, he had been off duty come six o'clock that night, and yet here it was, probably hitting midnight, and he was stuck doing paperwork.

Allen had no doubt this was revenge for the role he had played in the Dark Streets investigation several weeks back, and his defiance of Superintendent Dang.

From across the bullpen, Allen's fellow homicide inspector, Ao Cheung, approached him carrying a cup of coffee. He was set to work the night shift and had just arrived. Ao was a big bear of a man, sporting a beard and hairy arms. Even the larger-sized uniform looked tight across his chest and stomach.

"You look busy."

Allen scowled. "Don't remind me. Dang's got me going through every report issued during the day shift before submitting them to him."

"That many, huh?"

Allen nodded. "Most of them petty violence. Lots of vandalism and street fights. A few shopkeepers have been assaulted. One rape reported today, too. I don't want to think about how many *weren't* reported."

Ao raised his bushy eyebrows into his receding hairline and leaned forward, propping his thick arms on the back of Allen's chair. "Things have been getting worse and worse the past month. Rumors are it's hell outside the Eastern District, in Twisted Viper turf."

"I can't say that surprises me," Allen said, thinking about all that he knew about Johnny Hwang. "Hwang doesn't have the same self-control and altruism Wei has."

Allen regretted using Wei's first name the moment he said it. He tried his best to distance himself from his familiarity with the Dragons. It was bad enough he had a known history of being involved with the war against the Nine Stars nearly six years ago and that his nephew Winston was now a full-fledged member of the Dragons. A target sat firmly on his back; he'd been removed from the Anti-Gang Task Force for it.

"You close with the Dragons?" Ao asked, voice lowered. There was no hint of reproach in his voice, no judgment, no indication that he was fishing for information to use against Allen later.

Of all of his fellow officers on the force, he trusted Ao the most. He was a genuinely good man who, like Allen, had come up through the ranks through sheer will and determination. He was also far more interested in protecting the people of Hong Kong than departmental politics, which immediately set him above the pack. Most of the inspectors there would kill for a promotion. They all had their eyes on the top seat and would do whatever it took to get there.

"There was a time when I was," Allen admitted carefully. As much as he trusted Ao, it was always better to be cautious. Some lessons learned on the streets never went away. "I don't think I can say that now. More so than the rest of the force, probably, but it's not like I'm in their inner circle or anything."

He didn't say his older sister, Constance, was; he would keep her out of things as much as he could. She might be older, but he felt like it was his duty to protect her and her son, the way he hadn't been able to protect his brother-in-law.

"Do you think it's going to come to a turf war, like before?"

Ao's face showed how clearly he remembered those days; the idea of it happening again must've truly scared him, and after all Allen knew he'd seen on duty, not much would do that by then.

Allen completely understood. He didn't only live through the war with the Nine Stars, he was in it. He'd experienced firsthand the brutality of a turf war. He never wanted to go through that again.

"I don't know." He tossed his pen down on his desk. Fuck the reports; Dang could take them and just be happy they got touched. "It seems like Hwang wants it, that's for sure. But Wei Tseng, he's fought one of them before, and I can promise you he's not eager for another one."

"Things have been really hot around here since Yang collared those redpoles." Ao finally took his weight off the back of the chair. "Not that I'm complaining. The more of those bastards we get off the streets the better this city will be."

"Getting the redpoles is just the start, though. This city won't be safe until we bring down Hwang and the entire organization—and you can bet your ass Hwang's not going to go down easily."

Allen stretched back, clasping his hands together high over his head. He eyed Ao's coffee and decided he could use some himself. Even though Ao already had a full cup, he followed Allen to the coffee pot eternally brewing police-station grade—in other words, disgusting—coffee.

As he poured his coffee, Allen glanced at Ao. There was something in his face that said he had something to say but wasn't sure how. Allen didn't press; Ao would say it when he was ready to do so.

"Did you hear about Dang's speech to the Anti-Gang Task Force yesterday?"

The moment he heard Dang's name Allen just knew he wasn't going to like what he heard. "No; no one from the task force talks to me much. I don't know if it's on Dang's orders, or if they just don't want the stigma of being seen with me to rub off on them."

Ao looked around to make sure no one was paying them any attention. When he was satisfied the conversation was simply between them, he stepped closer. To anyone who passed by, it would just look like they were engaged in conversation, maybe about a case. No one would think twice.

"Apparently he told them they need to be careful and think through their moves in targeting the Twisted Vipers. Told them to make sure they've considered all the possibilities—maybe the devil you know is better than the devil you don't."

Allen felt his mouth drop open. If he'd still been pouring his coffee, it would've spilled. "Is he actually advocating that we keep the Twisted Vipers in power?"

"He says he's advocating caution for the good of the people." Ao made a noise deep in the back of his throat, showing just what he thought of *that*.

The warning Wei had once given him swam into Allen's memory. *Your boss is dirty.* He'd taken it with a grain of salt, then—Wei and Dang didn't have the highest opinion of each other, after all. But with the way the Dark Streets investigation ended, he realized Wei was right. This new nonsense reaffirmed that.

"Things are getting really interesting in here," Ao murmured.

Allen nodded his agreement. "Tell me about it. It's getting to where you can't tell where the allies are on the streets or in here." As he spoke, Inspector Leung, a newly promoted member of the Anti-Gang Task Force, walked by. After Leung had shot a man dead when he'd had no weapon, Allen was sure Leung was Dang's man through and through.

"Well, we know we can trust each other, at least," Ao said.

"That's something." Allen patted him on the shoulder.

Ao's cell phone rang then, bringing their conversation to an end. Allen wondered who it could be so late. He didn't know whether Ao was involved with anyone—Ao never talked about his personal life—but he didn't think anyone he was seeing would call him while he was on duty.

Ao hung up the phone quickly, his face stony. "We've got shots fired and an officer down at a karaoke bar called Indulgence."

Three

CONROY HATED DEALING with the police, especially uniforms who resented their overall lack of authority, but he didn't have much of a choice. He'd called emergency services, and his hands were still caked with Richard Yang's slowly drying blood., the red burning into his brain. It would linger there, along with the bitter, coppery smell long after he'd rinsed his hands clean. The officers insisted he stay there and wouldn't let Wei near him until Homicide arrived on the scene.

Wei had been his second call, considering who was responsible for the shooting. It was a damn bold move on Hwang's part, and the fact that he was willing to do it didn't speak well to his state of mind. The Dragons had been relying on the fact that Hwang wasn't stupid, but his actions tonight threw that assumption into doubt.

Conroy looked again at the gore on his hands and clenched his fist. It was the blood of a good man, someone who truly cared about the people of the community, as much as Wei or the Dragons did. It was that caring that had gotten him killed, no doubt.

His loss was a heavy blow to the district.

"How much longer till the real police get here?" Conroy asked the young officer near him. Instead of an answer, Conroy received a scowl.

How the fuck can Wei stand there so fucking calmly? The Dragons' leader waited outside the police perimeter, arms crossed over his chest, just watching. At his side were Chris Ma—who'd been drawn out of Indulgence with everyone else when the police sirens were heard, even over the sound of the singing inside—and Tony Lau, the oldest of the Dragons.

Tony always had a Zen air about him, like he'd discovered the secret of life and patiently waited for everyone around him to do the same thing. He'd lived a hard life on the streets, and Wei and the Dragons depended on his forty or so years of experience.

Tony looked calm, like Wei, but Chris, probably in part because he was still drunk, wavered between looking confused and shaken. Every now and then Tony would lean in and say something to Wei, who would nod.

Finally, a black sedan, the type driven by inspectors in HKPD, came to a stop beside the three police cars there. The ambulance had come and gone; once they'd declared Yang dead, the body'd been left there for the coroner and Homicide.

"Oh, fuck me." Conroy groaned under his breath when the inspectors exited the car. One was a mountain of a man, but it wasn't him who caught Conroy's attention. He hated the police in the best of circumstances, but add in Allen fucking Hong, and his night had gone from bad to worse.

At least the feeling was mutual. The moment Hong's eyes went to him, a sort of ripple passed over his face; his features became serene, expressionless. Conroy supposed feeling nothing was easier than dealing with the roiling mass of emotions being in each other's presence caused. Conroy couldn't just turn it off, though, and his anger and resentment bubbled just beneath the surface.

"Why did I know I'd find a Dragon here?" Hong sighed, as if they were some constant thorn in his side.

It was a sentiment he expected from the slimy, corrupt piece-of-shit Dang, but getting it from Hong was too much.

"What, were all the other officers too busy collecting your boss's kickbacks to show up?"

Hong said nothing, though his partner's mouth went thin, visibly restraining his words.

A shout went up from the cops behind Conroy, and he turned to see Wei, Tony, and Chris approaching and skirting a wide path around Yang's fallen body. The cops pursued them until Hong gave a small shake of his head, and the officers fell back to the perimeter, though they shot angry glares toward the Dragons over their shoulders.

"What the fuck happened?" Wei demanded.

"You shouldn't be here, Tseng," Hong said, though he didn't sound anything but tired.

Wei looked at him like he'd said something ridiculous. "A cop is downed on my streets, and you think I'm not going to be here?"

"Your streets?" Hong's partner repeated, snorting.

Wei ignored him completely.

"Well," Hong prompted. "What happened?"

Conroy looked to Wei. "We can talk about this back at—"

"No, we're going to talk about this here and now," Hong interrupted, his voice cold steel. "And you're going to talk about it with *me*, not with Tseng."

"You giving orders now?" Conroy asked hotly.

"Open your fucking eyes, Conroy," Hong hissed, taking a step closer. The suddenness of the movement made Conroy want to take a flinch back; it was a miracle he didn't. Something in the way Hong said his name sparked something in Conroy, stirring up memories he'd much rather leave in the past. "A cop is dead, here. You think that HKPD is just going to back down and let the Dragons handle this in-house? You're out of your fucking mind!"

"We've seen how HKPD handles things, haven't we, Hong?"

"That's enough, Conroy," Wei said, his expression stern. "Hong's right on this one. Just explain what happened."

Conroy considered arguing, but knew better. Sure, Wei had no problem with the Dragons expressing their opinions in private, but here, especially in front of Hong and his partner—who watched this exchange with hawkish interest—Wei wouldn't stand for it. Reluctantly he explained his encounter with Yang, going out to return his hat and his shooting at the hands of Johnny Hwang, while Hong's partner filled out the report.

"He just reached into his jacket and pulled out a gun—a nine-millimeter, I think. He pushed it right against Yang's chest, over the heart, and pulled the trigger. Then he turned around, cool as he could be, got back into the car, and drove away."

"Did he see you?" Tony asked, his face grim.

"I don't see how he didn't," Conroy admitted. "If he did, he didn't show it. Just got in the car and…" Conroy looked down at his blood-caked hands and his words caught in his throat. For a moment his brain ceased to function and he felt like he was standing in a wind tunnel. He focused on his breathing and forced himself to continue. "He just left, like he wasn't in a hurry or anything."

"You're sure it was Johnny Hwang?" Hong sounded doubtful. "It was Hwang and not one of his redpoles?"

"Yes, I'm sure it was fucking Johnny Hwang. You think I don't know what he looks like?"

Hong's partner shook his head dismissively. "No way Johnny Hwang comes out and does this guy in himself."

"Yang *was* the inspector in charge of the investigation into Hwang's redpoles," Hong pointed out.

Conroy couldn't cover the surprise from Hong's answer—his easy acceptance of Conroy's word as fact.

"Still." Hong's partner remained unconvinced.

"Well, while you two figure that all out" Conroy said loudly, bringing attention back to him, "*we're* going to go actually do something about this."

"Like hell you are," Hong said. He turned from Conroy to Wei. "You've got to stay out of this, Wei. I mean it this time. Dang's already gunning for you. The last thing we need to do is give him more ammo. Besides, whatever you do now is probably going to push the district into another war, and I don't think any of us here want that."

For once, all six men standing there, Dragon and law enforcement alike, agreed on something.

"Fine," Wei conceded, though Conroy could see it irritated him to do so. "For now, anyway," he added. "But let me be clear, Hong: the Vipers start making any other moves in my territory and I'm not going to have a choice."

Hong nodded gravely. "I understand."

Hong's partner held out the form he'd filled in for Conroy to sign, and Hong turned away. "Come on, Ao. Let's go pay a little visit to Johnny Hwang."

On his way out, Hong motioned the medical team forward. They hurried to the body with the swift, skillful movements.

"We need to get the guys together, Wei," Tony said quietly.

"I told Hong we wouldn't act, and I meant it."

"No, Tony's right, Boss," Conroy said, and Chris nodded his agreement. "We don't have to do anything, but we do need to get ready in case *they* do something first. I've got a bad feeling about this."

"Yeah, me too."

Four

JOHNNY HWANG LIVED in a penthouse apartment in Wanchai. It looked over most of the expansive metropolitan area and loomed above a street filled with vibrant nightlife, from midnight noodle shops to bars and two very popular clubs.

Allen had seen photos of it as part of observations in the Anti-Gang Task Force, but grainy shots taken at night didn't do it justice. It was hard not to be impressed by the size of the building, taller than any other around it.

As soon as Allen and Ao walked into the lobby—all tall pillars and open space, designed to give the impression it was even bigger than it actually was—three men in suits moved toward them. Allen eyed them warily; they weren't concierge.

They wore suits, but they were hard men of the streets, Hwang's bodyguards. Each was buff and muscular, looking like they'd be well-suited for the rugby field if they hadn't become triad, effectively selling their soul to Johnny Hwang for money, power, drugs, and sex.

One had a completely bald head, a scar along the left of it that might have come from being cracked with a baseball bat. The second had spiked-up hair dyed yellow-blond, a perpetual smirk on his face. The third could have stepped out of a suit advertisement on a billboard or magazine, his hair perfect in a way that reminded Allen of Conroy.

The thought was accompanied by a mental flinch. Why the fuck was he thinking about Conroy Wong at a time like that? That was ancient history, and better off left there, too.

"I'm going to need you two to leave immediately," Blond said, his threatening tone a stark contrast to his polite words. "This is a private building."

Allen flashed his credentials. "We're here with Hong Kong Police Department. We're going up to see Hwang."

"Mr. Hwang is a busy man," Perfect Hair said dully, like he was a puppet and could only say the things programmed into his voice box. "You'll have to make an appointment."

"Oh, we heard how busy he's been tonight." Ao spoke as he returned his credentials to his pocket. With that, he barged right by the three men, Allen right behind him. The action caught the three men off guard. They no doubt expected them to scurry away, since that was what most people did. Even if they had been prepared for the motion, though, Ao was still bigger than them. He would have gotten by.

"Stop!" Allen didn't see which one of them yelled, but it didn't matter. He wouldn't waste any more time with Hwang's muscle than he already had. Unfortunately, the elevator needed a key card to reach the penthouse.

"It's always something," Allen muttered. "Hold the door, Ao."

Ao pressed his finger against the open button and held it there. Allen waited for the first of the three guards. It turned out to be Blond.

"I won't ask you to leave again." He crossed his arms over his chest in a gesture attempting to look intimidating and failing.

Allen pinched the bridge of his nose and let out a long sigh before speaking. "Listen, it's late and I haven't been home since six this morning, so you'll forgive me if I'm a little impatient. You're going to hand over your key card for the elevator here, and then you're going to go sit down somewhere and shut the fuck up, or my partner and I are going to take you and your two buddies here in for that gun I see poking out behind your jacket. Who knows, I might even decide I need to defend myself from you if you so much as move. Now, I won't shoot to kill—" Allen's hand fell to the Smith & Wesson Model 10 at his side. "—but I will take out a kneecap."

Blond blanched. His eyes flitted to the other two on either side of him, who scowled. They would leave it to him, then, no doubt so they could lay the blame at his doorstep when Hwang got pissed. Blond finally acquiesced, pulling the card from his front pocket and pressing it against the elevator.

The elevator moved smoothly and damn near silently; there was no background music, barely a hum of the engine at work.

The door opened into Johnny Hwang's apartment, a wide space decorated to mirror a B-rated drama—lots of marble surfaces, gold-trimmed picture frames, expensive art pieces, a vase that belonged in a museum and not some man's home.

They were greeted by four more men in suits, standing in an intimidating half circle around the elevator entrance.

"Quite the welcome party," Allen mused, taking them in and doing a quick mental risk assessment. The odds weren't good; Allen and Ao were stuck in the confined space of the elevator, while the men had lots of room to spread out. If guns were fired, Allen and Ao would have no escape. In a hand-to-hand situation, they'd be at a disadvantage, as well; Ao's size would make it difficult for either of them to maneuver properly.

"It's all right, gentlemen," Johnny Hwang said from behind his bodyguards. He wore dark green silk pajamas, amusement clear in his eyes. Allen didn't believe for one moment the man had been in bed; not a hair was out of place and he looked wide awake. He suspected Hwang had been waiting for them, especially if he'd seen Conroy at Indulgence.

The four bodyguards parted, two to either side, and Allen and Ao exited the elevator. Allen wasn't stupid enough to believe his badge would protect him here, but he refused to allow Hwang the pleasure of seeing him on edge.

"I must say I wasn't expecting visitors at this hour," Hwang said as they approached. Halfway through the wide space of the foyer was a second level, a slight step up from the foyer, just ahead of a doorway that led further into the penthouse. Hwang stood there waiting for them. "However, I am always happy to play host to the wonderful HKPD. What can I do for you fine gentlemen?"

Ao looked at Allen and rolled his eyes. *Give me a break*, the gesture said. Hwang caught the look, judging by the way the edge of his smile turned down a little, his eyes hardening.

"We're with HKPD Homicide." Allen flashed his credentials once more. "This is Inspector Cheung. I'm Inspector Hong"—There was a warning in Hwang's voice, a tone that spoke of more than just having heard his name in passing.

Allen wasn't surprised, though; Allen had very little dealings with the Twisted Vipers during the street war with the Nine Stars, but it was common knowledge that he was involved with the Dragons, just like it was common knowledge that, while hating the Nine Stars and wanting them gone, the Twisted Vipers sat back and did nothing—probably in case the Nine Stars won the war.

No one would want the wrath of the Nine Stars to come raining down on them, not when the rain was made of bullets and blood.

"Well, then, we can skip introductions," said Allen in a clipped voice. "Great. Let's get right to it: where were you this evening?"

"Want to give a specific time frame, or do you just want me to go through my entire calendar?"

"Just tell us where you were," Ao snapped.

"There is no need to be rude, Inspector." Hwang's polite man of wealth veneer slipped a little, something of the harsh edge of his true self creeping in, the cold-blooded killer peeking from behind the curtains. "I had an early lunch at the Palace—I'm sure you've heard of it? You can check with the staff there. I was there until eight. Then I had a business meeting in Victoria Harbor—"

Something illegal, no doubt, Allen thought, though he didn't bother attempting to pursue it. If they could catch him, Hwang wouldn't have brought it up.

"After that, I was here all evening."

"Really now?" Allen feigned surprise. "I'm a little confused, then, Johnny. How about you, Cheung?"

"Definitely confused," Ao agreed.

"You see, Johnny—I may call you Johnny, right?—we have someone who is confident they saw you outside Indulgence."

"Not only did they see you, they're certain they saw you shoot and kill a man," Ao added.

"Not just any man, Johnny, but Inspector Yang—a man who, if I'm not mistaken, recently arrested three of your men?"

Johnny made a melodramatic shocked face that would have done the actors of any Western soap opera proud. "Inspector Yang is dead? That's so unfortunate. His death is a great loss to our fair city."

"Spare me, Johnny. So, you're saying you didn't know anything about his shooting?"

"Of course not! I'm mortified at the implication, Inspector!"

"And what about our witness who ID'd you?" Ao asked.

"Well, I'm afraid he—or she—must be mistaken."

"You're a pretty recognizable figure in town, Johnny. Do you really think someone just mistook some random guy for you?"

Hwang's smile was more genuine this time. "You know, Inspectors, I once heard a girl in a bar swear to her friend that she saw some famous *gweilo* singer—part of some boy band from the UK—out and about. She was adamant about it. Used the same argument you just did as well, that he's so famous she couldn't possibly be mistaken. Her friend didn't believe her and did some research. Turned out the guy was filming a music video in the States at the time, so couldn't be there. She was mistaken. As is your supposed witness."

"In that case then, you wouldn't mind joining us at the station to ask you a few questions in a more formal setting?"

"Now? It's rather late, Inspector—"

"Oh, come on, Johnny, we insist."

Five

"I STILL DON'T understand why he would go do something like this himself," Ao said, watching Hwang through the two-way mirror of the interrogation room. "It's a huge risk. Seems stupid to me."

"Maybe he didn't think it was a risk," Allen suggested. The exhausted feeling he'd had from working more than eighteen hours straight was gone now that they were here. He actually felt energized, excited. They'd never had a chance like this before, to put the head of one of Hong Kong's triads behind that table. He couldn't wait to get in there, but he wanted to keep him stewing just a bit.

"Why wouldn't he think it risky?" Ao asked curiously.

"Hwang's territory is completely subservient to him, around people who see gang violence every day and don't report it. He's undeniably in charge."

"Yeah, but he was in the Eastern District," Ao argued. "And he had to have seen that Dragon guy, Wang—"

"Wong," Allen corrected impulsively. "And that could have a simple explanation, too. The discord between HKPD and the Dragons is common knowledge; my best guess would be that Hwang counted on that to keep Conroy silent."

"Would have been safer to just shoot the *puk gai*," Ao muttered.

Allen had called Conroy that—and much worse—in his own mind an uncountable number of times, but hearing it from Ao made him squirm a bit, uncomfortable.

"Shooting Co—shooting Wong would bring Wei Tseng down on him—trust me, I've seen that firsthand; it's something that even Hwang fears." Allen remembered very clearly how fierce Wei's wrath could be. There was no taking Wei lightly, particularly with his triumph over the Nine Stars.

"But Hwang *wants* a street war, right?"

Allen nodded, studying Hwang through the glass. He sat in silence, eyes flicking to the mirror occasionally. He was the perfect mask of calmness, as if waiting for a business partner at his favorite restaurant and not potentially being charged with murdering a cop.

"Oh yeah, he wants the war. But he wants it on *his* terms, not Wei's. He won't strike until he's ready."

"Well, if we can make these charges stick, he won't have a chance to strike at all." Ao pushed his chin to either side with his fist, popping his neck. "Even if it means spending more time talking to that smartass Dragon, it's worth it."

Allen had no doubt who he was talking about. "Conroy Wong has some problems with authority. Always has."

That earned him a raised eyebrow from Ao, and he wished he'd kept his mouth shut. "You know him pretty well, then?"

I used to, he thought. "We ran in the same circle during the street war. Now come on, let's go and loosen Hwang up before his high-priced lawyer gets here."

Allen let Ao go ahead, taking a moment to school himself. He didn't really think that anything would come of their interrogation; breaking Hwang required more than a little pressure. Still, they had to try, and there was always the slim chance they might get lucky.

Ao barreled through the door and then crossed to the other side of the table in two strides. Allen came in behind him at a slower pace, sticking to the walls and observing.

"Ah, so we're done playing the waiting game?" Hwang crossed his legs and placed his hands on his lap. "I was looking forward to seeing how long you thought I'd last before I was ready to talk. If this is all, I'm insulted. I imagine a teenager could last longer."

"Not everything is about you, Hwang," Ao barked. "We've got a lot of things on our plate, so if you don't mind, let's make this quick."

Hwang's eyes narrowed, but his accommodating tone never slipped. "Of course."

Ao presented a photo of Indulgence to Hwang. "You know this place?"

"Well, the sign says it's called Indulgence." Hwang studied the picture with utter indifference. "I think I've heard about it, though; a karaoke place in the Eastern District?"

"Have you ever been there?" Allen asked from where he leaned against the wall.

"Me?" Hwang chuckled. "No. As you're no doubt aware, Inspector Hong, I don't often venture to the Eastern District."

"Okay, does *this* look familiar?"

Ao placed another photo down, this one of the crime scene shots of Yang's body.

Hwang looked at the picture and then met Ao's gaze steadily. "I don't understand your question, Inspector."

He's too damn careful, Allen thought. *He's not going to provide us with any openings.*

"It's a simple question, Hwang. Does what you see in this picture look familiar?"

"The man, yes," Hwang said, the first sign of impatience creeping into his voice. "I've seen him on television and know his reputation. Like I said back at my house, his loss is tragic. I fail to see what this has to do with me."

Allen stepped away from the wall, shortening the distance to Hwang. "You have pretty good reason to want Inspector Yang dead, don't you, Hwang?"

Hwang's expression was perfectly practiced surprise, as if he stood in front of a bathroom mirror and made faces to teach himself to mimic normalcy so people wouldn't see the sociopath beneath the facade. "I do?"

"Don't play games!" Ao banged his fist on the table. The suddenness of it was almost enough to make Allen jump, but Hwang didn't so much as blink. "Everyone in the city knows Yang was responsible for busting three of your men."

"Is that what the rumor mill is churning out these days?" Hwang examined his nails. "I hadn't heard that."

"Bullshit," Ao growled. "Three of the top redpoles of the Twisted Vipers don't get brought in without you knowing it. You lost three good men to Yang's investigation. Surely that pissed you off."

"I'm a businessman, Inspector. No matter how good an employee might be, they are still replaceable."

"But money isn't," Allen said, patting Hwang on the shoulder. He could feel the muscles clench beneath his hand, bunching as if Hwang worked to restrain himself from a physical outburst. "Your operation had to have taken a financial hit when the news broke, right? A man like you, sure you can replace manpower. But money? No. Fucking with your money is the only cardinal sin you have. Isn't that right, Hwang?"

"You know, Inspector, I hear that it is all the rage in America for police officers to leave the force and start writing crime novels." Hwang planted both feet firmly on the ground again. His posture, his expression, the tone of his voice, it all plainly said that he was bored. "Given the creativity with which you just spun that tale, I'd say you might want to give that some consideration."

Three short raps on the door to the interrogation room interrupted them. Johnny Hwang smiled.

"I believe that's for me."

Sure enough, a moment later his lawyer came in. He was a man as doughy and round as a pork bun, with a bad comb-over of dark wispy hair, a weak chin, and watery eyes. "I'd like to ask that you direct all future questions for Mr. Hwang to me, gentlemen," he said. Even his voice was weak and phlegmy; with the pair of Coke-bottle-thick glasses perched on the end of his blob of a nose, he reminded Allen of a character from an American cartoon. "Come on, Mr. Hwang, let's go."

"He's not going anywhere," Allen said firmly, pressing a hand against Hwang's shoulder and forcing him into his seat again. "We're holding him pending charges."

"You're going to just end up wasting twenty-four hours of Mr. Hwang's time," the lawyer protested.

"Twenty-four hours?" Allen flashed the lawyer a toothy smile. "Oh, no. We're investigating him under triad-related murder, which, as you know, is now considered by the Hong Kong Special Administrative Region to be an act of terrorism. We can hold Hwang for up to fourteen days."

"Fourteen days?" Hwang repeated, twisting to face his lawyer so fast Allen suspected he might give himself whiplash. "Is this true?"

"I'll fight it," the lawyer said stoutly, tilting his barely there chin up.

"You're welcome to try and waste more of Hwang's money," Allen said obligingly. "But no lawyer has ever been successful in their attempt."

"You've got to get me out of here, Liu," Hwang growled.

"I will," the lawyer assured him, though he didn't sound that confident, at least not to Allen's ears.

"Well, while you work on that, we're going to get Mr. Hwang settled in his new accommodations." Allen turned to the mirror. "Come on in, guys."

Two uniformed officers came in behind the lawyer. One of them already had his handcuffs out and ready to snap closed around Hwang's wrists.

Allen expected Hwang to rave and howl as they dragged him off, but he was stoically silent. If looks could kill, though, they'd have a murder on tape right there.

"You'll regret this, Inspectors," the lawyer said. "I'll own the HKPD when I'm finished."

"This isn't the first time we've heard that," Ao said dismissively.

The lawyer left then, mumbling under his breath.

Right on his heels, Henry Dang, Superintendent of the Eastern District Precinct, came in, glancing over his shoulder at Hwang's departing lawyer.

"He didn't react so well to us keeping Hwang," Ao explained.

"He's not one to trifle with, gentlemen," Dang warned. Allen wondered for whose benefit he was telling them that, their own or Hwang's. "You need to be careful in this investigation."

"Are you asking us to drop it?" Allen asked, cautious not to sound like he was making an accusation. They'd already had one confrontation after the Dark Streets case, and he didn't want to make the target on his back even bigger. He was one hundred percent certain of Dang's corruption, but he had to tread carefully. Henry Dang was a powerful man and would be a formidable enemy.

"Of course not," Dang huffed, puffing his chest out a bit. "I'm saying be careful. It was going up against Hwang that got poor Richard where he is now, after all."

Six

IT WAS NEARLY four in the morning when all available Dragons made it to their meeting space over Coffee by Constance, owned and run by Hong's sister. It also doubled as a safe house at times, so there was a bed and a refrigerator Constance kept stocked with food.

Winston and Steel were among the last two to arrive, and Conroy was pretty sure he knew what they'd been up to before coming, too. They walked to where Conroy stood near the door.

"'Sup, Conroy?" Winston slapped Conroy on the shoulder. "Shouldn't you be babysitting the fresh meat?"

"Isn't it past your bedtime?"

"We were in bed," Steel grumbled.

"Yeah, but I doubt you were sleeping, so suck it up." Conroy ignored Steel's lascivious look and turned his attention to Wei, who was speaking to Constance and Noah in a hushed voice. Their faces were grave. Noah looked more afraid than anything else, but he was plainly trying to hold it together for Wei. Constance just looked determined.

Wei finished with them and turned away—after putting a lingering hand on Noah's shoulder. Something passed unsaid between them, nevertheless understood by both men. It wasn't something he would ever say out loud, something he could barely admit to himself, but Conroy envied Wei and Noah their connection. Hell, Steel and Winston, too.

Conroy had plenty of fun with hookups and one-night stands, but sometimes he wanted more—and he thought he'd had it at one point.

He shoved those thoughts back into the dark vault at the back of his mind where they belonged. Nothing good came from those thoughts. The past was the past, and it might as well stay there.

Constance moved to the back of the room to stand next to Mimi, the newest Dragon. She was still in the process of recovering from getting shot by the hired assassin who'd been targeting Dark Streets racers in order to start a war between the Twisted Vipers and the Dragons. A woman with her spunk, Wei recruited her while she was still in the hospital bed.

Wei let out a short whistle, drawing everyone's eyes immediately. All conversation ceased. Wei briefly explained what had transpired in front of Indulgence to the gathered Dragons. As he did so, Conroy noted the unease that grew on everyone's faces.

"What the hell does all of this mean, exactly?" Walker Teng asked when Wei finished. "Where does it go from here?"

"Too soon to tell," Wei said.

"I think everyone is looking at this the wrong way," Conroy stated. "We've taken off the head of the snake. The Twisted Vipers are going to be weak without Hwang. He's the power and brains. Without him, they go back to being a bunch of *puk gai* squabbling over territory."

"You're assuming the charges will stick," Constance interjected. "They rarely do for men like Hwang."

"You think he's going to get away with killing a police officer?" Conroy asked incredulously.

Constance shrugged. "That's what usually happens. And even if they do, I think it will lead to just as many problems for us. We'll be left with a bunch of illegitimate leaders who desperately want to prove their worth. What's the best way to do that? Taking down the Dragons. Remember Leo Tong? Now imagine ten or fifteen of them all at once."

"I see your point." Conroy threw up his hands in surrender. "I still think we'd have an easier time with those idiots than with Hwang."

"Either way means a fight for us," Chris added. "We all know there wasn't gonna be a happily ever after with us and them."

Everyone nodded; Chris was right.

"There's one thing I don't think we've given proper thought to," Tony said. The man was worlds and above smarter than all of them, and there were probably a million things he'd thought of that no one else had.

Conroy became impatient. "Well, are you going to tell us what it is, or are you going to make us stand here and guess?"

"The Blue Suns."

Conroy and the others winced. Wei didn't. Well, Wei and Noah, but that was to be expected.

"Who are the Blue Suns?" Noah asked, frowning, probably because of the collective reaction to the name.

"The Blue Suns are the most powerful triad in the New Territories," Tony answered. "They operate out of Kowloon, but their sphere of influence takes up all of Mainland Hong Kong, and probably into China as well."

"They've been the top dogs in the triads for a long time," Smile Kang added from where he stood apart from the others, as usual. His remained as stoic and emotionless as always—which earned him the ironic nickname. "At least two decades. That's a major win in the world of the triads. Being at the top means you've got all the others gunning after you, wanting your position, the money you get, your influence. There have been plenty of attacks from the other triads, and the Blue Suns either wiped them out or absorbed them. Every time."

"And what does that have to do with the Twisted Vipers?" Noah asked.

"The Blue Suns have no control over the island," Wei explained. "They've wanted to take control for a long time, but the Nine Stars made sure it didn't happen. Ever since they fell, it's been the Vipers and the Dragons who keep them from making a move."

Noah nodded like he was starting to get the picture. Conroy couldn't help but feel proud of him. For a foreigner having been thrown into this environment not too long ago, he'd adapted quickly to his new life.

"But if the Twisted Vipers look weak, or the Dragons do, then the Blue Suns might decide to make a move on the island?"

Wei nodded. "It's a threat we've been under for a long time."

"That just means we have to handle this sooner rather than later," Conroy said, shrugging away the concerns about the Blue Suns. Worrying about a triad-equivalent boogeyman did nothing to solve the imminent threat. "We take down Hwang and the Vipers before the Blue Suns can decide to test the waters."

Wei gave Conroy a funny look, and Conroy cursed inwardly. *Goddamn it, that's his* let's straighten something out *face. He's going to call me aside any minute now...*

"Conroy, step outside with me for a minute, yeah?"

Wei was the boss, though, and Conroy did as told.

Outside the eastern sky was beginning to turn gray, the first hint of dawn's approach. The air was closer to cold than chilly, and for a moment, Conroy luxuriated in it, even though he only wore the short-sleeve button-down and jeans.

"There a problem, Boss?" Conroy asked casually, leaning against the railing that overlooked a small courtyard. Conroy appreciated the privacy; it meant he was open to a real conversation and not just giving orders. He'd still be talking to the boss, but with no one else listening, he'd let Conroy say his piece, too.

"You tell me," Wei replied, coming to stand next to him and propping his arms on the rail. "You're not taking this seriously enough, Conroy. This isn't a joke. This is a big deal."

"I get that it's a big deal, Wei. What do you want me to do, hide in my room all night and cry? That's not how I deal and you know it. If it makes you feel better, I'll sniffle a little bit, though."

Wei snorted and clapped Conroy's shoulder. "What I want is for you to actually think for once. I know you like a good fistfight—"

"What, you think I'm going to go off running after Twisted Vipers? Sure, I like a good fight, but I'm not suicidal. Besides, no way any Twisted Viper *ong lan gau* would take me on in a fist fight. They're too fuckin' scared."

"Damn right." Wei pushed away from the rail. "Now let's go inside and get this meeting over so that we might manage to get some sleep by noon."

Seven

THE MEETING LASTED until midmorning, and nothing was decided. They would continue to beef up their presence along the border between Twisted Viper and Dragon territory, and they'd redouble their recruitment efforts, but no real action plan existed.

Conroy knew Wei well enough to know he wouldn't leave that to committee. One of these days he would sit down with Tony, Conroy, maybe Chris or Smile, but that would be it. When they had a plan, they would put it to work. Wei understood that a camel was a horse built by committee, and you couldn't win a war that way.

Conroy was too tired to get behind the wheel and decided to walk home. Wei suggested he crash at the meeting place, but he knew some of the younger members would be there all day, and he'd never get any sleep, so he turned him down. Besides, he slept naked, and he didn't think any of the guys would appreciate him traipsing out to the toilet naked.

He always slept better in his own damn bed anyway.

Conroy's apartment wasn't anywhere close to as nice as Wei's was; he lived in a five-story brick building that didn't have an elevator and half the time didn't have functioning air-conditioning during the summer. Whatever it was, though, it was home. He'd been living in the same building since before the formation of the Dragons. It was shitty and rundown, but it was his.

It was hard to see the building until someone was practically on top of it; it was dwarfed by larger buildings around it, particularly the twenty-story apartment structure behind it.

Conroy had a love-hate relationship with the apartments behind his; on the upside, it rose up on the east side of his building, where his apartment happened to be. That meant the morning sun didn't wake him.

The downside was that the small veranda he had for hanging his laundry was also on that side, and without the sun, his clothes took much longer to dry. That and the building had come up so close to his that he could sometimes hear the music or television in the other building, especially in the summer when most people kept their windows open to tempt in breezes.

Still, if that was the worst of it, he couldn't complain. It was a price he was willing to pay for his home.

He did his best to power through the exhaustion, but by the time he came within visual distance of his apartment, Conroy was swaying on his feet. It had already been a long day before he'd agreed to go out with Chris—when he had thought he could depart and be in his bed by a comfortable two or three in the morning instead of pushing noon.

Even now, the best he could hope for was four hours; he couldn't sleep through the night because Wei was going to need all hands on deck in case shit really did go down with the Twisted Vipers.

I hope that Wei puts someone else with the would-be Dragons today. He forced himself to put one foot in front of the other again. *Otherwise those kids are in for some unpleasantness.*

"You've never looked more beautiful than you do right now," Conroy muttered to the building as he reached the front. The moment reminded him of all those nights and mornings stumbling home, bloody and bruised after confrontations with the Nine Stars. The only difference was that back then, he wasn't stumbling home alone.

No use rehashing the past, he told himself, driving the thoughts away and instead thinking of how good it would feel to crawl between his bedsheets.

He didn't notice the man leaning in the doorway inside the building entrance at first, probably due to his exhaustion. The man looked like anyone else off the street, and since he wasn't wearing a suit, Conroy didn't immediately take him for a Twisted Viper. More likely he was just some gangbanger they had found on the street and sent to do their dirty work. Using unaffiliated bangers would give the Vipers some deniability if the cops got involved.

The lurker was caught off guard, judging by the way he came away from the door too quickly, letting Conroy get a little too close. The man— really not more than a boy, maybe nineteen, if that—had a round face, the baby fat barely melted away yet. He was scrawny, supporting Conroy's suspicions.

Conroy could have knocked him on his ass if he wanted, but refrained. He doubted the kid had been sent after him to take him out, so he decided to conserve what was left of his energy. If he punched this kid now, he might not make it up to his bedroom.

"You...you Conroy Wong?" The kid's voice was high, a tremor of fear inside it. He was trying to sound confident, put on a show, but it was plain to Conroy.

Who the fuck did they send? Conroy squared his shoulders, straightening his back so he grew to full height. He towered over the kid, who couldn't have been more than five six. "Yeah, who's asking?"

"That don't matter." The kid forced his voice deeper... It made him sound ridiculous. "I got a message for you."

Conroy put on his best *I couldn't be more bored if I tried* face. "Oh? From who?"

"That—"

"Yeah, yeah, that don't matter, either," Conroy interrupted. "Just give me the goddamn message so I can go to sleep."

The kid squirmed, like he hadn't expected Conroy's reaction. He didn't know the man's reputation, then. "The message is, 'You need to make sure to keep your fuckin' mouth shut, if you know what's good for you.'"

What kind of amateur hour bullshit is this? He was almost exhausted enough for it to be funny; he had to hold back the laughter, because he was afraid that in his state if he started he wouldn't stop. *I knew the Vipers were down some of their brainpower with Hwang out of the picture, but I didn't realize he was the* only *one with brains!*

"Okay, kid, I received your message. So go on, get out of here."

"Hey, I ain't no kid!"

Conroy ran his hand through his hair. The product was fading from sweat and time, and it had that gross, oil-slick feel that made him desperate for the shower.

"You know what? Let me give you a piece of advice, kid. You want to act like a man, a big shot? First rule of the streets is don't be stupid. Comin' here, not knowing who you were meeting, that was stupid. If I'd been someone else, you might have got shot up before you even had a chance to say your piece. You're lucky I'm such a nice guy.

"Now, in return for my life advice—" Conroy grabbed the kid by the front of his too-big shirt and pulled him closer. "—I want you to go back and give a little message to whoever sent you here."

"Didn't you tell me I shouldn't do stupid things?"

"It's only stupid until you ask yourself one thing," Conroy said. "Who are you more afraid of right now: them or me?"

The guy gulped audibly, like that bird in the old American cartoon when he realized the cat was looking at him with that hungry look. "Wh—what's your message?"

"Tell him to *fuck. Off.*"

Eight

IT FELT LIKE Allen barely hit the pillow before the next morning—or later that morning, since it was damn near four when he finally got home—arrived. Still, he got up at six thirty and made his way to the precinct by seven. If he had been on a normal schedule, without an active case, he wouldn't have been to work until late, but investigations took precedence over everything else.

Ao was there, looking like he'd gotten a full eight hours and then some. It made no sense to Allen. The man could nap at his uncomfortable desk chair for forty minutes and be well rested. He wished he had that ability.

He'd gotten used to operating on little sleep as a police officer, but it wasn't his preferred mode of being. Give him twelve hours of sleep any day.

"You're looking beautiful as always," Ao observed, giving him a teasing grin. "I can tell this is going to be a great day."

"*Diu lei,*" Allen replied, only half-serious.

"Clearly someone doesn't want their coffee." Ao spoke like a teacher dealing with a misbehaving student. "It came from an actual coffee shop." Ao stepped aside to reveal two tall Styrofoam cups on his desk, bearing the mark of a coffee chain that had bled into Hong Kong from Korea.

Allen practically drooled at the sight. "I take back every bad thing I thought about you in the past ninety seconds."

"You're going to have to do a little better than ninety seconds." Ao stepped between Allen and the coffee as Allen reached for it.

Allen resisted the urge to hiss like a territorial cat; that would only give Ao more leverage.

"Fine," he said when he knew his voice would come out normal. "I take back every bad thing I thought *or* said about you in the past seventy-two hours. Happy?"

Ao made a big show of considering it, stroking his beard thoughtfully. The ridiculousness of the movement nearly caused Allen to laugh outright, but he knew saying anything would only earn him an equally ridiculous come back.

He'd rather not get into the facial hair envy conversation *again*.

"I guess that'll do," Ao said at last before stepping aside to let Allen scoop up one of the identical containers.

"Any idea where you want to get started on this case?" Ao asked, sitting down on the edge of his desk and enjoying his own coffee.

"Who said I was lead on this?" Allen protested. "I wasn't even technically on duty. You were the one who got the call, so it should be you."

Ao shook his head emphatically. "Like hell. You know how much trouble this case is going to bring? No way I want to put my neck out there to hang."

"Gee, thanks." Allen wasn't surprised that it would end up being him left out to dry. Given what Dang thought of him, he would likely take the blame for any mistakes whether he was lead or not. He didn't say that to Ao, though.

"The first thing we need to do, I guess," he said when he'd thought it through, "is talk to the others in the Anti-Gang Task Force. We need to find as much as we can about just what Inspector Yang was investigating and how deeply the ties went to Hwang himself. There might be something more there we're not aware of."

"Maybe," Ao agreed, like that was that. Then again, if Allen was going to be lead on this one, then that *was* it. "You all right going to talk to those guys? I mean, after Dang pulled you from the task force..."

"Don't remind me," Allen muttered, but not loud enough for Ao to hear. To him he said, "I'm fine. There were understandably some potential conflicts of interest there, with my family connection."

"You're the one who oversaw the end of the Dark Streets crap," Ao protested. It was a nice feeling, Allen found, having someone get indignant on his behalf. "That case wouldn't have ended the way it did if it weren't for you."

Allen knew the importance of his role in the Dark Streets case. He also understood that the role had led to Dang's uncompromising anger. Regardless, some things were best left unspoken, even with someone you trust.

Allen sat at his desk, determined to at least enjoy his coffee before he began. In less than twelve hours the case had already proved to be complicated. He anticipated—with no small amount of trepidation—many long nights at his desk in the near future.

That was the job, though, and he'd damn well do it, especially since this time it was a cop murdered. The fact that this could change the balance of power on the island in the Dragons' favor, well, that was just a bonus.

Allen disliked the idea of the Dragons existing, not because of what they stood for, but because they were necessary. That was one point Wei could never understand. Wei accepted the inevitability of their existence, but not Allen. People needed to start putting their trust in the police. The rule of law was everything. It was a continuous cycle, a Mobius loop that Wei lived in, where the only thing that made the Dragons' existence inevitable was that the Dragons existed in the first place.

He'd joined the police force to protect his family and friends, protect Constance and Winston and Shelby—and of course Wei and the others. He wanted to do that by creating a city that didn't *need* the Dragons to protect it, that didn't need to turn to anyone other than the police to keep them safe.

Allen didn't know if Wei could live in that world, though. His entire life had been about the triads in one way or another, Allen knew. First living under their thumb and then fighting them. Protecting people was in his very makeup, part of his DNA. That would never go away. Maybe Wei Tseng wasn't made to live in a peaceful world.

Maybe now that he's got something other than the Dragons to live for, though... Allen thought of Noah for a moment, Wei's American lover. He'd caused a change in Wei, a definite change for the better.

"Allen? You ready?"

Allen started at Ao's words. He hadn't realized he'd let his mind wander. Ao had already finished his coffee and stood over him, ready to get started.

Allen nodded, embarrassed, and downed the rest of his coffee.

The Anti-Gang Task Force had an area set around for them on the second floor, away from everyone else. Notices and information about various triads and their members—which were important targets and which weren't, which might be persuaded to flip on their boss if given the right incentives—lined the wall

Allen wasn't surprised to see a portion of the wall dedicated to the Dragons. He was proud, in a way, to notice that not one of their members were marked as potential flips.

The team consisted of eight inspectors aside from Yang, and they were present, huddled around a table and discussing something in quiet voices. Allen assumed they were discussing Yang's murder.

"Excuse me, gentlemen," Ao said in his naturally booming voice. The inspectors all turned toward them, expressions ranging from curious to dismissive.

Allen locked eyes with Inspector Leung and grimaced. Leung was Dang's man through and through. He'd killed an unarmed man without hesitation, and Allen suspected it was on Dang's orders. Someone had hired the man to kill Twisted Vipers and Dragons under the cover of the races. Allen knew blame rested on Henry Dang.

Leung didn't bother hiding his dislike of Allen, either; he curled his lips back into a sneer. "What is Homicide doing up here?"

"We've got a few questions to ask," Allen said coolly. He maintained the minimum amount of professionalism required. Leung was newly promoted to inspector, however, and Allen had seniority, so he didn't have to try all that hard.

"This is about Richard, yes?" The question came from one of the older inspectors on the team—a squat, potato-shaped man with a face who looked like he'd been punched in the face several times. Given the man's reputation for engaging in bar brawls when drunk, Allen figured he had.

"That's right. We're investigating his murder."

"Shouldn't this be an Anti-Gang Task Force case?" Leung asked. "Considering your prime suspect is the leader of one of the island's most vicious triad?"

"Not our call," another inspector said. He looked to be younger than Yang, but not by much. Allen knew him well; Inspector Dao was well respected on the force and had been around longer than most. Now that Yang was gone, Allen couldn't think of anyone who had more years on him.

"Thanks for your understanding," Ao said. "Obviously we are aware of the connections between Yang's murder and the task force's investigation of the Twisted Vipers. What we're trying to figure out is if there's a deeper link, something we can use as evidence of clear motive for Hwang to have done this."

"We need to connect Hwang to Yang with more than just circumstantial evidence," Allen added. "We need to show the two had some sort of personal involvement."

"You can check Yang's desk," Dao said with a shrug. "Yang didn't much talk about what he worked on when it came to these investigations. Wasn't the sharing sort."

"He had a meeting a few days before he died," Potato added. "No idea who it was with, though. He had the details of the meeting written down on a Post-it on his desk. Left work early that day, too."

Ao joined the inspectors and began asking them routine questions while Allen made his way to the desk Potato indicated. It was messily kept, paperwork all over the place, various Post-it notes in a variety of colors. Despite the cluttered desk, Yang's had meticulous handwriting; each Chinese character written with such precision they could have been printed by a computer.

He was also deliberate about his record keeping, too; each little square of paper had a date written on it. Allen found the most recent one, dated three days prior. It read: *7:00pm, Mrs. Chu's Noodles, Temple Street Night Market.*

The Temple Street Night Market was out in Aberdeen. "Hey, Ao," he called to his partner, waving the paper. "Looks like we've got our first lead."

Nine

THERE WAS NO one else in the meeting room of the jail where Hwang was being held. Henry Dang had been very careful in making the arrangements. Only guards who were on his payroll were around—duty shifts had been adjusted, vacations suddenly taken. The jail had been put on a sudden lockdown, each and every member of the population back in their cells, any available guards Dang didn't implicitly trust sent to keep an eye on the inmates—all so that when Johnny Hwang entered the wide space, only Dang and people he trusted would be any the wiser.

Seeing Dang standing there, Johnny Hwang sneered. A flash of hatred, hot and powerful, flew through Dang. How he'd love nothing more than to watch this man die in a pool of his own blood—preferably slowly and with much pain. Dealing with this man was the cost of doing business, though, and Dang knew all about that.

"Henry goddamn Dang. I was wondering how long it would be before you dragged your sorry ass here." Hwang flopped unceremoniously into a metal chair bolted to the floor. He held out a hand, and one of the guards provided him with a cigarette before lighting it for him.

Seeing the way these men, supposedly *his* men, treated Hwang alarmed Dang. Had he been mistaken of their loyalty all along, or had it changed, suddenly? Perhaps he was simply reading too much into it. He had told them to take care of him, after all.

"It took time to make the necessary arrangements," Dang said, hating how apologetic his voice sounded, even to his own ears. "I can't just drop everything and rush here during visitor's hours, now can I?"

"You really want to hold on to that job of yours, don't you, Henry? You like the perks you get from it, yes—particularly the part where you receive large sums of money from me in order to keep the police *off* my activities?"

Dang chuckled nervously. "Come on, now, Johnny—Mr. Hwang." He corrected himself after seeing the ugly glint that entered the gangster's eyes. "I was handling the matter. The charges against your people wouldn't have stuck. I was making sure of that."

"Maybe I didn't like your pace, then," Hwang said coldly. "Maybe I got impatient."

Dang could feel sweat breaking out on his forehead, but he didn't dare wipe it away; he didn't want to draw attention, though he had no doubt Hwang had noticed the perspiration already. Men like Johnny Hwang could probably smell fear.

"I wish you could have controlled yourself a little longer," Dang said. "After the incident with Inspector Yang..."

"Take care of it," Hwang snapped. "I don't care how—just take care of it."

Dang held back a glib retort, instead saying, "A police officer is dead, Mr. Hwang. There will be people who want answers—people in my department as well as my superiors. It cannot look like I am interfering with the investigation!"

"Do you know what question I find myself asking myself more and more, Henry?"

The sudden change in Hwang's tone made Dang uneasy. "I'm afraid I don't, Mr. Hwang."

"I ask myself why I need you. Why do I keep you around when you seem to be absolutely no good to me?"

Dang's eyes widened. He feared Hwang thinking him less than useful. He knew that the moment he ceased to be useful Hwang would have him taken out—an accident of some kind. Maybe he wouldn't even kill him; Hwang had plenty of evidence of Dang's corruption from their years of interactions and financial transactions.

No, it was imperative that Hwang need him.

"You keep me around because you need me, Mr. Hwang. It's getting harder to operate your businesses, isn't it? Imagine how much heavier the pressure would be if I weren't doing everything I could to keep the heat off you. How many times have they come after you and nothing come of it? How many times have I helped clean up your men's messes?"

"Which anyone in your position could do," Hwang said dismissively. "However, I suppose you're right. I do need you—until I have time to groom your replacement, at least. But I want you to make sure you hear me and take my words to heart, Henry: take. Care. Of. This. I don't want to waste any more time than I already have in this jail."

Hwang rose then, signaling the end of the meeting. It was a power move—Hwang's way of showing him he was still in charge, still running things even from behind bars.

"Oh, and Henry?"

Hwang glanced at him from the doorway.

"One of mine will be checking on you every now and then. I hope you will have good news to share with me soon."

Ten

THE SOUND OF his phone ringing managed to somehow pierce the cloud of sleep clinging to Conroy. For a moment he was completely disoriented, per usual. He lay facedown on his bed, his head buried under the pillow and his bedsheets wound around his naked body.

A cogent thought finally managed to get through his skull. *The phone. Answer the damn phone.*

"What?" His voice sounded gravelly and strange.

"Rise and shine, sleeping beauty," Chris Ma said. Conroy pictured the grin on the other man's face and decided punching him would be a good idea. "I know you need your beauty sleep, but Wei needs you back here."

"Fuck you," Conroy retorted while sitting up. He stretched his arms and took the phone away from his ear momentarily. When he was finished, he said, "We both know that even on a minute of sleep a night, I'd still look a hell of a lot better than you, anime hair."

"Just get your ass down here." Chris hung up.

Conroy sighed and began the process of untangling the sheets from around his legs, made more difficult by the fact that he always slept with one leg uncovered, so when he moved, the sheets got wrapped around him in some pretty weird ways at times.

Conroy finally managed to look at the time. It was half past four. He'd slept for about four hours. He went through the "morning" routine quickly—shower, dress, take a moment to eat a bowl of rice and Japanese *natto*—fermented beans—and then headed out.

With his car still at Constance's, he had to go by foot. He hadn't minded it this morning when all he wanted to do was get to a bed, but now he wished he'd driven home. He felt naked without it, like he was missing a limb. The other Dragons—minus Winston, who understood— all told him it was just a car, but it *wasn't*; it was *his* car.

He'd worked his ass off for the money to buy it, and now worked his ass off to keep it pristine, just like it had been when he'd bought it. He took pride in his car.

Never leaving her behind again, that's for sure. He could see the wisdom of Constance refusing to let him drive, but that didn't mean that he'd liked the choice.

He walked three blocks before he realized he had a tail. *Damn, second time in just a few hours I ain't paid good enough attention to what's around me.* Conroy blamed it on his tiredness, but that was no excuse and he knew better. No, he'd been lazy. The peace of the past five years had made him soft, as it often did men of war.

He wasn't concerned, not with only one man on his heels. The Vipers were probably keeping tabs on him now, after what had happened. Maybe the police, even. He doubted Hong would do that, though. Besides, this guy didn't look like the sort of guy the police would hire.

Conroy paid careful attention to him. The man succeeded as an efficient shadow, always staying a nice distance back, not walking directly behind him, letting people get between them so he didn't look suspicious.

Conroy was just better—good enough to spot him.

He considered going out of his way to lose this guy, to take the long way, find some crowded, well-traveled street to fade into. It would take too much time, though, and he needed to get to Wei.

The quicker option would be to speed up, take a side alley, and then confront the *puk gai* there. A good scare should send the guy running, especially considering his predecessor.

Ahead, a narrow alley, barely wide enough for two people to walk side by side, connected two streets. It seemed like as good a place as any, so he ducked into it, going about halfway between the two streets before he stopped and waited, leaning against the wall and propping his foot up against the brick.

He wished he had a cigarette. It was a habit he partook in every so often, now much less frequently than he used to, but sometimes the urge hit him in the strangest of times.

He waited a full minute before he realized his follower hadn't appeared. Maybe the guy knew he was onto him, and so he hung back?

Or maybe Conroy was being paranoid to begin with and nobody was following him. He made his way back to the alley entrance. Just before he stepped out, three figures stepped in. Conroy took an instinctive step away, carefully observing the men and gauging the threat as quickly as he could.

The man in the center was undoubtedly the leader. He was near Conroy's height, maybe a few centimeters shorter. His face sported a sort of stretched look, like he'd had plastic surgery. His hair was shoulder-length, tied back into a tight ponytail. He was dressed in casual clothing, but it was expensive stuff. This was no average gangbanger here.

The man to the left had been following him. He was a scrawny thing, constantly shifting his weight. A kid, like the first at the apartment. The guy to the right, though, definitely a Twisted Viper, some muscle. He was short, only about five-five, but he had the physique of a bodybuilder.

"If you three are lookin' for a little fun in the alleyway, I think it's a bit early for that," Conroy remarked, keeping his attention on the guy in the center. "Wait a few hours, it'll be dark enough nobody'll see you."

The leader pulled a face. "How vulgar," he said. His voice held the hint of an accent Conroy couldn't place. "I believe there is a discussion that needs to be had between us, Conroy Wong."

"Conroy Wong? Never heard of him."

The man rolled his eyes. "Aren't we a bit old to think that ruse would work?"

Conroy shrugged. "It always worked for Scooby-Doo."

"Just cut his ass, Jiang," the short-but-muscular guy said impatiently. "You just gonna let him mouth off to you like that?"

"He doesn't know any better," the man called Jiang said. "Bad manners in those who never learned good ones is only to be expected. Bad manners in those who *have* learned them, like some people—" The warning was clear. "—is unacceptable."

"I didn't mean nothing by it, Jiang," the guy said quickly.

"Listen, I've got a lot of shit on my plate, so if you want to say something to me, just hurry up and say it for fuck's sake."

Jiang sighed and pinched the bridge of his nose. "I've tried being reasonable. Clearly that's not going to work with you—not that I should have expected it to, considering you *are* a Dragon. I can't say that thinking has ever been your strong suit."

Conroy let the barb pass, knowing a reaction was the point of it—any excuse to initiate violence. Conroy wasn't going to oblige. "Just say it."

"We sent an associate to talk to you earlier, so I imagine you have an idea what this is about. We need you to consider the potential ramifications of your choices, Mr. Wong. Speaking out could be very bad for business. Might upset the delicate balance of power on the island. I'm sure you can appreciate how unfortunate that might be."

"Listen—Jian was it?"

"Jiang."

"Right, right. Jiang. You're here to tell me that I need to keep my mouth closed, right? You sent a kid to do that already. Don't you think this is overkill?"

"Considering the kid you're referring to came back with a less-than-polite message from you, I wanted to make sure there was no miscommunication between us."

"Oh, I'm pretty sure we understand each other clearly. You want me to keep my mouth shut about your boss offing a cop, and I want you to fuck off. See? Crystal clear."

"You might wanna watch your mouth," Muscle snapped

"Yeah, my grandmother used to tell me my mouth was going to get me in trouble one day."

"Sounds like a wise woman," Jiang said through pursed lips.

"Maybe," Conroy allowed. "Although she wasn't wise enough to not pick up an opium habit, so maybe there isn't much to say for her advice. Either way, my message to you all is the same: fuck off. Oh, and I hope that dog-fucking boss of yours rots in prison."

Jiang had the switchblade in his hand faster than Conroy had ever seen anyone draw one, including Chris.

"You'll keep a respectful tone when you talk about Johnny Hwang," he snarled. "I guess you need to be taught a lesson, given a little taste of what you can expect if you don't learn to *keep your mouth shut!*"

Jiang lashed out at him then. Conroy stumbled back, barely escaping the sharp blade. Jiang didn't hesitate, though; he kept going, pressing his advantage. Conroy dodged two more swipes, and then a third scored a long, burning cut along his left side.

Conroy pressed his hand against the cut instinctively, unsure of just how deep it went. He never took his eyes of Jiang and remained on the balls of his feet so that if necessary, he could beat a hasty retreat. He hated the idea of running away, but he was outnumbered, and with that switchblade, odds did not favor him.

Only an idiot stayed and fought a battle he had no chance of winning.

Jiang didn't attack again, though. He took in the blood on Conroy's shirt and made a noise of mild satisfaction. "I hope you let this stand as a reminder to you, Mr. Wong. Next time we won't be so polite."

Conroy waited until Jiang and the other two were gone before he pulled out his phone, careful not to get blood on it, and called Wei.

Eleven

ALLEN MADE HIS way to Aberdeen to visit the Temple Street Night Market midafternoon while Ao stayed behind to ask more questions of the Anti-Gang Task Force. Allen didn't envy him the gig; he'd asked questions all morning, and they weren't forthcoming with answers and avoided a lot of the questions related to whatever they might be investigating.

Allen couldn't get out of there fast enough.

Aberdeen wasn't his beat, so he lacked familiarity with the area. The *ye shi* was well-known throughout the island, though, so it wasn't too difficult for him to make his way there.

The title of night market was a bit of a misnomer for Temple Street; the market—or parts of it—didn't close. Most night markets didn't get set up until well into the evening, in areas where traffic wouldn't be hindered by their presence—side alleys and backstreets and such—but Temple Street Night Market had an entire labyrinth of space to set up, alleyways and courtyards that crisscrossed, forming the crux of the market. That area remained open at all times.

There were several signs set up telling him exactly where he could find Mrs. Chu's Noodles. It was too early in the day for a noodle stall to be open, so Allen hung around, questioning some of the few vendors around.

Allen had no luck asking them about Yang; even after carefully studying his picture, none recognized him.

He lingered, keeping an eye on the stall belonging to Mrs. Chu. She must make good money, to have her own permanent stall installed in the market. Most of the vendors there brought their own and set them up every morning.

It was very unlikely that Johnny Hwang would meet with Inspector Yang somewhere that he wasn't one hundred percent comfortable, and that would mean trusting the staff to be discreet and a place on Twisted Viper payroll.

Aberdeen was a little farther south than Allen thought Hwang's influence reached, but he was clearly wrong. Somehow, he—and the HKPD as a whole—had missed the growth of Hwang's control.

Around four, a stout-looking woman appeared and began opening Mrs. Chu's Noodles. Wanting to get to her before she began seeing to customers—he'd noticed quite a few people start making their way toward the stall as she entered—Allen hurried over, credentials already out.

"Excuse me. Are you Mrs. Chu?"

She gave him an appraising scan, head to toe and back, before she answered. "What do you think?"

Her tone made it clear she was one of Hwang's. Not openly hostile, but not cooperative. Still, he had to try. "Do you recognize this man? Maybe a customer from a few days ago??" Allen flashed her the picture of Inspector Yang].

Mrs. Chu barely looked at it. "You think I know the faces of every customer who comes through here? I do a lot of business; I don't have time to go around memorizing every face."

"Okay." Allen changed to Hwang's picture. "What about this guy?"

Not even a hint of a reaction when she looked at the picture; her face remained as stoic as ever. She was definitely good and loyal to Hwang— and it wasn't loyalty from fear, either. It seemed to reside in a deeper emotion.

"Don't know him, either."

"I'm pretty sure everybody knows him," Allen said lightly.

Mrs. Chu finally brought her full attention to bear on him, one meaty fist on her hip, the other clutching a long metal ladle. "You calling me a liar?"

"Of course not, ma'am. Just trying to cover my bases."

"Well, you go cover your bases with someone else," she snapped. "I've got hungry customers I need to prepare for."

Allen knew it would be pointless to ask her any more questions, so took her advice. First he checked with the customers to see if any were there when the meeting took place, but none were. His hope ran thin. The lead seemed to be a dead end. Turning to leave, he saw a young woman setting up a clothing stall—no doubt knockoffs being passed off as the real thing, normal Hong Kong market fare.

From where stall sat, the woman would have a good view of Mrs. Chu's Noodles.

"Excuse me. I'm Inspector Hong with HKPD. I was hoping I could ask you a few questions."

She eyed him warily for a moment, clearly uncertain.

"It's not about your goods, I promise."

She relaxed as soon as he said that. "Sure, sure. Go ahead. You don't mind if I keep setting up while you do, though, right? I need to be ready by the time the big crowds come through."

Allen nodded. "Are you here every night?"

"Yep." She hauled a box up and began unloading various T-shirt designs. "Figured it was a good business plan—set up by the noodle shop, that way if a customer happens to spill their bowl, there's a new, clean shirt right here for them."

Allen grinned. "That is a pretty good business model."

"It doesn't hurt that Mrs. Chu's sees more of the crowds than almost anywhere else in the market," she admitted. "Why do you ask?"

"Well, a few days ago, around seven at night, did you happen to notice either of these men dining at Mrs. Chu's?"

She took the pictures from Allen and studied them, frowning slightly. "Yeah, I saw them."

"Both of them?" Allen pressed.

"Both of them."

"Were they here together?"

"The young one showed up first. Sat there for a good twenty minutes eating noodles before the other one came. He didn't eat anything. They just talked for a few minutes, then the old guy left. The other guy looked real mad when he left."

"So you don't have any idea what they might have been talking about?"

She shook her head. "They sat at the far end, over there. I couldn't hear them if I wanted to."

"Thanks for your time. Can I get you to write your name down here for me? And a number where I can contact you."

"Is this necessary?" she asked as she took the notebook Allen offered.

"I'm afraid so." Allen waited as she reluctantly wrote. When she handed it back, he returned the notebook to his back pocket. "You have a good night, ma'am."

As he approached his car, his phone began to ring. He thought it was Ao at first, but the caller ID displayed Constance's name. She rarely called him, especially during the day. Warning bells went off in his head.

"Constance, everything okay?"

"You need to get to the coffee shop, Allen. It's Conroy."

Twelve

CONROY KEPT HIS arm raised above his head, wincing as Constance applied an antiseptic-covered cloth to his cut. His shirt had been peeled off—ruined, and he liked that one, too—and Wei, Tony, Chris, Smile, Winston, and Steel were there.

"You said he was called Jiang?" Tony asked when Conroy finished explaining what had happened.

"That's what the other *puk gai* called him, yeah," Conroy said. "Shit, Constance, what are you doing? Cutting me open more?"

"You're the one that didn't want to go to a doctor, Conroy," she replied, never taking her eyes off the wound. "It's got to be cleaned out. It's not too deep, but it's got to be treated. So get over it, sit there, and talk to Wei."

Winston snickered.

"What are you over there snickering at, punk?" Conroy growled in his direction. Winston had the good sense to stop smiling very quickly.

"If it was Jiang, then the Twisted Vipers mean business," Tony said, giving Wei a meaningful look. "He's Hwang's most brutal enforcer, his right-hand man."

"So he's Hwang's Conroy," Steel said.

Tony gave him an impatient look. "Yes, if Conroy were a psychopath with a particular love of knife work and inflicting pain on others."

Steel thought about it for a moment. "So like Conroy."

Conroy made a move as if to grab Steel. "*Hou sei la lei!*"

"Sit still," Constance snapped. Conroy did as told, but he gave Steel a glare he hoped made it clear that the moment he could get up, the guy was dead meat.

"If Hwang has Jiang involved, then it's serious," Tony went on.

"They're just trying to scare me," Conroy said. "Nothing to freak out about."

Tony clearly thought differently. "No, my friend. They don't use Jiang for intimidation."

Conroy glanced at Smile. "What do *you* think, man?"

The others also turned to him. Smile knew the Twisted Vipers inside and out, having once run with their crowd before the Nine Stars fell.

"Tony's right. I remember Jiang. He's a crazy sonofabitch, no restraint. Sending Jiang wasn't a bluff; it was a warning. He doesn't make idle threats."

"That's great," Conroy muttered.

As if the universe were conspiring to make the day top-ten bad, Allen Hong came in through the door in a rush, surprising all of them, Noah on his heels.

"I tried to stop him, or at least slow him down," Noah said, glaring at Hong. "But I'm pretty sure it's illegal to knock a police officer on his ass."

"You could try." Hong's words lacked any venom.

"Trust me, he'd succeed," Winston said. The relationship between Hong and Winston was still strained, a little awkward, but they were fixing it, working on making it better. Conroy didn't begrudge Winston that. They were family, after all. There wasn't a whole lot of shit in the world more important than that.

"What the hell is this *puk—*" Conroy took one look at Constance's face and swallowed back the insult. "What the hell is Hong doing here?"

"I called him," Constance answered.

It took a lot for Conroy to control the irrational anger that built up in his chest. The idea of any of the Dragons turning to Hong pissed him off. They didn't need him—he'd turned his back on them, never once looking back. He'd thrown away everything—the Dragons, Conroy—all so he could join the police.

Conroy couldn't explode in anger, not at Constance, so he decided to play it safe and keep his mouth shut.

"What happened?" Hong moved toward Conroy, clearly trying to examine the cut on his torso. Conroy glared, but Hong didn't retreat.

Damn it, Conroy thought. *I must be losing my touch.*

"I had a run-in with some of Hwang's boys outside my apartment," Conroy answered reluctantly. "One of them thought he'd try to carve the Zorro 'Z' into my chest."

"Is he all right?" Hong asked his sister gruffly.

Probably worried about losing a witness, Conroy thought.

"Nothing too serious." Constance finished her task and then pulled several bandages and medical tape out of her emergency kit. "He didn't need stitches, thankfully. Probably should have a doctor look at it to make sure it doesn't get infected, but he's flat-out refusing to go."

"Typical," Hong snorted.

"I *am* right here, you know. Just get me bandaged up so I can get out of here, Constance, okay?"

"Sure thing, Conroy," Constance said sweetly, applying the bandage with more force than was necessary and making him suck in a breath from the pain. "That doing it for you?"

"You're a cruel woman sometimes, Constance, you know that?"

She applied the second bandage much gentler than the first. "Don't you ever forget it, either."

"Not a high chance of that happening," Conroy assured her.

"How serious was this threat?" Hong asked.

"It was nothing; just a lot of hot air," Conroy said stiffly. "I'm not afraid of those punk-ass bitches."

"You need to take this shit seriously, Conroy," Wei said. His tone, his expression—it was all business and anger. This was the second time Vipers had come into his territory, and this time they'd attacked a Dragon. "They sent Jiang with a message."

"Jiang?" Hong's face went white.

"You know the name?" Tony asked.

Of all the Dragons, aside from Winston, he was the one who remained most civil with Hong. Conroy didn't know why, though age and will to hold on to grudges may play a role. Or maybe it was just him wanting to be peacekeeper, like always.

"I remember hearing it a few times on the force, yeah. Always associated with some of the worst deeds the Vipers are responsible for. He's one sick fucker, Wei. It sounds like the Vipers are going to go all-out to make sure that the case against Hwang falls apart. With no weapon and no other witnesses, all they have to do is get Conroy out of the picture and Hwang walks out a free man. He gets away with murder—with killing a cop."

Wei cursed. "Johnny Hwang going behind bars is the best chance we've got of establishing real peace on the island. We all know he was gunning for us, hard. There's a chance that whoever comes into power won't have the same hard-on for us that Hwang does."

"Putting Hwang behind bars is the best hope we have of getting rid of him without starting an all-out war," Tony agreed. "And then it still might come."

"If you want Hwang behind bars, then I need Conroy safe," Hong said.

"I am safe," Conroy growled.

Constance finished applying the bandages with some medical tape, and Conroy came to his feet. "Winston, will you check and see if there's any shirts I can fit in the back? Don't want to walk around here shirtless all day and make you guys jealous."

"I think we'll manage, man," Chris said dryly.

"What I mean is I want you protected," Hong said.

Conroy blinked, thinking for a moment that perhaps he'd imagined it, and this man *hadn't* just said the stupidest thing anyone had said to him. The look on Hong's face said it all: he knew what he said, he knew how Conroy would react to it, and he'd said it anyway.

"Protected? You want me protected, Hong?" Conroy closed the distance between himself and the inspector in two wide strides. "I'm not some damsel in distress waiting for a white knight to come riding in to rescue me. You might have me confused with Noah."

"Hey!" Noah cried, indignant.

"Sorry. No offense."

"Offense taken!"

Hong sighed, the sort of sound parents made when they were trying to be rational with unruly children, which only stoked his anger further.

"There's procedure, Conroy, protocol. You're the witness to the murder of a cop, committed by a high-profile triad boss!"

Conroy stepped closer until they were almost toe to toe. "I'm also a Dragon."

"That puts you in even more danger!" Hong exploded unexpectedly, backing away from him. "Not only are you a witness, like I said, but you're also the right-hand man of the Dragons, who the Twisted Vipers are well on their way to war with! Killing you would be like a two-for-one special, do you get that? They *will* try to kill you!"

"He's right, Conroy."

Conroy did a double take, shocked, to say the least. He'd expected agreement from Constance, maybe even Tony, but not from Wei. Wei, more than anyone, understood Conroy's beef with Hong, knew just how deep it went.

He must be more worried than I thought.

"What is it you had in mind, Hong?" Wei went on.

"This is fucking crazy, man," Conroy huffed. Wei ignored him.

"Well, normal procedure would be to put him under twenty-four-hour police escort."

"Twenty-four-hour—Wei, you hearing this bullshit?"

"Conroy…"

"No, Wei, seriously. You good with having *fucking cops* hounding us all day?"

"Of course I'm not," Wei snapped, his tone telling Conroy he was getting dangerously close to crossing a line.

"I said that was normal procedure, not what I recommended doing here," Hong said, rubbing his eyes with the palms of his hands. "I figure a hybrid of procedure and new methods would work best."

"How about you just take your procedure and fuck off?" Conroy sneered. "Let the Dragons handle this. It's our business."

Hong arched an eyebrow. "Your business? Conroy, a police officer is dead—a very well-respected police officer at that. You're out of your goddamn mind if you think HKPD is just going to let you handle this 'in house.'"

"It isn't Jiang's style to take on a whole group," Smile offered. "He bides his time, waiting until he can get his target alone."

"See?" Conroy gave Smile a nod of thanks. "I'm safer with the Dragons."

"During the day, maybe, but what about at night? You live alone."

"Yeah, but I'm rarely there *alone* at night," Conroy said, making sure Hong knew exactly what he meant. He might have been seeing only what he wanted to see, but it looked like the corner of Hong's mouth twitched downward a millimeter.

"Well, now you'll never be there alone at night." Hong's voice was flatter than before, so maybe Conroy wasn't imagining it after all. "Come night time, I'm your escort."

"No way." Conroy waved his hands emphatically. "No. Nuh-uh, not going to happen."

"Sure it is," Hong said. "Or you're going to go into protective custody. Those are your two options, Conroy. Take it or leave it. And don't bother looking to Wei for help," he added sternly when Conroy looked to the Dragons leader. "This might be his territory, but it's my case."

"For fuck's sake, fine!" Conroy surrendered, disgusted with the turn of events. "I don't know what I did to fuck up my karma so badly, but this better put it back in balance."

Thirteen

ALLEN HADN'T EXPECTED his idea to be greeted with enthusiasm on Conroy's part, given their past, but a tinge of pain resounded in response to the sheer revulsion Conroy'd exhibited. He didn't know why; he knew what the Dragons thought of him, what their opinions were.

Wei treated him with cold indifference now, for the sake of Constance and her family, but it wasn't enough for Allen to convince himself they didn't despise him. And if it had been, this here, well, it would have set the record straight once and for all.

He shouldn't have been so surprised, but observing Conroy's reaction to his instructions to return by sundown was more of a stab than he'd expected.

"Are you okay?" Constance asked him, drying her now clean hands on a dish towel. She always had an eerie sense of exactly how he felt, no matter how much he tried to hide it.

"I'm fine," he told her, hoping she would let it go, even though she would know it for the lie it was.

"That's good," she said casually while putting the dish towel down and fixing him with a knowing look. "I was beginning to think you'd lost your mind, but since you say you're fine, nothing to worry about there, right?"

Allen sighed heavily. "Don't, Constance."

"Don't what? Don't tell you when I think you're about to do something really stupid? You and I both know I'm not going to do that. Call it my sisterly duty."

"I'm not a little kid anymore, Constance. You don't have to be so damn protective of me, you know." He loved his sister dearly, and she him, but she'd always had this burning desire to shield those she loved from pain, from the world itself. Even though she had to know it was impossible, she still tried her best. Even though Allen was a police officer, well-trained to take care of himself, she still pulled the big-sister routine with him.

"You're not a little kid, but you *are* my brother. No matter how much you hate it, I'm always going to be protective of you. You're my family. You're stuck with it just like Winston and Shelby are."

"And how thrilled we all are for it," Allen teased. "Seriously, Constance. I'm all right."

Her face made it clear she didn't believe him. "I know you're doing your job here, but do you think this is really a good idea?"

"Is what a good idea?" Conroy asked, forcing himself not to squirm as he sat on the couch next to her.

"See, when you pull the whole 'I don't know what you're talking about' routine, I know you think I'm right."

"I can't know you're right if I don't know what you're talking about," Allen maintained stubbornly, hoping that if he held to that long enough Constance would drop it and move on.

"Is assigning yourself to be Conroy's babysitter through all of this *really* the right thing to do?"

"It's my job, like you said. Besides, you know Wei would never allow anyone else to do it. Give a cop that much access to the Dragons? No way in hell. I'm surprised he agreed to let *me* do it."

Constance gave him a shrewd look. "Since when do you need Wei's permission to do anything?"

Allen ran a hand through his hair before answering. God, Constance could really ride a horse to death.

"I'm trying to keep things as civil as I can. For you and for Winston. We're finally starting to fix our relationship, and I don't want to screw all of that up by pissing off Wei. Besides," he added ruefully, "I don't trust any other cops. I don't know who might be on Hwang's payroll."

"You don't know how long this will last, do you?"

"No idea. Might be weeks, might be months." *Months.* He tried not to let the thought sink its hooks into his mind. If he thought too much about it, he'd drive himself crazy.

"And you're okay with that?" Constance asked. She had her head tilted toward him, the curtain of her dark hair falling over the other shoulder.

Allen didn't meet her eyes, knowing what she would see in them if he did. "Investigations take time," he said with a shrug. "There's not much I can do."

"That's not what I meant and you know it. Are you going to be able to spend time in close quarters with Conroy Wong after everything?"

"That's ancient history," Allen said, his mouth suddenly dry.

"Uh huh. Look, you two have history together. Neither of you really like how it turned out—"

"If by that you mean Conroy hates me, then yeah, you're right," Allen snapped, surprised by his own bitterness. He was responsible for this, so he didn't have any right to be angry. "It doesn't matter, though. I have a job to do."

"Is this about the job?" Constance asked delicately. She didn't flinch when Allen turned suddenly blazing eyes on her, but the corners of her mouth turned down.

"What else would it be about, Constance?" Allen's voice was taut, like a bowstring stretched back to an archer's ear.

Constance straightened. "I don't know, Allen. Maybe this is less about the job and more about Conroy?"

"Why would it be about Conroy?"

"I just—I don't—" Constance hesitated.

"Don't stop now," Allen said. He sounded alien to his own ears. "Why would it be about Conroy?"

"I'm not sure...that you're over him," she finished in a soft voice.

A bubble of near-manic laughter erupted. "You think I still have a thing for Conroy? After more than five years? Come on, Constance. That's ridiculous. We weren't even together for very long in the first place."

"That's true," she said, "but relationships forged in fire like yours was, they tend to deepen quickly. Just look at Wei and Noah."

"I'm not still pining after him, Constance," Allen told her. "I let go of him a long time ago. Besides, I was the one who left, remember?" He reached and took his sister's hands. "This is just work, Constance. I know that."

The look on Constance's face told him all he needed to know, but at least she didn't say anything, and he was grateful for that. He didn't know how long he could keep up the argument.

Constance squeezed his hands, and he clung to them for a moment, enjoying the comfort he drew from the contact. He released her hands suddenly, cleared his throat, and stood up.

"I should be getting back to work. I'll see you when I come back later."

Fourteen

CONROY'S JAW ACHED from clenching it—his hands too, clinging to the steering wheel so hard his knuckles were white.

Awkward silence filled the car as he drove. Wei sat next to him in the passenger seat, Chris and Steel behind them. No one brought up what had just gone down, and Conroy appreciated it.

He couldn't believe Wei had agreed to have him babysat by a cop—and not just any cop, but goddamn *Allen Hong*. Wei knew their history better than anyone, him and Constance. It almost felt like a betrayal, Wei putting him in that position.

Conroy couldn't help but send a glare Wei's direction.

Unfortunately for him, Wei caught it. "Listen, Conroy..."

"It's cool, Boss," Conroy said quickly, eyes flicking toward Chris and Steel in the rearview mirror. "Don't worry about it."

"No, it ain't cool, Conroy. Stop running your mouth and hear me out. I know you don't like this idea, but it was the best option."

"Best option for who?" Conroy knew he sounded like a petulant child.

"For all of us," Wei seemed like he was trying to be patient. "We don't need the police breathing down our necks—you know that. I know you don't think it's such a big deal, but I'm taking the Jiang threat seriously. If Hwang is willing to gun down a police officer in front of witnesses, then these guys would have no problem killing you. I don't want to risk your life."

"Then I'll bunk with some of the Dragons," Conroy offered.

"I can't spare any for guard duty. With Hwang in jail, the Twisted Vipers are going to start doing shit, and you know it. I need as many bodies on the streets as I can get."

"Then put me on the streets!" Conroy cried, louder than he wanted to. He was very aware of the way Wei's eyes narrowed and the wide-eyed gazes of Chris and Steel in the backseat.

"No," Wei said, his tone brooking no argument or questions. "I know this is uncomfortable, but you've got to get over it. Put your personal issues aside. Hopefully this nonsense won't take too long and we can get on with our business."

Easy for you to say. You're not the one who'll be spending the night with him.

Just the thought of it all made his blood boil. It was bad enough being forced to have a babysitter, as if he couldn't take care of himself, but to have it be Hong of all people? That was just adding insult to injury.

And also put him in danger of going to jail for assaulting a police officer.

Wei's mind was made up, though, so Conroy remained silent. Didn't mean he couldn't glower though, so glower he did.

"That face isn't going to put anyone at ease, you know," Steel said from the back. "Looks like you're ready to punch someone out."

"Yeah, and if you're not careful, it's going to be you."

"Whoa, Conroy. Chill," Steel said, eyes widening.

"It wasn't too long ago that you were the one running around like you just wanted to pick a fight," Wei remarked, their eyes meeting in the mirror. It was mild, but it was without a doubt a rebuke, and Steel stopped talking.

The awkward silence returned, but only for a moment before Wei's phone rang. Wei didn't say anything, just listened. After nodding his head several times, he swore loudly and hung up.

"Conroy, we need to get to the *ye shi.*"

Conroy didn't bother asking which night market; there were several in the Eastern District, but only one the Dragons frequented, near the public bath they used. That *ye shi* was known as a Dragon hangout.

Conroy also didn't have to ask if it was serious; Wei's face was dark, storm clouds rolling in on the horizon of his eyes.

Conroy drove as fast as possible given the late-afternoon traffic, and it still took them nearly fifteen minutes to get there. Exiting the car, Conroy could hear cries and shouts coming from the night market on the other side of the buildings to their right.

What the hell is going on over there?

The four of them took off at a run for the alleyway serving as the entrance. Conroy had just the slightest apprehension going into the alley after what had happened to him earlier, but he wasn't about to get intimidated, not when he was needed.

It took a moment for him to process what he saw when he entered the night market. It wasn't too crowded yet, daylight remaining, but there were still a large crowd of people, not counting the vendors setting up their stalls. All of those people were running in all directions, dodging and shoving each other, climbing over stalls, crying out in panic.

"What the hell—?" Conroy couldn't find the source of the chaos initially, and then he saw them: six men, definitely not Dragons, sporting triad tattoos along their arms and necks, each carrying a weapon—baseball bats, crowbars, a thick piece of rebar. They were trashing the place, taking swings at the crowds as they ran by, wrecking stalls, and throwing merchandise around.

"*Hey!*" Wei yelled, his sharp, commanding voice managing to be heard over the noise. The men stopped briefly in response. "What the fuck do you *puk gai* think you're doing?"

"Look who's here." One of the four sneered. He had a crowbar, and even from a distance, Conroy could see the Twisted Viper tattoo on his forearm. "You fuckers looking to have some fun, then?"

Conroy cracked his knuckles, feeling the familiar anticipation before a fight building up in him. It would do him some real good, working his anger out on these *ong lan gau*. The poor bastards didn't know what they were in for.

Conroy didn't wait for Wei's lead on this one; he knew exactly what he had to do. He made for the nearest Viper, who'd turned over a pork bun cart and battered the exterior with a dinged-up metal baseball bat. Conroy's sudden movement surprised the guy. He'd barely got the bat raised to manage a weak swing.

Conroy caught the swinging bat with one hand and landed a punch square on the bastard's jaw with the other. The blow sent him sprawling onto his ass without the bat. The man spit blood and glared at Conroy.

Conroy tossed the bat aside, reaching down and hauling the Viper to his feet. He punched him twice more, once in the stomach and then again in the face before releasing him to fall back over the pork bun stall he'd been vandalizing.

Eager for more, Conroy looked around and decided his next target. Chris had backed one of the remaining five men into a corner and was dodging swings from a piece of rebar. A second man was moving in on him, crowbar at the ready.

Conroy charged the crowbar-wielding Viper, jumping over several tossed-aside boxes of T-shirts on the way there. This guy was more alert than the first, though; at Conroy's approach he stopped advancing on Chris and drew back the crowbar. His first swing nearly caught Conroy's head and would have if he hadn't darted away to avoid it. A second downward swipe clattered loudly against the concrete as it struck where Conroy's right foot had been moments before.

Conroy kicked, hard, hitting the *puk gai* in the stomach. That guy was more dangerous *and* more prepared; with that crowbar, Conroy was going to have a hell of a time getting in close enough to take him out. He cast his eyes around for a weapon, anything, and his eyes fell on a round piece of PVC pipe, probably broken off an awning pole of one of the stands.

He scooped it into his hands just in time to fend off another overhead swing of the crowbar. The impact reverberated all the way up Conroy's arm to his shoulder, making him wince. He heard the PVC crack, even saw white chips fly about, but it didn't break entirely.

Conroy took a few warning swings with the PVC pipe, keeping his adversary at a distance. He would have to be very careful about this, unless he wanted to end up with a broken bone courtesy of this ugly bastard.

Somewhere nearby he heard a cry of pain followed by a crash. It wasn't hard to find the source; Wei had sent the Viper who'd spoken when they'd arrived crashing into a table that had been stacked with crates of bootleg DVDs and CDs.

The sound disrupted Conroy's opponent, and he took his chance. Conroy stepped up, drawing back the PVC pipe as hard as he could before striking his opponent in the arm holding the crowbar, just above the elbow.

The crowbar clattered to the ground as the man let out a howl of pain. Conroy laid him out with a right hook, a feeling of satisfaction jolting through him, powerful enough to override the pain in his fist from its encounter with the bastard's face.

He stood over the downed man, hoping he would get up, for any excuse to continue wailing on him. That little encounter barely deserved to be called a fight; his desire to beat the shit out of someone hadn't abated in the slightest. Unfortunately, this guy wasn't getting up anytime soon.

Conroy started to help Chris, but as he looked, Chris had the Viper doubled over and a rough knee to the stomach was enough to put him down entirely.

Steel was a bit too wild when it came to fist fights, too reckless, took too many risks. He had a busted lip already but continued to grin; the Viper before him was in far worse condition. In a few minutes, Conroy doubted he'd be able to see out his left eye, and his nose sat awkwardly on his face then, off-kilter.

Steel looked about ready to knock him out cold, but Wei stopped him. The fight was over because Wei was done. The Vipers had been stomped, and Conroy doubted any of them would be making a play for the market again.

"Listen real good right now, motherfucker." Wei took the last standing Viper's shirt in his fist and drew him in until they were nose to nose. "You go back and you tell Jiang and the rest of those *ong lan gau* that the next time they make a move on my territory, their men won't be coming back to them in such good condition. Clear?"

The spineless Viper nodded his head rapidly, looking terrified. Wei released his shirt forcefully, spitting to the side. "Get your friends out of here before I decide not to be so forgiving."

Conroy watched them collect themselves and stagger off, wishing Wei hadn't been. Here, in this situation, on these streets, he wouldn't question Wei. Still, he couldn't help but feel that this wasn't the end, but the beginning.

Fifteen

ALLEN HAD BARELY walked through the doors of the precinct before his cell phone rang. He sighed, stopping in the large lobby and stepping out of the way of flow of traffic. The number on the caller ID was Leung's. Allen figured he should answer. He couldn't think of a reason for the call, didn't know what to expect.

"This is Hong." He hoped Leung would keep it short.

"Hong, this is Leung. We got a call from someone who said they found a gun in an alley in Siu Sai Wan. Figured it might have something to do with the Yang shooting, so you should be the one to take care of it. I'll send the address in a text."

"All right, I'll get there as soon as I can. Send it on over. Are there any uniforms on the scene?"

"No. The woman who found it called it in to the triad hotline, probably assuming that it was triad related."

"Okay, I'm on my way."

Allen had a strange feeling, but that was no doubt more to do with the necessity of interacting with Leung than anything else. He didn't trust that sonofabitch at all. A murder weapon was an essential part of any prosecution; without it their chance of getting a conviction was cut in half, and he needed to follow all leads.

Siu Sai Wan was about a ten-minute walk from Indulgence, close to the ocean. The air smelled of fish and salt, a smell Allen always found comforting. He loved the ocean, the quiet strength of it, the way its gentle beauty could turn to mighty, powerful rage. It was something he could appreciate, a reminder of his sister.

The alley was just a stone's throw from the ocean; he could hear seagulls as they called from the late-afternoon sky. It was almost peaceful, if he ignored the fact that he was on his way to collect a possible murder weapon.

Allen made his way to Indulgence first and followed the path to the alley. There were quite a few places that a gun could have been discarded readily.

It didn't make sense for Hwang to have discarded the weapon. Allen tried to follow the reasoning in his mind—it would have been easier if Ao was with him, a second perspective to bounce ideas off of, but his partner was busy pursuing other avenues of investigation, talking to old informants the Anti-Gang Task Force had connected to the Vipers.

Maybe Hwang discarded the gun because there was heat on the whole organization, and to get caught in some raid with a gun that killed a police officer would be damning. It also might have been because he knew the police were coming his way, since Conroy was a witness.

He reached the location and found a woman standing at the entrance, looking around nervously.

"You Inspector Hong?" she asked before he could open his mouth to speak.

"I am," Allen said, taken aback.

"The man I talked to on the phone said you were coming. I found the gun over there." She pointed down the alley.

"How did you come across it?" Allen asked, studying her closely. She appeared to be in her midforties, thin, someone who lived a life of poverty or damn near it. Her hair had a greasy luster, her skin was sallow, and her eyes dulled to the world.

"I come through this alley every day on my way home from work," she answered. "I work up at the fish market down that way. I sell fish cakes. They're good, too. The fish cakes, I mean. Business is tight, so I don't have a car or a bicycle. I walk. Right through this alley on my way home. I damn near tripped over it, otherwise I never would have noticed it was there."

"Did you touch it, move it at all?"

"No, no. I knew better than that. I don't got much money, but I'm not stupid, Inspector."

"Of course not, I didn't mean to imply that you were," Allen said gently. "I'm going to go have a look at the gun, okay?"

"Can I go now?" The woman was antsy; she probably didn't trust the police any more than Wei and his Dragons did.

"Actually, no. I'm going to need to get a formal statement from you when I collect the gun. Just be patient, ma'am; we'll get you home as soon as we can."

She sighed but nodded. Allen made his way down the alley until he spotted the gun. Whichever of Hwang's goons had discarded it—he highly doubted Hwang had done it himself—hadn't taken much care in doing so. It looked like they'd just thrown it down the first dark alley they'd come across, not caring that it could be discovered.

The wiser course of action would have been to throw the gun into the ocean—they weren't far from it, after all. Maybe they were just in a rush to get rid of the weapon, in the wake of Yang's shooting.

Allen crouched down to examine the gun carefully without picking it up. It was a 9mm, just like the kind they suspected had been used to shoot Yang. The coroner's report would be coming back the next day, but Allen and Ao didn't need it to be sure. They'd seen enough gunshot victims.

"I'm one step closer to locking you up, Hwang," he muttered, slipping a pair of gloves on, taking an evidence bag out of his pocket and sealing the gun inside it.

"I'm going to..." He trailed off when he turned back to the entrance to the alley and saw the woman had left. She must have been more spooked by the idea of talking to the police than Allen thought.

That was okay; he knew where she worked if he needed to find her. Right then he needed to get the gun logged in to evidence. He couldn't wait to see the look on Hwang's face when he told him they had the gun.

Sixteen

CONROY LEANED AGAINST the window of Coffee by Constance, unable to stop himself from glowering. The sun had gone down, and Allen had let Constance know he would be there soon.

"Come on, Wei," he'd pleaded. "You can't tell me this is a good idea! Don't make me do this."

"We need the police on this one, Conroy," Wei had explained. "And Hong is the only one I trust. If we don't go along with this, he's going to put the police on you twenty-four seven. That's the last thing we need. I'd rather have you out of commission at night than in protective custody for the foreseeable future."

Conroy couldn't argue with that, and so he resigned himself to his fate. He would just have to deal with Hong. That didn't mean he had to like it, and he would make sure Allen knew that.

When Hong's car came to a stop in front of the coffee shop, Conroy didn't hurry to get in the car. He remained against the window, hands stuffed into his pockets. Hong rolled down the window and stared at Conroy, face showing no indication of his thoughts.

Conroy waited until he knew Hong would be annoyed by his delay and then meandered over, climbing into the backseat behind Hong.

"This isn't a taxi, you know," Hong said shortly once the door closed.

"That's what it is to me." Conroy settled back on the seat in an over-exaggerated motion. "We're not friends, Hong, and I'm not here because I *want* to be. If Wei hadn't told me to do this, I wouldn't be here right now. Just remember that."

Hong's gaze lingered on him in the rearview mirror for a moment, but Conroy turned away to look out the window. The car finally got moving.

You can handle this, he told himself. *Just pretend he's not here.* That was more difficult than it sounded, though. He couldn't help but notice Hong behind the wheel. History and things long unsaid hung in the air between them, almost palpable. They were simply in the car together, and he already felt the pressure of Hong's presence. With every kilometer they traveled, Conroy's mood grew darker.

He'd avoided Hong's presence as much as humanly possible the last five years—which hadn't been so difficult, considering until recently the inspector was *persona non grata* with the Dragons. It was only after the *gweilo* Noah showed up that Hong had become involved in their lives again.

No choice; have to tolerate him for Constance and Winston's sake. Conroy could do a lot for his family, even deal with Hong—in small doses. But this, this took it to another level. He was about spend the entire night, and every night for the foreseeable future, with Hong.

Hopefully he'd have plenty of Twisted Viper ass to kick to keep his rage in check. Constance would not be happy with him if he put Hong in the hospital.

Conroy drew himself out of his thoughts long enough to pay attention to the direction Hong drove. He didn't know what he'd expected, but when he realized they were coming up on Hong's apartment building—the same place he'd been living for nearly ten years—he was surprised.

They got out of the car, not speaking to each other, though Conroy thought Hong looked like he wanted to say something. He hesitated for a moment before leading the way into the building.

Memory tugged insistently at Conroy. The last time he'd shown up at the apartment, he hadn't had the courage to go in. He'd just stood outside, staring up at Hong's window until he could no longer handle the feelings swirling inside him, and left.

Not that he'd talk about that with Hong.

"Might be a little messy," Hong muttered when they reached his door, and he unlocked it. "I wasn't expecting to have guests when I went to work this morning."

"Here I thought the word for someone being taken somewhere against their will was *captive*, not guest," Conroy sneered, stepping inside past Hong.

The place looked much like Conroy remembered it, even after all these years. Hong hadn't so much as relocated the couch. No surprise; the last time Conroy had been inside the apartment—months before his final visit—there hadn't really been a lot of time for anyone to spend at home. They were always rushing out at all hours to deal with whatever turns the battle with the Nine Stars took. And now that he was a cop, Conroy didn't imagine Hong spent much time there, so why bother changing anything.

"I get it," Hong said dryly. "You don't want to be here. Okay. There's not really much we can do about that now, though, so let's just make the best of it."

"Agreed—if by 'make the best of it' you mean do our best to pretend the other person isn't here. Let's just stay the hell out of each other's way."

Hong's jaw tightened, and his eyes took on a detached look Conroy had often seen from cops, the look of someone viewing a situation through their professional filter. That was probably best; this was all business, after all.

"Fine. You know where the shower is. There's the kitchen. I'll get some blankets and a pillow for you to put on the couch."

Conroy grunted. He flopped down on the couch, searching for the remote to the television. His own place didn't have cable, so he fully intended on taking advantage while there.

He glanced over to see Hong go through a clear daily routine. He removed his gun and hung the holster on what looked like a specially made hook near the door. His keys went on a smaller hook next to the gun. He'd always been meticulous about things like that, and on more than one occasion in the past, he'd chided Conroy for the way he'd throw his keys down on the coffee table when he'd visited late at night for—

Not a helpful line of thought, that. Conroy stopped himself and directed his attention back to the remote hunt.

He found it and forced his eyes to the television, where some variety show was showing a series of funny clips and watching various celebrities Conroy had never heard of react to them. Hong passing in front of the television, unbuttoning his shirt, drew his eyes from the screen temporarily before he willed his gaze back to the screen. A minute or two later, the sound of the shower starting came from the back.

Conroy wasn't particularly hungry or thirsty, but he decided to use the kitchen anyway, since it was Hong's. Unfortunately the refrigerator had a rather small selection. There were three eggs, a container of butter, three blueberry yogurts, two unopened containers of tofu, one unopened container of *natto*, and a head of cabbage. At least he had beer— imported Japanese beer, at that. Conroy took a can of Asahi from the fridge.

He had more luck on the food front in the pantry, where he found an unopened bag of potato chips, a loaf of bread, a box of cereal, and beef jerky. He took the potato chips and the jerky and then returned to the living room.

On his way, something on a small bookshelf tucked in the corner of the room caught his attention. He hadn't noticed the bookshelf before; it was the one new addition to the place, the only way it had changed since his last visit.

Conroy put the things he'd scavenged on the coffee table before returning to the bookshelf. Like he'd thought, it was a small Mickey Mouse figurine, one Hong had bought nearly six years ago when the two of them had taken a trip to Hong Kong Disneyland.

Conroy picked it up, turned it over in his hand, and examined the porcelain. It had aged fine, he guessed, though the paint of one gloved hand looked a little faded, and the material of his overalls started to throw off threads.

Why did he keep this? Conroy stared at it. It had no value whatsoever. It had been a stupid impulse purchase, so Hong could remember their time together. It had been a good day, with great weather. They'd been able to distract themselves from the darkness their lives had descended into with the street war, at least for a few hours.

Still, what reason was that to hold on to a memento from a failed relationship? It couldn't have any other memories associated with it.

The discovery made Conroy wonder what else Inspector Hong might have been holding on to.

The sound of the water turning off alerted Conroy to Hong's imminent return. He returned Mickey to his place on the shelf and went back to the couch. By the time Hong emerged from the shower, shirtless and in gray sweatpants, Conroy's beer sat open and he'd started to chow down on the potato chips and jerky.

Conroy resisted the urge to ask Hong the array of questions circling his mind. Answers were tricky things, and Conroy knew this answer might not sit well with him. Instead, he let it lie.

Hong stood there for a moment, looking at Conroy on the couch, helping himself to his food and drinks. He looked like he wanted to say something, but when he spoke, all he said was, "I'm going to bed. Goodnight."

Conroy kept his focus on the television, though his ears strained to catch the sound of the bedroom door closing, feeling like something else, something just as heavy, had been added to the pile of things that lay between them.

Seventeen

THE DREAM EVAPORATED seconds after Allen awoke. Whatever it had been, though, it left him out of breath, body quivering in a cold sweat.

He threw his blankets off and lay there, staring up at the ceiling and waiting for his breathing to return to normal. He turned his head and looked at the time. The clock read 4:58 a.m.

He tried to will himself back to sleep, but he couldn't. He was still tired—it tugged at him, a burning sensation in his eyes he couldn't escape even when he closed them.

Allen couldn't remember his dream, but he couldn't shake the feeling it had something to do with Conroy. He was hyperaware of Conroy's presence in the living room, as he'd been all night. It had been difficult to fall asleep in the first place, listening to the television in the other room.

He remembered Conroy used to go to sleep with the television on, needing the background noise, but it had been a long time since he'd had to deal with that, and he was woefully out of practice. Now he couldn't hear it, so he guessed Conroy'd woken up at some point in the night and turned the television off.

He'd told himself for the last five years that he was over Conroy, that he'd moved on from that whole part of his life the day he'd made the decision to join the police. He'd had no problem maintaining his beliefs all this time, mostly because he'd barely had any contact with Conroy or the Dragons. What few encounters they'd had were tense and cold, and Conroy barely did more than glare at him.

No, it was plain enough for anyone to see where they stood.

Being around Conroy was awkward, bringing up memories better left in the past. This was work, though, and he'd endure a few moments of awkwardness if it meant putting Johnny Hwang behind bars for good.

How could Wei and the Dragons not see he did his best to protect the people of the Eastern District, too? They couldn't see past their own feelings, and that was part of what made him know he'd made the right decision when he'd walked away from that life. It was dangerous, thinking you alone had the right answer. Wei had become convinced that only he knew how to protect these people—only he had their best interests at heart, and anyone who didn't agree with his methods didn't care about the people.

He couldn't blame Wei. He'd lived a hard life, and the corruption in the police department made life difficult—and led to the death of Allen's brother-in-law. Wei wrote the police off entirely after the death, but Allen knew they weren't a lost cause. The corruption could be removed, like a cancer, and the police could be restored to what they were meant to be.

No matter how well-intentioned Wei's actions, no matter that he thought only of the people of the island, he was in the wrong. He couldn't fight against the existence of the triads while maintaining his own group outside the law. He prayed Wei would one day come to see that.

Allen let out a great sigh and opened his eyes once more. There was no way he'd be able to get back to sleep just lying there. Maybe if he got up, drank some water, and then went back to bed, his body would figure out it still had some time to rest before he had to rejoin the waking world.

Allen climbed out of bed and made his way to his bedroom door, keeping quiet so he didn't disturb Conroy. The last thing he wanted to deal with was Conroy's casual, cold hatred. It was somehow a million times worse than if he'd just rage against him.

A long rectangle of blue light fell over Allen when he opened the bedroom door. So, Conroy hadn't cut the television off, just muted it.

It was surreal, creeping through his own apartment in the pre-dawn dark, trying not to disturb a man who hated him so much he could barely tolerate being under the same roof. Allen could almost believe the entire thing was another dream.

The occasional snore came from the couch, reminding him of Conroy's presence—as if he could forget it. He made his way quietly to the kitchen, giving the sofa a wide berth as he did. He didn't want to wake Conroy, but not out of consideration for the sleeping man; he didn't want to deal with the man's ill-concealed disgust, not this early in the morning.

He didn't need to turn the light on to get a glass and fill it with water. He'd been hoping the water would quench his thirst and make it easier for him to sleep, but he was fast losing hope of that.

Conroy's unmissable presence reminded him of *why* he was there, which got an entire other world of worries and concerns running through his head, fears that the hell he'd lived through five years ago would be repeating itself on the streets soon.

On his way back to the bedroom, he decided to turn the television off. The remote rested on Conroy's chest, and Allen stopped mid-reach for it, taken by the sight of him.

Conroy slept on his back, head turned away from the television, an arm thrown over his face, and his other hand resting on his abdomen. The glow from the television made his features stand out.

Conroy slept naked, Allen recalled, but his underwear remained on now. The thin fabric drew his attention first, filled by a pretty hefty bulge—that part Allen hadn't forgotten, even after five years. Conroy had one of the best cocks Allen had ever seen, long and veiny, not too thick, the perfect girth, paired with a set of well-shaped balls.

Conroy's was the only cut cock Allen had ever been with that way because his parents were devout Christian converts, his father even becoming a pastor.

The muscles of Conroy's stomach, chest, and arms were on full display, and Allen couldn't help but look at them in admiration. Conroy had the sort of body men dreamt of, the kind that could only be honed from hours in the gym. Allen always appreciated the work Conroy put into his body, even if the man's primary motivation was vanity.

It took Allen a minute to realize he was staring at Conroy, a man who hated him, and—to make it that much worse—he had a hard-on.

Shame burned hot through his chest and face. Here he was, perving on a sleeping man—a sleeping man who hated him and who he, by all accounts, should hate as well.

His erection remained despite his mind's attempt to punish his actions.

He decided to just leave the television on—it couldn't run the bill up too high, could it?—and go back to bed. It wasn't worth all of this to take the remote from where it rested between the swell of Conroy's pecs.

Just as Allen started to straighten up and return to his bed, his phone rang from his bedroom. Allen was a heavy sleeper once he finally got to sleep, so he had to have the phone's volume as high as it would go to have any chance of hearing it.

"Fuck," he muttered, startled by the noise. He regretted it the moment the word slipped from his lips.

Conroy jerked awake, squinting in the harsh light of the television, clearly bewildered to find Allen standing over him. "What the fuck are you doing?"

Maybe it was because he was half-asleep, but the words lacked the usual derision they carried when he addressed Allen.

"I was just cutting off the television," Allen explained over the loud sound of his phone. He'd selected the most obnoxious ringtone. Now he regretted his decision.

The realization of his remaining hard-on brought enough horror to finally flag his erection, though it was probably too late.

"What's that noise?" Conroy asked, irritation and disdain slowly seeping back into his voice, proportional to his return to wakefulness.

"It's just—it's my phone," Allen explained, trying to find a casual way to stand that didn't show his now semi-erection tenting the front of his sweats.

"Well, whatever it is make it stop," Conroy grunted. "Do you know how hard it was getting to sleep on this god-awful couch?"

Allen, who'd fallen asleep on that couch more times than he could count, did know, and it had never been too hard for him. Forgoing a response, he returned to his bedroom, adjusted the material of his sweats until his deflating cock wasn't so visible, and answered the phone.

Only work would call so early, and seeing Ao's name didn't surprise him.

"You've either got really good news right now, or really bad news," Allen said when he answered the phone.

"I need you to get down to the precinct as soon as you can." The weight of Ao's tone lacked promise for the good news idea.

"Bad news, then." Allen sighed. "Okay, just give me time to get dressed and I'll be there."

He didn't like the idea that he was being summoned to the station before six in the morning. Ao wouldn't have done so if he didn't have a damn good reason, and he dreaded discovering said reason.

He dressed as quickly as he could and returned to the living room, intent on getting out of there. *Fuck,* he thought, glancing at Conroy. *I forgot about* him. He was supposed to keep an eye on Conroy. His plan had been to drive Conroy to Constance's shop when he went in to work. That didn't look to be an option today.

Nothing for it; he had to wake him up and talk to him. "Conroy, wake up." He stood over him, hands on his hips. "Conroy. Conroy!"

"What?" Conroy all but spat the word, turning his head to glare at Allen.

"Something's come up—that was work calling me in. I've got to get there as soon as possible. I'll call Wei later; you need to wait here until a Dragon comes and gets you."

Conroy continued to look blankly at him, showing no indication he'd even heard what he'd said.

"I don't have a lot of time here, Conroy—do you understand?"

"I'm not a fucking elementary schooler, Hong," Conroy growled. "I have ears, and I can hear just fine. I can understand what you're saying."

Allen had to fight back sharp words; they wouldn't make a difference anyway. "Fine." He grabbed his gun and keys and stormed out of his own apartment.

Eighteen

CONROY TOSSED AND turned on the couch after Hong left, trying to get comfortable so he could go back to sleep. It was way too early to wake up. He couldn't manage to do it, though. Every time he closed his eyes, he thought about what he'd woken up to, Hong standing over him, his dick clearly hard.

Had he been touching himself standing over Conroy's sleeping form? Or had the sight of Conroy's body just turned him on so much he couldn't help but get hard?

Not that Conroy could blame him; he knew he was sexy, and he knew from experience that Hong liked his body. That particular rabbit trail of thought led to places Conroy didn't think it wise to visit, memories of his past with Hong.

If he thought about it objectively, removing his current feelings for the *puk gai*, and only thought about their sex life, it had been good. Hong was an attentive lover, and best of all, he was versatile.

Yes, as much as Hong's betrayal had hurt, Conroy could still admit he'd been good in bed.

The memories brought Conroy to annoying stiffness. He was not about to sit here and beat off when it was a bastard like Allen Hong who got him hard. Those times were behind him; Hong had made his choice and his loyalty quite clear.

Conroy's life would have been so much easier if Hong had been a bad lay.

Frustrated, Conroy grabbed the pillow that Hong had given him, covered his face, squeezed his eyes shut, and tried to force himself to sleep. He didn't understand how some people—like Tony or Wei—could basically will themselves to sleep. Conroy, on the other hand, could toss and turn for hours and never fall asleep. It was like the harder he reached, the more it eluded him.

It didn't help that the pillow, the couch, it all smelled like Hong. That was why he had elected not to use the blanket he was given, despite the relative chill in the apartment. Conroy had always preferred being cold to being hot, so it didn't bother him so much.

Finally he had enough. He sat up, tossing the pillow across the room, where it landed and slid over the hardwood floor and came to a stop in front of the refrigerator. He reached for his clothes, which he'd tucked safely out of the way under the coffee table, and barely managed to catch the remote before it slid to the floor.

Once he finished dressing, he checked his phone. It was pushing five forty-five, still too early to call any of the Dragons. Still, he couldn't stay there; he'd drive himself crazy. He'd prefer to chase sleep in the comfort of his own bed.

Before he left, he considered sending a message to Wei to let him know where he went, but decided to wait. He didn't want the message to wake Wei. The boss was angry in the morning; he knew that from personal experience.

When he got to the street, a light fog lingered from the night before, hovering a foot or so above the ground. He felt damp from the fog, which only amplified the bite of morning air.

It was bad enough he was leaving Hong's alone; if he walked back to his place—which was too far to feasibly do, anyway—Wei would be even angrier, so a taxi seemed like the best solution. Luckily Hong's apartment was on a busy street, so he didn't have to wait long before one came into sight.

He flagged it down and climbed inside. It was nice to be out of the fog, even if the driver kept the interior of the taxi too warm for his liking. It wasn't very far, anyway. He gave the driver his address and slouched back on the seat, taking some small pleasure at the thought of what Hong's face would look like if he returned to find Conroy gone.

He'd be pissed, but Conroy didn't care about that. He wasn't particularly concerned with Hong's feelings. Hong would probably go whining about it to Wei, though, and Wei would be annoyed, too. The best way to head that off was to get to Wei before Hong could. He'd have plenty of time. He wanted to change clothes and shower in his own place at least.

Conroy was glad to be out of the taxi once it reached his apartment; the heat, combined with the steadily grown smell of the taxi driver himself, who'd probably been in the car the whole night, had started to make him light-headed. He gulped in fresh, crisp air as he paid the taxi driver.

As he climbed the stairs to his apartment, he was surprised to find that he was actually getting sleepy again. Perhaps he'd actually manage to get another hour or two of sleep before catching up with the Dragons.

He dug his key out of his pocket when he reached the landing of his floor, ready to get the door open and get inside. When he inserted the key into the door, however, it swung inward without him even turning the key.

If he hadn't been so tired, perhaps he would have noticed that the door had been busted. Whoever had entered hadn't bothered to pick the lock, instead opting to kick the door in.

You've got to pay attention to what's going on around you, he told himself sharply. He forced his tiredness away, slowly opening the door, doing his best to make sure the hinges didn't squeak in case whoever had done this was still in there.

The apartment was mostly dark, the morning sun having yet to rise high enough to cast its light into the windows. Conroy entered, body tense and ready. He swept his gaze carefully over the main room, looking for any signs of the intruder or intruders.

Strangely enough, the apartment remained as he had left it. That told him whoever was there was there for him and not his things. The list of who could be behind it was very narrow, and this whole thing smelled of Johnny Hwang.

The man—or, more likely, his redpoles—must be getting desperate if they were making a move on him again. Maybe he'd scoffed at the potential danger he was in too quickly.

The living room clear, Conroy made his way toward his bedroom. His unease grew with each step. He stopped when he thought he heard the floorboards creak. There was a loose board near his bedroom door, a place he'd long since learned to avoid.

Someone was in his bedroom.

Conroy's fists were still sore from the scuffle in the *ye shi*, but he was always ready for a fight. Maybe he could get the drop on whoever was in his room. Hopefully there wasn't more than one. In the small space of his bedroom, he wouldn't have the space to fight two guys at once. It would be a disadvantage on both sides, but more on his than theirs.

As he drew closer, Conroy saw that the bedroom door was open. Just before he reached it, a broad-shouldered figure came out of the doorway into the hall, looking right at Conroy. He was a big brute of a man, appearing as if he'd used steroids to bulk up. His face had the look of a man who'd engaged in multiple fights, or else had something smashed against it repeatedly.

This man didn't hesitate; he moved for Conroy, using the narrow space of the hallway to his advantage. Before Conroy could properly react, the man had one beefy fist around his throat. He maneuvered Conroy around, slamming him against the wall.

Conroy tried to break the man's grip with his right hand, but his would-be assassin grabbed his wrist and pinned it to the wall, too.

"I've got a message from Jiang for you," the man said, his voice cold and grating. "You should have just been smart and kept your mouth shut, *puk gai.*"

Conroy pressed his right foot against the wall and used it to launch himself forward. The move was enough to throw the man off-balance, and Conroy was able to free himself from the man's hold. He brought his knee up hard into the man's groin, doubling him over. Conroy might have been outmatched size-wise, but he had plenty of experience defending himself and wasn't afraid to fight dirty. Survival was what mattered, and he'd take a cheap shot if it meant staying alive.

Conroy slammed his elbow into the back of the man's head with as much force as he could muster, ignoring the jarring pain shooting up his arm. He did it one more time for good measure, and the man collapsed like a heavy sack, body thudding to the floor with a nauseating noise. Shit was starting to get out of hand.

He pulled out his phone, intent on calling Wei, but decided against it. It would be easier to talk to him about all of this in person, anyway. He took a moment to make sure that the *gai tsan* was actually unconscious before he beat a hasty retreat.

Nineteen

THE EARLY MORNING shift change had just taken place when Allen arrived at the precinct. He passed several inspectors and officers looking tired and more than ready for their bed—though Allen knew a few of them would make for the nearest girly bar and have a drink or two to send off the night. Most of them rationalized it with the logic that they'd just left work, so it was still nighttime for them.

Ao was nowhere to be seen when Allen reached the bullpen. Allen sighed, hoping Ao hadn't forgotten he'd put in the call and gone home. People did strange things when they were tired, and Ao had pulled double duty the previous day.

Still, his tone hadn't sounded like it was trivial enough for him to forget about it and go home.

Allen was about to try calling him when Ao suddenly bustled past him, motioning with his eyes for Allen to follow. Allen cautiously followed.

Ao led him into the hallway that went to the back stairwell. He looked nervous, like he didn't want to be caught. Everything about his behavior put Allen on edge.

"What's going on, Ao? What's with all of this hush-hush shit? I feel like I'm in some bad spy movie."

"Internal Affairs." Ao glanced up the stairwell as if merely mentioning the department would conjure them, like ghosts or demons.

Allen's stomach lurched. Anything involving IA was bad news. While Allen didn't have anything against them for what they did—god knew the police needed someone keeping an eye on them, though they didn't seem to be doing such a great job of policing the police—but most IA people he'd met were completely arrogant douchebags, like they were somehow better than the rest.

"What about them?"

"They've been here all night. First they talked to all the people on the Anti-Gang Task Force. Then, about two hours ago, they called me in to have 'a little chat,' you know."

"What are they asking questions about? Yang's murder?" Allen didn't know why they would be investigating that, though, since it didn't fall under their purview. Unless they thought Yang was dirty? No, that was ridiculous. With the man's record, they'd have to jump to some pretty big conclusions to come up with corruption.

"They didn't ask anything about that, not directly. They were asking about *you*, man."

Allen felt dazed for a moment. Why would Internal Affairs ask about him? He'd never done anything to put himself in their crosshairs. Were they starting to think him suspicious because of his past? But he'd cleared every hurdle when they let him into the academy, and his past connection to the people who were now the Dragons had never been an issue before.

"What did they want to know?" Allen barely registered his own voice.

"At first it seemed real general—how long I'd been your partner, what I thought about how you conducted investigations. Then it got weird."

The sound of a stairwell door opening silenced Ao. He stared at the stairs, waiting for someone to appear, but no one did, and soon another door creaked open, farther away.

"How did it get weird?" Allen asked when the door clicked shut.

"They started asking if you had any personal stakes in Hwang going down, things like that. I told them we all had personal stakes in bringing that *puk gai* down, that pretty much every person living on the island should. That's when they got to the point and asked me if I believed you would ever falsify or fabricate evidence to bring Hwang down."

Sweat broke out across Allen's forehead. His breathing hitched, and he felt like his brain wasn't getting enough oxygen. "They don't seriously think I did that, do they?"

"You ever known IA to ask questions like that for no reason, Allen?"

Ao was right, of course. Allen needed to sit down.

"Don't worry about it," Ao said encouragingly. "No one in their right mind would think you were capable of doing anything like that. This is just Internal Affairs being their typical asshole selves, wanting to get involved now that something's gotten big. Even if they investigate you, it's not like they're going to find anything, so just let them do their thing and then go back under their slimy rock when they're finished."

Allen inclined his head, not trusting himself to speak in that moment.

"Okay, we should probably get back out there. IA might have suggested to not have any contact with you since you're under investigation. Besides, I'm tired as fuck after yesterday."

Allen nodded, still not able to get his thoughts collected. Ao must have understood because he just patted Allen's shoulder as he left the stairwell.

Nausea hit Allen suddenly, and he hurried to the men's restroom. He leaned against the cold porcelain sink, gripping it tightly with both hands, head ducked down.

Get ahold of yourself. This is just some misunderstanding, and once you talk to Internal Affairs it will all get sorted out. He desperately needed to believe that.

He turned the water on as cold as it would go and splashed his face. When he looked in the mirror, water dripping off the end of his nose, he didn't like the fear he saw in his eyes.

He didn't want to leave the bathroom, knowing full well that plenty of people out there had probably already been talked to by IA, and if they hadn't, they would have at least heard that questions were being asked. They would all be suspicious of him now, and even if they didn't say it, their faces would show it; of that he had no doubt.

Still, he couldn't hide in the bathroom forever. He wasn't that kind of man. If he had an obstacle ahead of him, he faced it head-on.

He took another moment to steel himself and dry his face before he left the bathroom. As soon as he emerged, he was face-to-face with two men dressed in suits. He could tell from their attitude they were Internal Affairs.

One was tall, his features telling Allen that one of his parents wasn't Asian. The other, though shorter, had broader shoulders and a heavy, brooding brow.

"Inspector Hong," said the shorter man. "I'm Inspector Wu; this is Inspector Leong. We're with Internal Affairs. We would like to have a few words with you, if we may have a moment of your time."

"What's this about, exactly?" Allen asked neutrally. He didn't want to be too confrontational and tip them off that he knew about their suspicions; if he did, they'd either know someone—probably Ao—had talked to him, or else they'd think the hostility was coming from a place of guilt or fear of being caught. Either way was bad for him.

"This will only take a few minutes," Leong said, his expression polite. These men were probably expert poker players. Allen would have to be very careful interacting with them.

Allen sighed and made a *lead the way* gesture. He followed behind the two as they led him to one of the interrogation rooms. Leong entered ahead of him and Wu held the door open for Allen.

"Not the friendliest of places to have a little chat," Allen remarked. Neither man said anything.

Allen leaned against the wall as far from the interrogation table as possible. He would remain equal as long as possible. Sitting down at that table would give them the upper hand, turning into an interrogation of a criminal and not an interview of a cop.

"We'd like to talk to you about the investigation into Inspector Yang's murder," Leong said, sitting on the edge of the table while Wu paced.

"That investigation's barely begun," Allen said carefully. "I don't know how much there is to talk about."

"You're the lead investigator, correct?" asked Leong, ignoring Allen's words.

"Yes." Allen was a cop; he knew the wisdom of keeping your answers short and simple. Never offer more in answer than the question asked.

"Do you not think it's a conflict of interest, giving your personal connection to the case?" That question, asked gruffly, accusatory tone unhidden, came from Wu.

"I wasn't aware I *had* a personal connection to the case."

Wu snorted. "Don't play dumb. Everyone knows about your connections to the Dragons."

"My connections to the Dragons ended long before the conflict between the Dragons and the Vipers existed." Allen didn't let his tone get defensive; he wouldn't give them a button to push.

"Is that so?" Leong crossed his arms over his chest. "So you don't have any contact with the Dragons now?"

Allen knew better than to lie. "I didn't say that. My sister has connections to the Dragons, so I do occasionally see them when I visit her."

"Your nephew is also involved in the gang, right?" Leong added.

"He is, but my relationship with him has been strained, so I don't know how helpful knowing that is."

"What we're trying to figure out, Inspector Hong, is if you have a personal motivation for wanting to take down Johnny Hwang."

Allen rolled his eyes. "It isn't enough that he's a murderer, a drug dealer, and killed a cop on top of it all? There has to be something else for me to want him off the streets?"

Wu came around the table then, approaching Allen. He moved in a predatory fashion, like a shark cutting through water, zeroing in on blood. "Just how badly do you want him off the streets?"

Allen didn't blink at the blatant intimidation attempt. "Probably about as bad as every other officer on the island, especially after he gunned down Inspector Yang. I think there's a room full of men upstairs who'd gladly do him in themselves."

"What can you tell me about this?" Leong's segue was abrupt. He picked up an evidence bag from the floor beside the interrogation table. It had been tucked out of Allen's sight until that moment. They clearly hoped the reveal would spark some reaction in him, but remained neutral. If he hadn't heard from Ao before IA caught him, he'd definitely have been surprised.

"That's a gun I logged as potential evidence in the Yang case," he said promptly.

"Tell us about how you came to have this gun."

Allen told them the story—the phone call from Leung, meeting the woman at the mouth of the alley.

"Your report doesn't name the woman," Wu pointed out. "Why?"

"Because she didn't tell me her name." Allen started to let his impatience show. "People in her situation don't exactly trust the cops—maybe you've forgotten that, since it's probably been a while since you've been on the streets. I was lucky enough to get her to stand around and tell me what she told me."

"Was that the first time you've met this woman?" Wu asked.

"Yes. Why the hell wouldn't it have been?"

"You find her story to be believable?"

"I don't know why she would have lied," Allen said in exasperation.

"Money, perhaps?"

Allen straightened just a little. "What the hell does that mean?"

"It means that it's possible someone paid her to say what she said, to make the phone call she made."

"And you think that someone is me." It wasn't a question.

"Would it surprise you to learn that this gun—" Leong brandished the evidence bag, as if Allen could forget what gun he was talking about. "—has never been fired? Not once."

"Yes, that would surprise me," Allen said. Who the hell would throw away a brand-new gun? When most people got rid of firearms, it was because they didn't want to be connected to them.

"Well, it hasn't. Which means it can't be the weapon used to kill Richard Yang."

"I think you already knew that, though," Wu added. "Didn't you, Inspector Hong?"

"Of course I didn't," Allen snapped. "I was just doing my job and responding to potential evidence in the case. I logged it like I was supposed to. It's not up to me to make a determination about whether or not it's the murder weapon. That's for the lab."

"It's convenient that you were the one who found the weapon."

"I didn't find it. I didn't even receive the original call. Inspector Leung of the Anti-Gang Task Force did. I just went because he suggested it might be connected to the case, considering the location of the discarded weapon."

It hit Allen then. He'd been set up. He should have known there was something suspicious about the whole thing when he'd gotten the call. He knew Leung couldn't be trusted, and yet he'd gone anyway. He should have taken backup.

That was the sort of amateur mistake that he knew better than to make.

"If you're going to accuse me of something, do it now," he said through gritted teeth.

"Don't worry, we're investigating your actions," Wu said slowly. "And if we determine you had anything to do with planting evidence, we'll take you down."

Leong stood up from the table and adjusted his coat. "In the meantime, you're off the Yang murder. You're going to be on desk duty until further notice."

"Fine," Allen growled. He didn't wait for them to dismiss him; he barged out of the interrogation room and stomped through the bullpen. There was no way in hell he was going to sit there at his desk, not as pissed off as he was.

When he passed Superintendent Dang's office, the door was open and Dang stood there, face a mask, watching him as he left.

Twenty

"DO YOU WANT some coffee?" Noah asked Conroy, yawning through the last word.

"No," Conroy replied from where he sat slumped on the couch in Wei and Noah's apartment. "I wouldn't say no to a beer, though. Just kidding," he added when Noah made a start for the refrigerator.

"So Wei's been out all night?"

"Uh-huh." It was plain from the short sounds of the affirmation just what Noah thought about that. "It's been happening a lot since the mess with the Dark Streets. I hate it."

"The boss has a lot of responsibilities on his shoulders," Conroy said, doing his best to sound comforting. He liked Noah a lot and thought he was one of the best things that could have happened to Wei. "It's not easy being him sometimes."

"It's not easy dating him sometimes, either," Noah said.

Conroy snickered. "Yeah, I imagine he keeps that ass sore, right?"

"*Ga tsan,*" Noah said, sitting on the couch next to Conroy with his cup of freshly brewed coffee. He turned to the news.

The news report was all in Cantonese, so Conroy knew Noah didn't understand most of it, but with the pictures and videos, he could get the gist.

"You know there's channels that do the news in English," he said.

"I want to hear it in Cantonese. I need to practice. What is this story about? Looks like some kind of fire?"

Conroy read the scrolling bar at the bottom of the screen. "Overnight warehouse fire claims four lives."

"Where was that at?"

"Twisted Viper territory," Conroy replied grimly.

"Why the hell would they be doing this in their own territory? It doesn't make any sense."

"I don't know if you've been given the best example of what life is like under triad rule, Noah. The Dragons do things differently. The triads like the Twisted Vipers, though, they rule through fear. With Hwang out of the picture—even if it is temporary—people might start thinking they don't need to worry about the Vipers anymore. This is probably some business owner who decided he wasn't going to pay protection money anymore, or a drug supplier who decided to abandon their deals and what's left of the Twisted Viper leadership is trying to maintain control. Set an example, you see? Show everyone what happens if they start thinking the Vipers might be weak."

"So what you're saying is that in some ways having Hwang in prison is worse than having him on the streets." Noah frowned. "This is a complicated world, man."

"Hwang is a scumbag, no question," Conroy said, rubbing his fingers against his forehead and hoping they could ward off the beginning of a headache. "But he'd established control over the Vipers, kept a check on their urges, kept them from running wild doing whatever they wanted. He directed their violence for his own means, but at least it was a little under control. Now..." Conroy shook his head. "Now I'm afraid of what might go down there. It's only going to get worse from here."

Noah's eyes widened. "How so?"

"The longer Hwang is behind bars and it gets more likely that he's going to be put away, then we'll start seeing redpoles getting ideas," Conroy explained patiently. He'd lived so long in the world that sometimes he forgot there were people who didn't know how things worked. He envied Noah that sometimes.

"His men are going to start thinking they have what it takes to assume his spot and become the dragonhead. And if anyone else makes a move—"

"Then one of the other redpoles will decide they'd be better in charge and make their own power play," Noah finished.

"Exactly." Conroy nodded grimly.

"Jesus."

Conroy could see on Noah's face that he understood something of what they were dealing with now. He wasn't surprised, really: Noah had already suffered at the hands of a renegade Twisted Viper redpole. His sister had been murdered, and he'd nearly met the same fate.

"How do we stop all of this?"

Conroy didn't know what to say. He'd mulled over that question, and unfortunately the more he thought about it, the more undeniable the answer became. "Not without bloodshed."

Noah tensed next to him. Glancing at Noah's hands around his coffee cup, Conroy could see his knuckles were white. His face, though, was a mask. He didn't show whatever it was he was feeling. He'd learned quickly.

Shortly after Noah's rescue from that asshole Tong, Conroy had taken him aside. "Looks like you're here to stay," he'd said. "I don't think that's a bad thing. I'm happy for the boss—and for you, for that matter. But you have to understand something: he's going to always be worried about you. Nothing we can do about that, really. But we can help alleviate it a little. You have to be strong for him, show him that you're fine. If he's worried about you being worried about him, that's just going to complicate his life, put him more at risk. You've got to be strong for him, even when you're terrified. Got it?"

Noah had nodded, face serious.

At least I know he got the message.

The news program came to an end, replaced by one of those morning talk shows where hosts sat around a table and talked to health experts and got cooking recipes. Neither of them said another word until Wei returned.

When Wei did finally come in, he looked exhausted but unharmed, and he was with Tony, which didn't surprise Conroy. Conroy would have liked it better if it had been him with Wei, of course, but if it couldn't be him, there was no one better to watch Wei's ass than Tony.

Noah didn't make a big deal about Wei's return, though he did pull him into a tight hug. "You two need coffee, right?"

"Please," Wei said gratefully, and Noah hurried to the kitchen to fix two mugs. Wei started for the couch and stopped when he saw Conroy sitting there. Conroy almost laughed at the look on his face—almost. "What are you doing here?"

Conroy hesitated to explain, seeing how Wei had clearly not gotten any sleep, but delaying it would do him no good, so he filled him in on everything that had happened that morning, with the exception of Hong's raging morning wood. When he reached the attack in his apartment, Wei let out a string of curses.

"We've got to do something about this shit." Wei sat on the arm of the couch, arms crossed over his chest. His expression softened for just a moment as he took the coffee Noah offered him. "Luckily, Tony and I thought up a plan."

"It's mostly your plan," Tony argued. "The crazy parts, anyway, and that's almost all of it."

"What's this plan?" Conroy asked.

"Do you want me to go to the bathroom or something?" Noah asked. He was no doubt used to being sent away when Dragons business was discussed.

"No," Wei said firmly. "I'm not going to have you hiding in your own home. I don't care if you hear this. The plan is to reach out to the people in Twisted Viper territories where their hold might not be so strong, places led by lieutenants with the least influence."

Conroy leaned back, having a hard time processing at the idea. Tony had been right about one thing, at least: it was crazy. "What's the point of it? What are we going to try to accomplish?"

"We're going to get them to join us. Hear me out," Wei added before Conroy could tell him just how stupid he thought that plan was. "These will be the people with the least to gain from Hwang's arrest. A lot of them would actually suffer as rival redpoles take the chance to expand their territories. Some of these people will be at risk."

"I've got to agree with Tony that it sounds crazy," Conroy said after considering it.

"Something's got to be done," Wei said, coming to his feet. "If it's not, then we're going to lose this peace we sacrificed for. I won't give it up without trying every option. Besides, I think there's something both of you are forgetting."

"What's that?" Tony asked.

"The Blue Suns."

A chill ran down Conroy's back all the way to his feet. Three simple words, that was it, but fear—true fear—rose in him.

"If they sense weakness, any at all, they'll come to take the island," Wei agreed, fists clenched. "They make the Nine Stars look like us. They're brutal, beyond violent. Human trafficking, sex slaves, drugs, assassinations. You name it, they do it. Any fight we have with the Twisted Vipers wouldn't even be a warm-up against them. We've got to do something, and soon."

"You're right." Conroy buried his face in his palms. "The crazy plan suddenly doesn't sound so unreasonable."

Twenty-One

ALLEN'S RAGE DIDN'T leave him as the day progressed. It simmered beneath the surface, bringing heat to his face. He decided the best way for him to blow off steam would be at the gym.

He went through his normal routine, and when that wasn't enough, he hit the punching bag until his arms went numb and he didn't have the strength to raise them again.

When he thought he might finally have a handle on his anger, he showered and returned to work, but only long enough to discreetly take pictures of his files on the Yang murder case under the pretext of assembling them to hand over to Internal Affairs.

He saw Ao several times in the bullpen, and their eyes met briefly every now and then, but he made no attempt to interact, not wanting to draw the attention of IA to him. With Allen being taken off the case, Ao had become the new lead investigator by default. He probably hated it, but it would help Allen, because it meant he still had a connection to the case whom he trusted.

As the afternoon wore on, Allen noticed that Leong and Wu kept finding reasons to be in his basic vicinity. Having their eyes constantly on him felt like a slap in the face, considering he'd joined the force to fight against its corruption from the inside—corruption like Henry Dang. How was it men like Dang continued to get away with their crimes while those charged with investigating corruption kept their focus on the wrong men?

It was a pretty shitty way for the universe to be. But wasn't that the way it always was? He wasn't one of those people who had a cheery outlook on life. As a homicide inspector, he saw horrendous murders, and before that, he'd seen the worst humanity had to offer.

There was little use in complaining about something he couldn't change, so instead he decided to focus on the things he *could*, and right then the thing he could change was bringing Johnny Hwang and his entire organization to the ground.

While still at the gym. he'd received a message from Wei telling him Conroy was fine and with the Dragons and would be at Constance's at sundown, and Allen headed out just the sky darkened. This was his only solid chance to take Hwang down, and he wasn't about to let that slip through his fingers.

He did his best to ignore the heavy gazes of Wu and Leong on him as he left. He didn't think they'd reached the point where they would follow him, but he didn't want to take any chances, so he paid close attention to who was behind him as he drove to Coffee by Constance. None of the cars flagged his attention.

On the way, he made a call to Ao's desk phone.

"Inspector Cheung," Ao said when he answered.

"It's me. Listen, Dang's behind this, without a doubt. I need you to keep me filled in on what's going on, but make sure Dang and IA doesn't catch wind of it."

"I don't know how much longer Internal Affairs will let me be lead investigator, given you're my partner. I'm betting they're going to find a way to take me off the case."

Allen believed Ao was right about that, and it would be the worst-case scenario. "You have to do whatever you can to make sure that doesn't happen. Don't defend me to IA or anyone else. You didn't know about the gun, so you've already got some cover there."

"I don't like this," Ao said.

"I don't like it either, but we have to keep on this. We can't let Dang control this, or Hwang is just going to end up right back on the street. This is our chance to make a huge difference on the island."

"*Dak, dak*, you're right. If anything new comes up, I'll let you know."

"Good. But make sure that Dang doesn't know."

"Right."

The coffee shop came into sight.

"Good. I've got to go, but keep me updated."

Conroy was sitting inside, eating one of Constance's strawberry pastries. Noah and Shelby were behind the counter, but no other Dragons were present.

"Uncle Allen!" Shelby smiled at him, coming around the counter and then giving him a big hug. Unlike Winston, she'd never pushed him out of her life, taking what their mother said in his defense to heart.

"Stop getting taller," Allen demanded in a playfully stern voice, examining her. She was growing like a weed, as the expression went, and soon she'd be as tall as her mother. "Although you're finally starting to look like you're going to be eighteen. Which, let me just say, I'm pretty sure you're lying about. There's no way you're already turning eighteen."

Shelby rolled her eyes. "That's such a stupid thing to say, Uncle Allen."

Allen glanced at Conroy, who looked exhausted. "What happened to you?"

"Some *puk gai* woke me up this morning," Conroy snapped. "Any other brilliant questions, Inspector?"

Allen pursed his lips but otherwise said nothing. To be fair, he had been responsible for waking Conroy, in a sense, and he also knew Conroy was just lashing out as his default form of interaction. He'd long ago accepted that any encounters he had with any of the Dragons—but particularly Conroy—would be this way.

"Don't be an ass, Conroy," Shelby said, taking the uneaten half of Conroy's strawberry bun away from him.

"Hey, I was eating that!"

"Well, now you're not. Unless you tell my uncle you're sorry."

Conroy glowered at her, but Shelby just shrugged, unintimidated.

"Well, looks like it's going in the trash." She walked it back into the kitchen.

Conroy turned his glare on Allen, as Allen expected. "That's your fault."

"Of course it is," Allen said wearily. "Come on, let's get going."

Conroy came to his feet slowly, no doubt to annoy Allen. "Where?"

"I don't have any food at my place, so I was thinking we could get some dinner somewhere before we go back."

Conroy looked taken aback. "Like at a restaurant?"

"That would be where people get dinner, right? Hey, Shelby," he called toward the kitchen. When Shelby popped back through the door, he said, "We're going to get going. Tell your mother I'll call her tomorrow."

The walk to the car took too long and not long enough. "Any preference for where we eat?"

"A place with food," Conroy answered. "Oh, and lots of beer."

As he drove, Allen thought about the potential of the Internal Affairs assholes seeing him with Conroy. It would complicate matters and call the testimony of their only credible witness into question. With that worry in mind, he decided to take Conroy to one of those hole-in-the-wall places that served cheap food and cheaper beer, frequented by old people who probably got every meal there.

Anyone would IA would stand out, and the restaurant was devoutly dedicated to the Dragons, which made it the safest place they could go.

They were greeted at the door by a stooped-back woman who smiled at them and led them inside. There were three tables crammed into the small restaurant the size of Allen's bedroom. Two of the tables were occupied, one by an old man and a woman probably his wife—the other by a table of men who looked like they'd gone there straight from work, still in their stained coveralls. Their laughs were quick and ready, the sound of men well into their beers. An old television set perched in the corner, showing some comedy show.

No one paid any attention to Allen and Conroy as they were led to the third table, tucked into the back corner. Despite having four chairs, the table barely had enough room for two.

"You look like you had a hard day," Conroy commented after their beers arrived.

Allen raised an eyebrow. "I didn't know you cared."

Conroy grunted. "I don't. Just an observation."

Even though he knew Conroy probably meant it, Allen mentioned his run-in with Internal Affairs—though not the details of the gun, that would just be humiliating, admitting he'd been so easily duped.

Conroy's attention perked up when Allen mentioned the fear that Hwang would go free if Internal Affairs kept interfering with the investigation, but he didn't see fit to contribute anything to the conversation itself.

Their food came eventually—two big bowls of noodles, dumplings stuffed with vegetables and then fried, and fish cake kept simmering all day.

To Allen it felt for a moment like the two of them were in a bubble, an island to themselves. The sound of the other customers, the woman yelling to her husband in the kitchen, the laughter of the television show's audience—it seemed distant, as if it were coming from the far end of a tunnel, and only he and Conroy were there in that restaurant.

Allen didn't know why, and didn't notice his actions initially, but as they ate, he studied Conroy, his features made somehow even more handsome in the hazy light offered by the dirty overhead fixture.

Damn it, stop staring, he told himself firmly. What the hell was his problem? It shouldn't be so difficult to keep his eyes off of the other man. It had been a problem ever since he first met Conroy, through Wei. Conroy was beautiful—someone would have to be blind not to see it. He knew it, too. While that could be problematic for some guys, it made Conroy confident but not arrogant, and that nuance made him all the more appealing.

He'd known the moment they met that he'd end up falling for Conroy, and in the weeks they spent together afterward, it had happened. He wasn't ashamed to admit that it was Conroy's looks that had first attracted him. Getting to know his personality later had only cemented it.

Looking at Conroy right now, Allen was reminded, like he'd been that morning, just how easily he'd fallen for him.

That's a dangerous road to go down. He wasn't going to delude himself; that was over; he'd made that choice and he couldn't change that now. He was happy with the choice he made, or so he kept telling himself. That was all anyone could hope for.

So why are you still looking at him? He decided right then that he was going to stop. Yet no sooner had he looked down at his noodles than he glanced right back at Conroy. Conroy focused on his food, but there was a smirk on his lips that made Allen think he was aware of the staring.

Face burning, Allen resisted the urge to groan aloud. He'd made an ass of himself twice in the same day. He was on fire.

Twenty-Two

Conroy stared out the window of Hong's car as they drove, legs stretched out, seat reclined almost as far as it would go. He was actually glad to reach Hong's apartment, much to his surprise, mostly because he was dying to take a shower

He acted casual, but he was very much aware of Hong's presence. He'd seen Hong staring at him again at the restaurant while he ate. He was used to being stared at, but by Hong? Conroy had convinced himself that this morning had been a fluke, but now he couldn't shake the feeling it was more.

Did Hong still have the hots for him? He thought that door had closed a long time ago.

"I'm going to take a shower," he told Hong as soon as they entered the apartment.

"Whatever," Hong said with a shrug, collapsing onto the couch.

Conroy lingered for a moment, watching. He looked like he'd had a rougher day than he'd let on, too. Conroy considered asking him about it, but forced away whatever flash of sympathy he felt by reminding himself that whatever problems Hong had because of his job were his own damn fault.

He enjoyed the shower, soaking in the hot water as steam slowly filled the room. He let his muscles relax. Conroy hadn't realized before then, but he was carrying a lot of tension in his body, had been since Yang had been shot right in front of him.

That wasn't true, exactly; it had been building for a while. A shower wouldn't clear it all, but it would at least help ease it enough.

After what might have been fifteen minutes in the tub, he began washing. He started with his hair. He thought twice about using Hong's shampoo, not wanting to smell like the other man if he could help it, but he didn't have much choice, so he just sucked it up.

He drew the line at body wash.

While immersed in water, he thought he heard the doorbell, but he didn't pay it much attention. It could have been the television, for all he knew, or the post arriving.

Soapy water dripping from his head and hands down to the shower floor, Conroy's thoughts turned once more to the way Hong had looked at him earlier. He doubted Hong realized how much blatant hunger was in his gaze. Allen Hong wanted him. He just hadn't realized it yet.

The thought should've disgusted Conroy, but instead it intrigued him. He was never really lacking in possible sex partners; when he was horny, he picked up his phone and found someone—either on the Unzipped app or at one of the various nightspots he frequented. He knew quite a few people who would drop everything and come running to him if he asked.

Sex with Hong had been on an entirely different level than these guys could provide, though. He could look at it objectively and say yeah, the sex had been incredible. He could separate the sex from the man, and if he was honest, he definitely missed it.

But why was he thinking about sex with Hong at all? A quick glance down at his hard dick answered the question. It had been a while since he'd gotten any, what with everything going on, and his dick was starting to get insistent.

For a moment he allowed himself to imagine what it would be like to fuck Hong again. How different would it be? He'd never had sex with someone he hated, but he'd heard it was damn good. The shower faded away as Conroy got into the fantasy.

When he realized he was touching himself, he snapped back to reality. He released his cock, breathing heavily and doing his best to ignore the throbbing in it.

Conroy turned the shower to cold. The frigid blast killed his remaining arousal. He dried off and started to dress, but his mind turned toward a more devious plan. It was Hong's fault Conroy was stuck there under the watchful eyes of a man he didn't want to spend five minutes with, much less hours every night.

If I'm going to be miserable, I'm going to make damn sure he is, too.

He exited the bathroom naked, towel in one hand, clothes in the other, and strolled purposefully into the living room. It was impossible to miss the large man standing there with Hong near the door. He also didn't miss the way Hong's eyes were all but glued to his naked body, an intensity in his gaze. He thought he might have heard the big man mutter, "Good lord," under his breath.

Conroy slowly dressed, watching Hong and his guest, as if daring them to say something about his nudity.

"I didn't know you had a friend over," the big man said, face slightly pink.

"Oh, we're not friends," Conroy said brightly. He knew exactly how his words made their arrangement sound. He doubted this guy would be too shocked; Hong wouldn't be the first member of HKPD caught with paid entertainment in his home.

"He's our witness against Hwang," Hong explained quickly, sending an exasperated look Conroy's way. "This is Conroy Wong."

The man nodded faintly. "Yeah, I recognized him from the dossiers. The face, anyway; the rest of it isn't in his files."

"Maybe it should be," Conroy said, pulling his shirt over his head. "I bet it would make your work life a lot more interesting."

"Oh, for fuck's sake, Conroy." There it was—Hong's cross tone. Conroy had succeeded in annoying him with barely any effort at all put in.

He was proud of himself.

"So, do either of you cop bastards know when I'm going to need to go and make a statement against Hwang or what?"

Hong and his friend grimaced.

"That's why Ao—Inspector Cheung—is here," Hong explained.

"Dang is working hard to make it seem like the Dragons are trying to frame Hwang and that Allen here is in on it."

A move like that from Dang didn't surprise Conroy. The implications behind the intended result heated his blood.

"You've got to be fucking kidding me! That *puk gai* is trying to pass it off onto *us*? That's the stupidest thing I've ever heard! He gunned a police officer down in public!"

Hong crossed his arms over his chest, his face wrinkling in distaste. "He's very influential. He's spent years crafting the right facade and connections, both legal and illegal. To most of the outside world, he looks squeaky clean—respectable, even."

"That stunt he pulled with the fake gun didn't help, either," Cheung added. "Clever sonofabitch"

Conroy cocked his head, lost. "Fake gun?"

"It's not important." Hong tried to keep his tone dismissive, that much was clear, but the way that Hong's bearing changed—his shoulders stooping slightly, his eyes turning downward, evading everyone else's—revealed it for the lie it was.

"Not important?" Cheung let out a harsh bark of laughter. "You've got IA up your ass now, trying to prove you're a dirty cop, and it's not important?"

"I know I'm not dirty."

Cheung rolled his eyes. "Yeah, because we all know *that's* what matters."

The revelation surprised Conroy. Hong's job was in danger? He thought Hong was a prick with absolutely zero loyalty to the people who mattered, but how anyone could think he was a dirty cop was beyond him.

"I saw the whole thing," Conroy insisted, surprised by how vehement his own voice was. "You've got an eyewitness."

"An eyewitness who happens to be a Dragon," Hong corrected. "That's not going to mean much for us, unfortunately."

"With what we've got now, there's no way to build a case," Cheung agreed. "At his first hearing, they're going to let Hwang go."

Hwang would be free, and the first thing he'd do, without a doubt, was wreak bloody vengeance on the Dragons. He'd become unstable, crazed, and he posed a threat now more than ever.

Conroy couldn't let that happen. He had a duty to protect the people of the Eastern District, and the Dragons. "What will it take to keep that *ga tsan* behind bars?"

"Evidence," Cheung answered. "Pretty much anything, at this point. The weapon, a confession, a witness who isn't a Dragon—"

"Wait," Conroy said, sorting through memories. "The night Yang was shot, I wasn't the only one outside. There was a girl out there—she looked like maybe she worked there. She stood just a few meters from me."

Hong and Cheung exchanged looks. "And you're *sure* she saw what happened?"

"She screamed when the gun went off," Conroy remembered. "So yeah, I'm pretty sure."

"Why didn't you say anything before?" Hong cried.

"I forgot about her, considering a man was shot in front of me," Conroy growled. "I'm mentioning her now."

"What do you think?" Hong asked Cheung.

Cheung considered for a moment. "If we get another witness, it will be difficult for Dang to claim bias or Hwang's innocence. Mr. Wong, had you ever seen the girl before? Is she connected with the Dragons in any way?"

Conroy shook his head. "We're not involved with Indulgence. I don't think Wei's ever actually been there before the shooting."

"Then that sounds like our best bet."

"Conroy, do you think you would recognize her if you saw her again?"

Conroy shrugged. "I can try, but no promises. I didn't even remember her until just now."

"It's a long shot," Hong said, "but at least it's a shot. We need to get down to Indulgence and see if we can find her."

"Let's go, then," Cheung said, but Hong put a hand on his arm to stop him, shaking his head. "What?"

"We can't run the risk of someone from IA seeing us together," he said apologetically. "If we find her, we'll call you immediately. You'll be the one to talk to her, that will all be by the book."

Cheung nodded, reluctance plainly visible. "Fine. But you better call me the moment you find her."

Cheung departed, and Hong turned to Conroy. "You ready to go to Indulgence?"

"Going to a karaoke bar with a man I can't stand to find a girl who witnessed the same murder I did? That's my idea of a great time."

Twenty-Three

IT AMAZED ALLEN how quickly places recovered from some traumatic incidents but not others. Indulgence looked as if nothing had changed from the day before the incident and now, like a man had never been gunned down in front of it.

Despite the relatively early hour they'd arrived, Indulgence pulsated with people. There was no such thing as a slow night for a karaoke bar.

"It's going to be hard to find one woman in all of this," Allen said to Conroy.

"What?" Conroy asked, pointing up at the ceiling to indicate he hadn't heard.

Allen shook his head. He didn't want to shout to be heard over the music, not when he was just going to get a snide remark in return, anyway.

It chafed that he was entirely at Conroy's mercy here; he had no idea who they were looking for or what she looked like. Conroy had tried to describe her on the way to the bar, but he hadn't had much luck. No matter how many times Conroy said it, Allen couldn't conjure an image of her in his mind.

He'd been forced into the copilot's seat, and he didn't exactly trust the captain.

The fact that Conroy had been willing to help them, had even seemed angry when he'd learned that Hong's job was on the line, complicated that distrust.

But no, the voice was just being ridiculous. He knew why Conroy was helping them, and it had nothing to do with him. He just wanted Hwang behind bars because that was what was best for the Dragons. With Conroy Wong it would always be the Dragons first. Allen had known that five years ago, and he knew it now.

"We should circle the room, talk to the female staff," Conroy said.

"And how am I supposed to ask for..." Allen sighed; Conroy had already walked off, engaging with a pretty girl with red-streaked hair, carrying a tray of drinks as she passed him by.

Allen stood there, feeling more lost than he had since his first day as a beat cop. He'd been thrown completely out of his element here. Before, he would have had the aid of his badge when it came to questioning people. When someone didn't want to give him the time of day, he would flash the badge and immediately his questions would get answered. He couldn't do that here, not without risking his activities getting back to IA or Dang.

He wasn't going to let inconvenience get in his way, though. His career was riding on finding this girl that Conroy saw there. He suppressed any nervousness that thought generated and made his way to the first female employee he saw.

"Excuse me!" The woman looked harried—she bore a tray with at least seven drinks on it and carried an order sheet with several different room numbers—but she gave him a polite, if impatient, smile. "I was just wondering if you were working the night of October ninth."

The woman's expression became guarded. "Yes. I work every night but Wednesday."

"Were you here when the...incident happened?"

"I was. I'm sorry, but I'm very busy right now."

"Did you happen to *see* what happened?" Allen asked quickly.

"No, I was inside working the VIP rooms," she answered. "If you'll excuse me, I need to get these drinks out."

Allen let her go. He didn't know why he felt so dejected about it all; he hadn't really expected the first girl he asked to be *the* girl.

He scanned the room quickly, ostensibly to find the next female employee he could talk to. However, the moment his eyes found Conroy in the crowd—it was like he was a beacon, burning so bright that Allen couldn't help but look at him—they stopped moving. Conroy leaned against a table and chatted with one of the employees—but not a woman, Allen saw.

Annoyance surged through him. He tried to tell himself it was because Conroy was clearly wasting time. Did he need to be reminded that they were there to flirt or plan hookups?

It's not Conroy's ass on the line, though, Allen thought bitterly. *Why should he care?*

Allen forced his eyes away and found another female employee making her way back to the bar with an empty tray. He hurried to her, posing the same questions he'd asked the first woman he spoke with, but she hadn't been working the night it happened and hadn't heard about any of her coworkers who saw what went down; all the news they had came from the news or second- or third-hand information.

Three more times he repeated the pattern, and three more times he came up with nothing. It didn't help that he had no idea how many employees Indulgence had, so he had no idea whether or not he'd spoken to everyone.

He found his sixth employee not far from where Conroy continued to converse with the same guy.

"I was wondering if..." Allen trailed off when he heard the guy with Conroy laugh in that over-the-top purposefully laughing to be flirtatious way. He looked over and saw that Conroy and the laughing employee were now standing much closer together than before.

"Did you need something, sir?" The waitress prompted him, shifting her weight from like she wanted to flee.

"Yes, er, sorry. I was wondering if you were working the night of October ninth."

Understanding came over her face. "You're the guy asking around about that. No, I wasn't. I've been on vacation since October first. This is my first day back. Sorry I can't help you."

Allen cursed silently to himself as she walked away.

"You, Shun," the bartender called out over the music, catching the attention of Conroy's companion. "Room 19 just pushed the call button. Stop trolling for dick and get your ass back there!"

Allen waited until the guy left before approaching Conroy. "I've spoken with six or seven employees," he said accusingly. "How many have you talked to?"

Conroy's sneer made him regret his tone. "Is that jealousy I hear?"

"Don't be an idiot. What you're hearing is *annoyance*." The words sounded defensive, even to his own ears, and did nothing to get rid of Conroy's expression. "We came here to find a witness, not line up your next meaningless lay."

"You think I'm not taking this seriously? Okay, Inspector, what have you learned from these seven people?"

Allen bit his lip. Conroy had a point. Sure, he'd talked to seven people, but he hadn't learned anything. "Okay, I've got nothing right now, but at least I'm trying!"

"I am, too. You've got your methods. I've got mine."

Allen was too familiar with his method. Anything he said then, though, would just be taken out of context by Conroy, twisted and doubled back on him, so he saw no point in responding. Conroy was Conroy, and Allen certainly wasn't going to change that.

"You just keep talking to the waitresses. I'll do my thing, and we'll see who ends up with the more useful information." Conroy gave Allen a slight push. "Now get out of here; he's coming back, and you being around will kill the vibe. Everything about you screams 'cop.'"

Allen bit back a retort and moved away from Conroy. As he made his way to the bar, he heard the waiter—Shun—ask Conroy, "Who was that?"

Allen sped up his pace. He stood at the bar and looked around, trying to spot another waitress. He'd spoken to them all. There were more in the area where the karaoke rooms were, off to either side of the main bar, but Allen wouldn't be getting back there without paying for a room, and he hoped to avoid that if at all possible.

The bartender came and leaned against the counter in front of him. "Can I get you anything?"

"Huh? Oh, no. I'm good, thanks."

Allen glanced back over his shoulder toward Conroy and Shun. Conroy's eyes flicked in his direction, and Allen scowled, turning back to the bar.

"Your boyfriend?" the bartender guessed sympathetically.

Allen stiffened. "What? No, god no. Just some guy."

"Uh-huh."

"I'm serious. We're not even friends, really."

"No, sure, I get it." The bartender made it clear he didn't believe a word of it, and Allen's glare sent him away to tend to someone else at the other end of the bar.

The universe was conspiring to piss him off recently. He didn't know what had he done, what action had damaged his karma in such a way that he had to make up for it by being forced into this terrible situation.

Conroy joined him at the bar a few minutes later, before his mood had a chance to darken any further. Allen noticed him tucking a piece of paper into his pocket and received a cheeky smile in return.

"Shun's number."

"Great," Allen snapped, sharper than he intended. "Mission accomplished. Wait, no, that wasn't why we were here at all."

"You want to hear what I've learned, or you going to keep being a smart-ass?"

Allen sighed. "You mean you actually got something other than the number? Fine, go on."

"Shun said that since the incident, there's one girl who hasn't been in—one who worked that night."

"You think it's her?" Allen asked hopefully.

Conroy shrugged. "No way to know until we talk to her."

Allen's sour mood faded, replaced by his subjective police officer mindset. "Okay, so how do we find her?"

"That's going to be a little tricky," Conroy said. "Shun couldn't remember her name. All he could tell me was that she's Vietnamese."

Allen's hope wilted, though he tried to remain optimistic. "Well, it's a start I guess. Now we need to just figure out who she is and where to—"

Allen's mouth clamped shut. He'd happened to glance over toward the door and spotted the absolute last person he'd expected to see in a place like this.

Inspector Leung.

"Fuck," he hissed, turning his back and hunching his shoulders down in an attempt to avoid attention.

"What is it?" Conroy asked.

Allen shushed him, grabbed his shoulder, and turned him to face the bar.

"What the fuck is wrong with you?"

"Inspector Leung just came in." Allen fought the urge to crane his neck to locate Leung. "He's one of Dang's. If he sees us here together, he'll get suspicious. We can't have Dang catching on to what we're doing before we've found this woman."

Allen peeked around, hoping Leung would steer clear of the bar. He had no such luck. From the corner of his eye, he spotted Leung's unmistakable form approaching the bar at the opposite end, which put Conroy between them.

Being on the Anti-Gang Task Force, Leung would recognize Conroy from his dossier. If Leung even glanced their way, it could throw a massive kink in their plans.

He caught Conroy's eyes with his own and did his best to indicate Leung's presence nearby. Thankfully, he caught on. Unfortunately, he took it as an opportunity to turn and study Leung, to take his measure.

Panic heightened with the movement. Everything was on the line, and the jumble of his brain made him act without thought.

He grabbed Conroy by the shoulders and jerked him forward, their faces coming together, and claimed his lips in a kiss.

Twenty-Four

CONROY COULD STILL feel the phantom remnants of Hong's lips against his own, even ten minutes after the kiss broke. He'd barely resisted his first impulse of punching Hong. Once they'd split apart, they'd stared awkwardly.

Conroy saw it again, then, that need in Hong's eyes. He wondered if Hong was truly oblivious or just trying to push it all away.

"I had to keep Leung from recognizing us," Hong justified as they left the parking lot of Indulgence.

"Whatever," Conroy said, not looking at Hong. *Whatever you need to tell yourself.* Sure, Hong probably *thought* that was why he did it, but there were simpler ways to go unnoticed—like just walking the fuck away. No, Allen Hong wanted to kiss him, and so he did.

"Better not try that again," Conroy warned him. "If you do, you'll be kissing my fist."

"Trust me, I won't."

If you say so, Conroy thought. He propped his arm on the car door beside him and winced. He'd been standing so close to that waiter, Shun, that the heavy smell of whatever cologne the man was wearing had seeped into the fabric of his shirt. He needed to change.

"We need to stop by my place," Conroy told Hong, finally looking his way. "I need some clothes, a toothbrush, that sort of thing, if this is going to take as long as it looks like it will."

"Fine." Hong put up no fight. He changed lanes near an intersection, ignoring the car behind him that honked its horn and turned in the direction of Conroy's apartment.

Conroy's building was quiet, despite it only being ten fifteen. The other people who lived there were mostly all safely tucked inside their apartments, likely sound asleep. They weren't much for the nightlife like Conroy was.

Conroy wondered as he made his way up the stairs if the Twisted Vipers had any more men lying in wait for him. If anyone was up there, they were probably expecting just Conroy, so they would be in for an unpleasant shock to find he wasn't alone.

Sure, Hong wasn't Conroy's first pick for backup, but the man could handle himself just fine—if he hadn't forgotten how to since becoming a police officer.

Where's kick-ass Noah when you need him?

At his door, Conroy hesitated after inserting the key, earning him a strange look from Hong. Conroy glowered in return and pushed the door open.

The place was a wreck. Someone—or several someones—had gone through and done a thorough job of smashing just about everything they could.

Conroy took in the mess that was once his home, not sure what exactly he was feeling. Regret? Sadness? Anger? Hong, though, was pissed, judging by his reaction.

"What the hell happened here?"

"My guess is Hwang's boys came back."

"*Came back?*" The intensity in Hong's voice caught Conroy off guard. He looked to him and there was true anger on his face. His muscles had gone taut with barely restrained rage, veins bulging in his arms, and his jaw clenched so tight Conroy could imagine his teeth breaking from the pressure. "What do you mean *came back?*"

Conroy reluctantly filled him in on the morning's run-in.

"Why didn't you tell me about this before?" Hong demanded, eyes bugging in his head a bit.

Conroy gave him a scathing look. "Why would I?"

Hong took several deep breaths before he spoke again, his voice sounding strained. "I know you don't like me, Conroy, but this isn't just about you anymore. My job is on the line here! Everything I've worked for is at stake. And you know what? The Dragons aren't going to be able to bring Hwang down alone. You need me, just like I need you. If Hwang gets out, do you think he's going to go back to the way things were? He's coming for you, Conroy. For all the Dragons. This is bigger than whatever bad blood there is between us!"

"I know that," Conroy snapped. "I know what Hwang is capable of, Hong. You don't need to lecture me on it."

The worst part was Conroy knew Hong was right. The attack wouldn't have happened if he'd listened to Hong. "Let's just drop it; it's not like we can do anything to change it now. I'll get some things."

"Wait." Hong held up a hand and made his way to the back of the apartment.

Conroy rolled his eyes but said nothing. If there was someone there, they'd likely have come out when they heard the two of them talking. Then again, if there *was* someone there, it would be nice to not be the one on the receiving end of the attack for once.

Conroy remained in the front of his apartment and began to clean, though he quickly gave up. It would take hours to put the place back in order, and he didn't have the time—or energy—to do it right then.

"There's no one back there," Hong said at last, emerging from the back. "Who knows if they'll come back, though. You should go get some clothes or whatever it is you need, and then we're getting out of here. I'll have Ao send some people around to try to see if we can get some prints in the morning."

"No way," Conroy protested. "I don't want cops rummaging around in my apartment."

"It will help build believability in you as a witness," Hong argued. "There's a reason the Twisted Vipers want to silence you."

"No," Conroy said. "There's no way to prove the Twisted Vipers are involved in this. Do you think Dang wouldn't find a way to weasel out of that, too? It's a waste of time. We need to focus on finding the waitress."

Hong looked like he wanted to argue—Conroy wouldn't be surprised; he'd always been one of those people who was convinced his way was the right one. He was stubborn as hell. Then again, so was Conroy. He didn't back down where anyone was concerned, except for Wei.

"Fine," Hong said through gritted teeth. "Just get what you need."

Conroy grabbed his gym bag and started tossing clothes into it. He stopped in the bathroom to collect his hair products, knowing Hong had none.

"Okay," he said once he'd finished packing, bag hoisted over his shoulder. "Let's get out of here."

Once back at the car, Conroy tossed the duffel bag into the backseat and climbed in. He hated sitting on the passenger side. Winston liked to comment about how it was one more way Conroy needed to be in control. Hell, he was probably right. Conroy could think of few moments more powerless than sitting in the passenger seat, with absolutely zero ability to influence the car itself.

Hong driving just made it that much worse. The idea of relinquishing even that much control to Hong made his stomach turn.

He didn't say anything, not wanting to let Hong know that he had the higher ground at that moment. Instead he drummed his fingers impatiently on his thigh, watching in the rearview mirror as a set of headlights pulled out of the parking lot behind them.

"Still have that thing about letting other people drive, huh?" Hong asked. Conroy glared at his own reflection in the window. *Observant* puk gai. "Do you want to drive?" he pressed when Conroy said nothing.

What he wanted right then was to drive his fist into Hong's jaw, but that wouldn't accomplish anything—other than making him feel really good—so he just bit the inside of his cheek.

Conroy blinked against the sudden glare of the headlights from the car behind them. Whoever was driving, they were coming up fast behind them. He couldn't say for certain, but he was pretty sure it was the same car that turned out after them.

I didn't see anyone getting into their car, though. Considering recent events, the thought made Conroy nervous.

"Speed up," he instructed Hong. Before the man could protest, he added, "Just do it!"

Maybe it was something in Conroy's words that did it, or his own inner suspicions, but whatever the reason, Hong did as told and pressed down on the accelerator.

Conroy watched the car behind them in the rearview mirror. Just as he expected, the car sped up. *Fuck.* "We've got Twisted Viper company."

Hong's head jerked as his gaze went to the rearview mirror. "Are you sure?"

"Yes, I'm sure," Conroy snapped. "We need to lose them."

"I realize that, thank you!"

It seemed like the driver of the other car could hear them, because it sped up suddenly, trying to fly past them on Conroy's side. Conroy looked at the car—he half expected to see Jiang behind the wheel, or at least in the passenger seat—but the windows were tinted so black there was no way to see who was inside, or even how many people there were. All he could see was his own reflection.

Even that vanished as the window rolled down—both the front and back passenger's—and he found himself facing two rough-looking men. None of them appeared to be redpoles. There were no men in suits; the man in the backseat was shirtless, and the other two looked like normal thugs taken off the street, which they no doubt were.

But they were thugs taken off the street with guns.

"Hong," Conroy called, but Hong was a step ahead. Conroy jerked forward as the car came to a sudden stop. Unprepared, the other car continued forward.

Hong threw the car into reverse, aiming toward a side road while the car up ahead struggled to make a U-turn. Hong sped down the street, swerving to narrowly avoid a delivery man on a motorized bike.

Unfortunately, their lead didn't last. Conroy saw the headlights of the car coming down the same narrow road.

His itch to be in the driver's seat grew. *This is why I never let other people drive*, he thought darkly.

The car behind them caught up, accelerating dangerously fast for the narrow space they occupied.

Conroy alternated between watching the road ahead of them and the car behind. He cursed when he saw the front passenger lean out the window, gun in hand, and attempt to sight their car. "Turn left up here. Hurry!"

Hong didn't protest. He jerked the car left just as the gunman pulled the trigger.

The road Conroy sent them down was little more than an alleyway, barely big enough for Hong's car to get through.

"This doesn't give us a lot of space to maneuver." Hong clutched the steering wheel, knuckles a ghostly white. To his credit, he didn't slow down, as most people would.

"Trust me, that's a good thing," Conroy said. The gunman had no choice but to pull back inside the car as they followed Hong and Conroy. That bought them a little time. "At this rate, we're not going to lose them. You need to get us to a busy street."

"No," Hong refused. "I'm not going to endanger people's lives by leading a car full of gun-wielding triad members into their midst."

"Then I hope you have a better plan," Conroy quipped. "One that doesn't involve us getting shot."

"I might." Hong reached toward Conroy, and for a wild moment, Conroy thought Hong was going to grab his cock.

"Woah, what are you—"

Hong's hand bypassed Conroy and opened the glove compartment, where he had a gun concealed. Conroy clapped his mouth shut, hoping Hong would miss the real reason he protested. Judging by the disbelieving look on Hong's face, though, he knew exactly what Conroy had been thinking.

Hong hefted the gun, and Conroy eyed it critically. "You sure you know how to use that?"

"I think I remember."

They left the alley, and Hong slammed on the breaks, twisting the wheel simultaneously so the rear of the car drifted out and they faced the mouth of the alley.

It was a damn impressive move. He'd never said it to Winston, because it would have pissed the kid off—and Hong wasn't on his list of favorites, either—but Conroy always thought Winston came by his love of cars naturally.

"What the hell are you doing?" Conroy cried.

Instead of answering, Hong rolled down his window and pointed his gun. The car pursuing them screeched to a halt, trapped.

Through the windshield, the only window on the vehicle not completely obscured, Conroy could see the men—four in total, from the looks of it—arguing back and forth, one gesturing with his gun.

He wasn't expecting the resounding echo of the gunshot in the confines of the car. Hong had aimed not for anyone in the car, but the front tire, which gave way in a loud pop and rush of air. A second shot—Conroy was ready for it, this time—punctured the second tire, and a third shot went through the grill and hopefully did some damage internally.

With that, Hong hit the pedal and sped away.

Twenty-Five

HENRY DANG ADJUSTED his tie in the small mirror on the wall of his office for the fourth time. He wanted it to look absolutely perfect. He was going to be attending a gala that night, one that, according to rumor mill, the Chief Executive, the highest political figure in the Special Administrative Region, would also be attending.

It would be quite the accomplishment if he could manage a meeting, even briefly, with the most powerful man in Hong Kong. It would be very much worth the effort to curry favor with those in high places. The powerful made the best of friends; that was the axiom he'd lived his entire life by.

When the knock came at his office door, he sighed. He had the feeling this wasn't going to be something that could be dealt with quickly. Reluctantly, he returned to his desk chair and made sure he was comfortably settled before calling, "Come in."

It was Leung, as he'd suspected.

"What is it, Leung? Make it quick, too—I'm busy."

"Hong was at Indulgence, asking questions."

"I'm not surprised to hear he's been asking around the place, Leung. It would surprise me if he *wasn't*. What kind of questions is he asking?"

"He's asking after a woman who works there."

"A woman?" Dang repeated. The wheels in his mind turned. "Why would he ask for a woman?"

"A lover of Yang's, perhaps?" Leung suggested.

Dang dismissed that idea with a shake of his head. "He wasn't the type to have a mistress on the side."

Twenty-Six

ALLEN'S HEART HAMMERED in his chest even after they'd created substantial space and time from the alley. What he'd done was crazy. He was a police officer; he couldn't just go around firing his gun. And yet he hadn't thought twice about it, not this time.

He had no doubt his life, and Conroy's, had been in danger, so he didn't regret his choice. He'd make the same choice again if it meant protecting himself and Conroy. If it came down to it, he could do more than shoot out a car's tires. He'd proven before that he could take a life if it meant protecting the people he loved.

When the time and miles stretched far enough, Allen pulled the car into the parking lot of a closed restaurant.

"What are we doing here?" Conroy asked.

"I just need a minute," Allen said, trying to force his tense muscles to relax. He let his hands fall to his side, hoping Conroy wouldn't notice how they were shaking.

"That was actually pretty awesome," Conroy said suddenly, and for the first time in a long time, Allen didn't hear derision in his voice. "That drift out of the alley? Winston would have been proud."

Allen gave him a slight smile. "You think so?"

Conroy nodded.

The words meant a lot, considering how damaged his relationship with Winston had been for so long. He suspected Conroy knew they would, and that was why he had said them, which inspired a weird feeling of gratitude toward him.

Focus. "We need to get somewhere to lay low," he said. "They all got a clear look at me, and if the Vipers didn't already know I was involved with this, they do now. I doubt my place is safe."

"The place above Coffee by Constance?" Conroy suggested. "I've been saying this whole time I'd be safer there."

"That's out of the question," Allen said quickly. Just the idea of hiding out there made him feel queasy.

"Why?" Conroy challenged, some of that old disdain slipping back into his voice. "Don't want to be surrounded by Dragons?"

"That has nothing to do with it. You think the Twisted Vipers don't know that's a Dragon hangout? Right now that's probably all they think it is, but if we go there then they're going to eventually come looking for us, which is going to put my family in danger. Winston's a Dragon, and there's nothing I can do about that, but I'm not putting Constance and Shelby's lives at risk."

Conroy pursed his lips and nodded his understanding. It surprised Allen that Conroy let it go so easily, but it shouldn't have. Conroy understood how important family was to Allen, if he understood anything at all about him.

"What do you suggest then?"

"There's a motel the police sometimes use as overnight safe houses when we're protecting witnesses in high-profile cases, or as a meet point in sting operations," Allen told him. "I think our best bet will be to lay low there for a while. The Vipers won't know about it, and Dang wouldn't risk compromising himself by telling them about it, even if he suspected we were there. If he did, then it would be clear that there's a rat in HKPD, and Internal Affairs might turn their eyes his way."

Conroy groaned. "I hate staying in motels. The beds are uncomfortable, the bathrooms smell weird, and the neighbors always end up having really loud sex."

"Well then you know what it must be like to live next to you," Allen told him with a smirk.

"From what I remember, you were the noisy one," Conroy fired back. There wasn't much he could say in response, so Allen just shifted the car into gear and pulled back onto the road.

The motel had never looked good, even when it was newly built. It was a two-story rectangular structure, hosting eight rooms in all—four on the first floor and four on the second.

"*This* is where you guys bring witnesses you want to keep safe?" Conroy asked incredulously. "It looks like the setting of a bad horror movie."

"Well, it's this or sleeping in the car," Allen said, climbing from the vehicle. He was stuck with Conroy, on Wei's orders, and he wouldn't defy them. Allen was very aware of the fact that it was only Wei keeping Conroy safely under his watch.

The thought of what might happen if this fell through clawed at Allen. He'd lose everything he'd spent five years working toward. If Hwang got out, his career was finished. More importantly, there would be another war, and innocent people would lose their lives.

The office was a cramped space with an attendant behind a glass divider with a small dip in the counter for money and the keys to be dropped through. The room smelled heavily of cabbage, stale cigarettes, and old coffee, all under a layer of incense probably meant to hide the smells and failing.

"All we got is a full," said the man behind the counter. He looked Allen and then Conroy up and down. "I guess that won't be bothering you two *sei gei lou.*"

Conroy bristled. "Excuse me?"

Allen elbowed Conroy as he slid cash into the groove in the counter, enough to pay for three days. He wanted to punch the homophobic prick in the face as much as Conroy, but words were just that—words. "It'll be fine."

The man sneered at them as he dropped two keys into the slot. Allen took the keys and walked away, eager to get clear of the smell of the room and the ignorance of the man.

"Should have let me punch him," Conroy muttered, stalking out behind him.

"All that would leave you with is a hurt fist that smelled like cabbage," Allen said wearily. "He's not worth it."

"Maybe. But I'd definitely feel better."

"That I won't argue with."

Their room was the farthest from the office on the second floor. It was small, with a bed and nothing else but an old tube television inside a rickety stand and a small desk crammed against the window. The door to the bathroom was open, but the meager light shining in from outside the room didn't illuminate it.

Allen, who'd stayed in the motel before, didn't really relish seeing it again.

Conroy barged into the room past Allen, flipping the light on as he went. He dropped his duffel bag on the floor and immediately flopped down on the bed.

"Just like I thought—uncomfortable."

"You can always sleep on the floor," Allen suggested in as sweet a tone as he could muster, closing the door behind him and then turning the dead bolt. He hooked the chain as well, just to be sure. The door was flimsy and the lock looked like it would yield to the first strong kick or shoulder that came its way, but it was better than nothing.

Conroy snorted. "Fuck that. You dragged my ass here. The floor is all yours."

Allen opened his mouth to counter but decided it wasn't worth it. He wouldn't win, and he was tired. All he wanted to do was pass out. The next day they would find the witness and get on with their lives.

"Fine." He tossed one of the bed's two pillows to the floor and tugged the thicker blanket off the bed, ignoring Conroy's noise of protest. He was at least going to be comfortable. "Cut the light off, will you?"

Conroy sighed and rose from the bed, the box springs squeaking unpleasantly with every movement. The only light left in the room then was a pale sliver that came through the gap in the curtain blocking the windows.

"You think something bad happened to her?" Conroy asked suddenly.

"Happened to who?"

"The waitress from Indulgence. She hasn't been seen since the shooting. You think maybe Hwang's men knew about her?"

Allen pondered the question carefully. "It's a possibility we have to consider. The only answer I can give is I don't know. Maybe she hasn't come to work because of the trauma. Witnessing something like that is hard on anybody, especially if they've never seen it before."

Allen still vividly remembered the first man he'd seen shot—some random shop owner in the *ye shi*, gunned down by the Nine Stars because he wouldn't pay protection money. That incident was one of the catalysts that had led him to joining up with Wei to bring the Nine Stars down.

"All the more reason to find her as quickly as we can," he finished quietly.

He hoped she was still alive.

Twenty-Seven

CONROY SLEPT FITFULLY whenever he wasn't in his own bed. The fact that the paper-thin mattress he slept on currently continued to creak loudly every time he shifted his weight only made it more difficult. He kept waking himself when he changed positions.

Finally, after the sixth time, he gave up on the whole idea of sleep altogether. He sat up to look at the clock on the bedside table, its big red numbers glowing brightly in the dark room, and noticed a light from the bathroom. He figured Hong was using it and paid it no attention, lying back down.

As he lay there, he began to notice an unusual sound coming from the bathroom. He held his breath, straining to hear it. He got lucky and caught it at the right time: that was definitely a moan.

He sat up again. Was Hong in the bathroom watching porn and jerking off? His cock stiffened of its own accord, a symptom of him having been practicing unwilling abstinence with the threat of the Twisted Vipers hanging over the Dragons.

Telling himself he was just out to embarrass Hong, Conroy got out of bed as quietly as he could and hoped Hong was either so wrapped up in what he was doing he didn't notice the bed squeaking or else chalked it up to Conroy repositioning again.

Unsurprisingly, the door had no lock, given the conditions of the cheap place. He stood there, ear almost pressed against the thin wood, listening. This close he could hear the video clearly, along with Hong's heavy breathing. It sounded like the video had reached the good part, if the constant moans of the bottom were anything to judge by.

Conroy's hand strayed down to his cock, tenting the material of the boxer briefs he'd reluctantly agreed to wear so Hong didn't pitch a fit about him sleeping in the nude. The contact sent sparks right to Conroy's core, even through the fabric.

When he could stand it no more, Conroy threw the door open. Hong sat on the toilet, his right hand fisted around his cock while his left hand held his cell phone. He'd pushed his shirt up behind his head and slid his underwear completely off one ankle, though his left foot was still tangled in them.

Hong's eyes were wide, locked on Conroy. When he finally spoke, his words came out in an uncharacteristic stammer. "Co-Conroy! What—what are you doing?"

Looking at Hong in that moment, his face still flushed from his exertions, his cock in his hand, arousal swept through Conroy like a typhoon. He didn't care that it was Hong; all he saw was someone he knew was willing and was a hot fuck.

"Right now I'm trying to figure out what it is that got you going like this," Conroy said, stepping into the bathroom. It was a small space—with the door shut, two people might manage to stand comfortably in it—so a lone step found Conroy in front of Hong. He didn't miss Hong's eyes drifting to his tented underwear.

"Everybody needs to jerk off," Hong said evasively, not raising his eyes to meet Conroy's.

"And yesterday morning?" Conroy asked haughtily.

Hong all but flinched. His dick was still hard, though.

"I saw you; you were hard standing over me."

"That was just morning wood," Hong muttered.

"So you didn't get hard looking at my body?" Conroy ran a hand down his chest, the pads of his fingers rubbing against his nipple before reaching down, coasting along his stomach, until the tips of his fingers slipped beneath the waistband of his Calvin Kleins.

Hong followed his hand on its entire journey.

"Come on, Hong. You and I both know you love my body. *All* of it." He emphasized his words by slipping his entire hand into his briefs and cupping his throbbing cock. "Isn't that right?"

Hong didn't seem capable of speech, but his hand did the talking for him. He'd resumed stroking his cock with the slightest, likely unconscious movements.

"Yeah, I thought so." Hong pushed the front of his boxer briefs down and then tucked the waistband beneath his balls as he freed his cock. "You want this, don't you?"

Hong shook his head, coming to his feet and pushing past Conroy, careful not to let their bodies touch. His underwear trailed from his ankle.

"This is a bad idea," he said, running a hand through his hair.

"Why?" Conroy asked, following him out.

"Why? Because it's you and me, that's why."

Conroy went to the bed and sat in the rectangle of light coming in from the bathroom, reclining a bit and observing Hong with hooded eyes.

"That don't mean anything. It's just sex. We're both horny, and we know what we're getting with each other. We're cramped in this tiny room together, might as well at least get our rocks off while we're here. You ever had hate sex?"

Hong shook his head.

"Me neither, but I hear it's good. And you know *I'm* good."

Hong took several deep, shuddery breaths.

"Fuck it." He stepped forward and went to his knees between Conroy's legs, just like Conroy expected he would. In the small amount of time they were together, Hong hadn't been able to get enough of his dick.

He remembered exactly how good at sucking cock Hong was the second those lips closed around his cock. It was warm, wet heaven. He reclined all the way back and let out a moan.

"Fuck, I needed this," he breathed as Hong's lips worked farther and farther down his shaft. He didn't even care that it was Allen Hong of all people doing it—knowing that made it better, in a way. Here was a man who'd been out of his life for years, and he still went to his knees at the drop of a hat.

Conroy reached down and grasped Hong's head in both hands, holding him still and thrusting his cock deeper into his mouth.

Hong sputtered around his length but didn't try to pull away or stop him. It felt good to put some power into it, like he could work off some of the excess stress that had built up the past few weeks.

But Conroy wasn't in the mood for foreplay. He stood up, gently pushing Hong back so he could strip his boxer briefs off. He tossed them aside and reached down, gripping under Hong's shoulders and tugging him to his feet.

"Get on the bed," he instructed. Hong started to lie down on his back, but Conroy shook his head. "No. On your hands and knees."

Hong didn't hesitate; he got in position in the center of the bed and then looked back over his shoulder at Conroy, who climbed onto the bed behind him.

Conroy ran his hand along Hong's spine, pressing down when he reached the space between his shoulders. Hong got the message loud and clear, dropping from his hands to his elbows and arching his back. His legs slid wider apart as he did so, like his body hadn't forgotten what Conroy wanted.

Conroy slapped the firm globes of Hong's ass twice, once on either cheek. He slid his hand across them, thumb prodding at the muscled ring of Hong's entrance, testing it. He grunted appreciatively when the puckered opening quivered beneath his touch.

He left the bed and went to the nightstand, his cock standing out at a ninety-degree angle like some sort of obscene divining rod. He opened the topmost drawer, hoping his intuition was right, and it was. The drawer contained a small bottle of lube—enough for one, maybe two uses—and a three-pack of condoms.

Conroy snatched them up and returned to his position behind Hong, slapping his ass again and enjoying the way Hong hissed in a mixture of surprise and pain. He placed the condoms on the bed beside him and popped open the lube. It was one of those annoying kinds, where the stopper needed to be removed from inside the cap before it would squirt out, but eventually he got it flowing.

He squeezed a liberal amount out onto the index and middle fingers of his right hand and smeared it across Hong's hole.

"Jesus Christ, that's cold," Hong hissed, body tensing beneath Conroy's touch.

"Don't be a baby," Conroy chided, allowing his long middle finger to press beyond the tight ring and inside Hong to the second knuckle.

Hong was tight, but no virgin. He knew how to relax his body, and after a momentary reflexive tightening, his muscles loosened. Conroy began to move his finger in and out, plunging deeper each time until it was fully inside. Once Hong handled that with no problem, he added his index finger, stretching the inner muscles in preparation for the much thicker penetration to come.

Impatience got the better of Conroy, and he didn't do near as much preparation as he might have with a different partner. He knew Hong—knew what he could take.

Conroy managed to open the condom wrapper with one hand by holding it down against the bed and rolled the thin layer of latex down his dick. Another generous glob of lube was applied to his cock, and then he was lining the head of his cock up with Hong's waiting hole.

He told himself he was going to take it slow and easy, but the moment that exquisite heat enclosed the first inch of his cock, he knew that wasn't going to be possible. He plunged forward, driving every bit of his shaft inside him.

Hong threw his head back and let out a long, low, "*Fuck!*"

"Bet you missed this cock, huh?" Conroy smirked, trying to push farther into him and earning a grunt.

"Just shut up and do it," Hong growled.

"Whatever you say."

Conroy gripped Hong's hips tightly and drew out fully in one quick pull before thrusting fully back in once again.

There was nothing quiet about the groan of pleasure that drew from Hong's lips, and Conroy couldn't help but chuckle. "Told you that you were the loud one."

Hong buried his face in the flimsy pillow on the bed, muffling his voice, and Conroy picked up speed, setting a rhythm that grew faster and more frantic with each thrust. All the tension and stress he'd built drove into Hong.

The sound of flesh slapping flesh joined Hong's lewd cries of pleasure in an erotic harmony that was music to Conroy's ears. Everything with Hong felt the same as it had before; an electrical current seemed to dance through their bodies, ratcheting up the pleasure tenfold.

A new sound joined the orchestra of sex noises, and it took Conroy a beat to realize it was his own grunting. He couldn't help it. Every thrust took him closer to the edge. He could feel the pressure building in that spot just below his navel.

Conroy used his weight to guide Hong's body down until he was pressed flat against the bed, Conroy's knees to either side of his legs, his cock driving deeper at this angle.

"Fuck yes," Hong panted, tossing his head from side to side, his fists clenching the sheets and twisting them. He tried to push his hips back against Conroy, get him in deeper, but the position limited his ability to do more than lie there and take Conroy's cock.

Conroy pushed himself to his toes, driving his full weight into it. He wasn't going to last that much longer at this rate, but he couldn't stop himself. His baser, sex-driven side had taken control, and it wasn't going to stop until it reached its goal.

He pressed his forehead against Hong's sweaty shoulder, his long, deep thrusts turning to shorter, more frantic ones.

"I'm coming," he called just as his orgasm flooded his body and filled the condom.

When it passed, he carefully pulled out and rolled onto his back, condom still attached to his slowly deflating cock.

Hong rolled over, too, not close enough that they were touching, but close enough that Conroy could feel the warmth coming from the bare skin of his shoulder. Hong pumped his cock furiously, and about a minute after Conroy's, his own orgasm came. Come spurted from his cock, the first shot reaching his neck, the rest coating his chest and stomach.

Conroy reluctantly moved, reaching over to take the box of tissues from the nightstand. He took two, which he used to remove and wrap the used condom, and passed the box to Hong, who cleaned himself up.

The clock read nearly four in the morning.

"Well," Conroy said, voice hoarse, "guess we could get some sleep."

"I guess so," Hong said, something catching in his voice that Conroy couldn't quite place. Even after he spoke he remained in the bed, staring up at the ceiling.

"Well?" Conroy prompted when he showed no sign of moving.

"Huh?" Hong jarred, like he'd been on the brink of falling asleep.

"Aren't you going to get back on the floor?"

"Wha—? Oh." Hong sat up slowly.

Conroy snickered. "What? Did you think we were going to sleep together?"

"Don't be an ass," Hong snapped before rising from the bed.

"I'm not hearing a no." Conroy shifted until he freed the sheet from beneath him, pulling it over his body. The post-orgasmic glow faded, replaced by a comfortable sleepiness. He waited until Hong had gotten settled on the floor before he spoke again. "Turn the light off, will you?"

Twenty-Eight

IT HAD BEEN a long time since Allen had woken up so sore, and longer still since he'd been so conflicted. He wanted to convince himself the previous night hadn't happened, that he'd just had an extremely realistic and detailed sex dream, but the telltale twinge of pain in his ass every time he shifted his weight told it for the truth it was.

What the hell had he been thinking last night? If he hadn't already been horny and jerking off in the bathroom he never would have given in like that. Even as he thought it, he wasn't sure he believed it. Sure, horniness was a part of it, but he couldn't say that it was all or even most of it.

Conroy had this allure about him, always had. It didn't only affect Allen, though; he'd seen plenty of people taken in by the man's natural charm and charisma. Sure, he had the looks, which helped, but there were absolutely gorgeous people out there who didn't have the same air about them, and thus didn't have the same draw that Conroy Wong had.

Allen dug around on the floor until he found his cell phone. Seven thirty approached, and his phone needed to be charged. He didn't have his charger with him, so he'd have to wait until they were in the car.

He considered waking Conroy before he got in the shower but decided against it. The less he had to deal with him the better. The last thing he wanted so early in the morning was to deal with Conroy's casual disdain.

Allen wasn't fool enough to think their screwing the night before would in any way change Conroy's behavior toward him. It was just sex, taken where it was easily available. That was all.

Conroy was Conroy, and a night in bed certainly wouldn't change that, even if it was a really good night.

Allen made his way to the bathroom quietly. As he emptied his bladder, he noticed the dried come speckling his stomach and chest. Thinking about how sweaty he'd gotten the night before, he definitely needed a shower.

The crappy motel's showers were lukewarm at best. He tried to use the time to consider what the next step in the plan should be, but—much to his frustration—his thoughts kept drifting to the previous night's activities.

He had a pretty healthy sexual appetite, though some guys he'd been with had said it was a little much for them. Conroy had been a lover who could keep up with him and then some. Sex with Conroy had never been dull.

Conroy hadn't lacked excitement or energy back then, and based on the previous night's performance, it wasn't something he lacked now, either.

Hong turned his face to the shower spray, hoping the water would wash his mind of Conroy. He didn't need to be thinking about him. He needed to get his mind back on what really mattered: finding the second witness and putting Johnny Hwang behind bars. Cut the head off of the Twisted Vipers, and the body would die eventually.

He grabbed the bar of plain, unscented soap from its tray and lathered up, rinsing away the remnants of the previous night.

If only it was so easy to do that with the mind.

It took effort, but he forced his mind away from Conroy. He needed to call Ao and let him know how things had gone at Indulgence. He'd promised to keep him updated and knew he'd be anxious as hell if he was in Ao's shoes. Besides, Ao might have an easier time getting information since Allen was limited in when and where he could flash his badge.

They needed to identify the missing employee and track her down. Conroy's worries from the previous night, about whether or not she'd been discovered by the Twisted Vipers, ate at him—a constant niggling in the back of his mind. That was all the more reason they needed to move fast.

That and the fact that sharing this motel room with Conroy already led to consequences he hadn't foreseen. The sooner he put distance between himself and Conroy, the sooner he could clear the fog of Conroy-induced confusion.

He left the shower, determined to stay focused. He made sure to dress in the bathroom; he wasn't going to go out there as exposed—literally—as he'd been the night before. He faced the first obstacle to this new mentality the moment he walked out of the bathroom, though.

Conroy was awake, and he'd thrown the sheets off himself. He lay there, naked, semi-erect, and eyeing Allen. He didn't say anything, but there was a definite challenge in his gaze, a flicker of fire that made Allen think about the previous night.

"Good, you're awake." Allen did his best to slip into his no-nonsense voice. "Get in the shower and get dressed. We've got to get to work."

"I'm pretty sure I can think of some work for you to get to."

"I can too," Allen said firmly. "And I'd wager mine is more important than yours. Now get up and get in the shower before I decide to handcuff your ass to the bed."

"You say that like it's a bad thing."

I walked right into that one, Allen thought with a silent sigh. "Just go."

Conroy obeyed, though he took his sweet time getting up and sauntering to the bathroom. Allen exercised more self-control than he knew possible and kept his eyes everywhere but Conroy's ass.

While Conroy was in the shower, he used the motel phone to call Ao. When Ao answered, he filled him in on what they'd learned from the night before.

"This is starting to sound actually doable," Ao said, as though he couldn't believe it.

"Yeah, well, we're not there yet. Conroy is worried the Vipers might have gotten to her already, and I'm a little concerned about that, too. We need to find out who she is. Right now all we have to go on is that she's Vietnamese and works at Indulgence."

"What time will it be ready?" Ao asked suddenly. Allen figured someone had walked by Ao's desk, so he was pretending to have a normal conversation. "Well, I can't get there before six. Is that okay?"

Allen sat on the edge of the bed and said nothing, focusing on the sound of the shower behind him. With the water being as tepid as it was, he didn't imagine Conroy would be in there long.

"So what's the next step?" Ao asked in a low voice, indicating that the passerby was now out of earshot.

"If we want to know who this employee is, we need to talk to someone who'd know about employment records for the place," Allen said. "I'm guessing the owner could tell us what we needed to know, but I don't know who the owner is or where they might be."

"You could wait until open hours at the place," Ao suggested, no doubt purposefully not saying Indulgence so as not to draw attention. "Someone who would know who she was is bound to be there."

"Yeah, but I don't want to wait that long. If the Twisted Vipers *do* know about her, then time is a factor. If Leung hadn't shown up, we would have been able to get the information last night."

"Hold on," Ao said. "I'll let you know what you need to know. Give me a few minutes and I'll call you back. What's the room number?"

After ending the call, Allen sat quietly. He hated waiting, even if it was just for a few minutes.

Behind him, the bathroom door opened. He kept his gaze resolutely forward, focusing on the ugly pattern on the thick curtains in front of the window. Whoever had been the interior designer for this place hadn't known a damn thing, that was for sure, unless ugly was the *chic* look back when the building was first erected.

Allen could have guessed it would happen, but Conroy crossed into his line of sight, his cock at eye level, and stood there, hands on his hips. Allen turned his eyes toward Conroy's face.

They looked at each other silently before Conroy spoke.

"You going to move? I need to get into my bag. Unless you *want* me to stand here naked all day."

Allen looked down and saw that Conroy's bag was behind his legs. He got up quickly, sidling sideways so he kept amble space between them. He watched Conroy dress from the corner of his eye, unable to resist.

"Oh, Hong," Conroy called as he slipped his shirt over his head. His voice was casual, but something in his words gave Allen an unsettled feeling. "I saw the picture at your place."

"What picture?" Allen asked suspiciously.

"The picture from Disney."

Those four words were like a punch to Allen's gut. He hadn't thought about that picture still being out when he'd brought Conroy to his place. Not once had it passed his mind, and now he wished it had.

"Why do you still have it?" The question was posed as curiosity without malice, its absence something Allen was unused to. "I thought you'd have thrown it away by now."

How did he answer that question when he wasn't sure himself? Allen had never been able to bring himself to throw it aside, no matter how many times he looked at it and thought he'd be better off doing so. He considered it, convinced himself he would toss it, and then never went through with it, and so it stayed there in the same place he'd first put it when they returned from that day at Disney.

The jarring ring from the phone saved him from answering. He hurried to answer it, thinking that he needed to thank Ao for his timing and cursing pictures from Disneyland.

Twenty-Nine

"J‌UST REMEMBER TO—"

"For fuck's sake," Conroy snapped, leveling the full force of his glare on Allen, who was driving them to visit the home of the owner of Indulgence. "If you tell me to let you do the talking one more time, I swear I'm going to drop-kick you out of this car."

He'd heard it so frequently from Hong in the short time between the phone call from Inspector Cheung and then that he could believe Hong had taken it up as a mantra.

"If I thought you were actually listening every other time I said it, I wouldn't have to repeat it so much," Hong said defensively. "You have a big mouth—I think that pretty much all of the Dragons do; that's why Constance fits in so well—and that's fine when dealing with your brand of problems, but I don't think that's going to help us any here."

"You'd be surprised," Conroy started, though a nearby horn honking made him stop and start again. "You'd be surprised how many doors are opened when a Dragon is with you."

"And you'd be surprised how many businessmen won't give a shit," Hong countered, bringing the car to a stop at a red light. "From what I can tell, this Bao guy is one of those. He's been around since the Nine Stars took power."

Conroy shrugged. "We'll see."

Hong rounded on him. "No, we won't. Because you're going to keep your mouth shut and let me—"

Conroy growled in unison with a horn honking behind them; the light had turned green.

Conroy had been relegated the duty of navigator, since Hong drove. He glanced at the navigation app on his phone, monitoring their path.

Lan Bao, the owner of Indulgence, lived at the far edge of the Eastern District in a neighborhood that was technically Dragon territory, though Conroy had never been there, nor had he heard it mentioned. That was probably how he'd managed to stay clear of any of the power struggles in the district.

"Take the next right," Conroy instructed just as they came to the turn in question.

He barely restrained his chuckle as Hong cursed, turning the wheel and veering into a turn he barely made while the car behind them honked again.

"Could you tell me when the turns are *before* I need to make them?"

"Hey, I'm not telling you how to drive, so you don't tell me how to navigate," Conroy replied with a lazy grin. "Bao's house should be somewhere near here."

The cul-de-sac they ended up in had many narrow houses that looked like they'd been designed by Tim Burton, nothing quite straight as they rose into the air. Clothes hung from clotheslines outside of third-story windows. The sounds of dishes being washed and morning routines going on came from windows open to lure in cool autumn breezes.

"Okay." Hong brought the car to a stop near the mouth of the cul-de-sac. "But which one?"

"Maybe the one with the sign on it?" Conroy pointed to the house at the dead center of the cramped round. A sign hung above the door, Bao's name written in *hanzi*.

"Safe bet." Hong led the way to Bao's house. "Let me do the talking, Conroy. I mean it."

Conroy clenched his jaw and punched Hong in the shoulder. It was extremely satisfying and left him wanting to do it again. He hoped Hong would give him a reason to.

With one last glare in Conroy's direction—Conroy leered in return—Hong knocked on the door.

When the door opened, Conroy's eyes watered as they were instantly greeted with the unmistakable smell of durian. The man who greeted them in the doorway was stoop-backed and short, the top of his head coming to Conroy's chest. He had long, snow-white caterpillar eyebrows and a completely bald pate. He had to be close to eighty, if Conroy took a guess—though that might have been the bad posture throwing it off.

"What the hell do you want?"

Friendly one, isn't he? If his nose hadn't already been wrinkled against the smell of the durian, he would have wrinkled it just then in distaste for the man.

"Are you Lan Bao?" Hong asked in his politest civil-servant voice, the sort of tone that from others just dripped insincerity, but Hong could make believable somehow.

"Who the fuck wants to know?"

"With a mouth like that, I hope you're not someone's grandfather," Conroy said reproachfully. His own vocabulary wasn't far off from old man Bao's, but he was a hell of a lot younger. There was just something wrong about hearing old men cursing up a storm.

"I'm with the Hong Kong Police Department," Hong said, turning his head toward Conroy long enough to mouth quite clearly *sau seng*—shut up. "I was wondering if we could have a little bit of your time."

"I'd rather you didn't," Bao said.

Before he could close the door, Conroy reached out and pushed it open. The old man might have been feisty, but there was no way he was going to be able to close the door against Conroy.

"This guy might have made it sound like a request, grandpa. That's just his way. It isn't, though."

Bao looked Conroy over before spitting to the side with a dismissive "Bah! Last time I checked, cops couldn't come barging in wherever they want."

"Cops can't," Conroy agreed, taking an intimidating step closer to Bao. "But I'm no cop. I'm a Dragon. I'm here on Wei Tseng's business."

"Never heard of him," Bao said immediately. It was left unsaid, but there was without a doubt a *and I don't care* attached to the end of it. The man's attitude about *that* made Conroy angrier than anything else.

The people of the Eastern District owed Wei Tseng more than they could ever repay. He'd fought tirelessly to free them from the nightmare that was the Nine Stars and still fought to keep the peace and let them go about their lives untroubled by the triads.

"Maybe your memory's going," Conroy growled, taking a step toward the old man. Bao didn't blink, didn't back down; his gaze held hard, cold steel.

Hong grabbed Conroy's arm before jerking him back.

Conroy shook his hand away violently, glowering at him. He wanted to punch someone right then, and it would have felt good for that someone to be Hong.

"This isn't helping," Hong snapped at him in a low voice, stepping closer—the man was dumb or just suicidal, Conroy couldn't decide which. "You were supposed to let me do the talking."

"We both knew that wasn't going to happen," Conroy growled. "Not with this *puk gai* talking shit about Wei!"

"What did you call me?" Bao cried, trying to step around Hong, but Hong threw his arm out, holding him back.

"This is the problem with you Dragons," Hong growled, real anger flashing in his gaze. "You're so concerned with your goddamn pride that you let it get in the way of everything else! Who cares what one old man says? This is just some guy who runs a karaoke bar. That's it." Hong's eyes flashed to their surroundings. "A bar that's not doing too well, by the looks of this place."

Conroy knew his expression must have looked wild; he felt his eyes bugging out at Hong's words. "You don't know shit about honor, Hong. That's *your* problem. I'll be damned if I'm going to listen to your fucked-up take on the Dragons!"

"Are you seriously willing to let some stupid beef with this guy ruin our chances of putting Hwang behind bars?" Hong demanded, never raising his voice, which just pissed Conroy off more for some reason. "Is your pride worth that?"

Why did Hong have to be reasonable? Conroy would have felt much better if he had come out on top in the argument, but unfortunately the *puk gai* had a point. Wei wouldn't let some guy's ill-advised wise-ass comments keep him from doing what he needed to do, and Conroy couldn't let that happen, either.

But he'd be damned if he apologized. Instead he muttered something under his breath—not quite words, but enough to satisfy Hong. What he didn't say was that he had a hard time believing Hong would be able to get anything useful without kicking his ass for it, and even though he'd really like to wail on the old man, Conroy wasn't the type of guy who'd pick a fight with someone who couldn't defend themselves.

Wei would kick his ass if he did.

"You'll get nothing from me," Bao snapped, trying once more to close the door. Before Conroy could reach out to stop the door, Hong did so, though he did it with much less force and significantly more respect than Conroy had.

"I'm sorry that we're inconveniencing you—and that my friend here is a hothead—but this is really important." Hong's tone was honey, the sort of voice that would soothe a wild tiger and have it on its back for belly rubs. "We were hoping you could help us in an investigation."

Bao spat to the side. "Don't see how I could be any help to the cops."

"You remember a man gunned down in front of your club?" Conroy asked, voice simmering with pent-up rage. "The *cop* gunned down, I should say."

"I had nothing to do with that," Bao said firmly.

"No one said you did," Hong said cajolingly. "We were hoping you could help us find someone who may know something."

"Don't see how I could do that," Bao said.

"Maybe a few good punches to the gut will help clear your vision," Conroy suggested, cracking his knuckles.

"And maybe the same to you would help you school your tongue," Bao replied, looking completely unconcerned.

Hong shot Conroy a glare that quite plainly said *shut the hell up*. Conroy didn't have a good temper at the best of times, and this whole situation was making it worse. He controlled himself, though it was getting more difficult to do so. His nails dug into his palms, and he was sure he'd have permanent scars by the time this ridiculous conversation finished.

"We think one of your employees might have seen what happened," Hong explained. "We were hoping you could tell us who she is and where she lives. She's a Vietnamese girl, hasn't been to work since the shooting happened."

Conroy watched as a look of understanding came into Bao's eyes. The old bastard knew exactly who they were talking about.

"That's not information I can just hand out," he said gruffly. "There's rules to this, confidentiality and such."

Now he's just fucking with us, Conroy thought, impatience reaching its limit. Before he could grab the old man by his shirt and shake some sense into him, Hong began talking again.

"You would be doing the department a big favor," he said meaningfully.

"It would be good to have the police owe me a favor, I think." Bao smiled then, showing a mouthful of gold.

Maybe that's where all his money went.

"Okay, fine," Bao said at last. "I can tell you, but you owe me a favor?"

"So you'll give us information you already know and expect a favor in return?" Conroy huffed. "You ever heard of obstruction of justice?"

"That will be fine," Hong said, an easy smile on his face.

Pushover. This was police business, not Dragons, and he didn't give a damn if Hong went around throwing out favors and getting shit in return.

Thirty

BAO CAME THROUGH with information. He was an odious little man, but he'd given them the name they needed, along with an address. After a quick phone call to Ao, they were on their way to find one Trang Nguyen.

"Meeting that *ga tsan* really makes me reconsider ever going to Indulgence again," Conroy said as they weaved their way through the streets of Hong Kong. Even barely past noon, the streets were crowded, simply part of being the most densely populated city on earth.

"You mean the gang-related shooting out front didn't?" Allen asked, glancing at him for a second before returning his eyes to the road.

"Nah. I've gotten used to that." A smile ghosted across Conroy's face, gone as quickly as it appeared, but Allen noticed it nevertheless. Part of him thought—hoped?—it might be a sign that Conroy's icy veneer of hatred was beginning to thaw.

He wasn't going to hold his breath, though.

"What's the plan when we find Trang Nguyen?" Conroy asked, his right foot tapping repetitively. On anyone else, Allen would have thought it a sign of nerves, but on Conroy, he knew it for a sign of pent-up energy, that he was anxious for action.

He just hoped that eagerness didn't translate into trouble for them down the line. Conroy could control himself for the most part, but everyone had their limits, and Allen started to think Conroy was approaching his.

They needed to bring this situation to a close quickly. Allen didn't want to see what would happen when Conroy *couldn't* control himself. He was riding in the car with a wild animal who was barely restrained by a leash—one who was growing closer to snapping.

"The plan is to convince her to go talk to Ao as soon as possible," Allen said, anticipating the eye roll that came his way. "I know it's nothing exciting, but it's the best we've got right now. It would be better if Internal Affairs didn't know we had any contact with her; they'll think I'm trying to drum up more false evidence."

Conroy grunted. "About that. You're just going to let that *jin jang* set you up like this and then get away with it? What the hell's wrong with you?"

"It's not that simple, Conroy," Allen said, wearied by the thought of trying to explain departmental politics and the tightrope he walked to Conroy, a man who believed that any problem should be addressed directly.

Allen admired that attitude, honestly, and it had even been his own way of thinking for a long time, but once he joined the force, he'd realized things didn't work that way everywhere. The Hong Kong Police Department was a separate world from what he'd known on the streets, which meant the rules were different. If he intended to stay on the force—which was where he truly believed he could do the most good—then he needed to learn to follow the code.

Conroy had never faced that adapt-or-fail situation. He lived in the world of the streets. Even though it was different life now, with the Nine Stars gone, the rules still remained the same, for the most part.

"Seems pretty simple to me. He set you up. You should bust his ass for it. You can't let him get away with it."

"That's easier said than done with him in Dang's pocket."

Conroy's lips curled back. "I wish we could bring that *puk gai* down while we're at it."

"Don't worry. He's going down," Allen promised. "I don't care what it takes. Henry Dang is going to crash and burn for everything he's done."

"Is that smoke?" Conroy asked suddenly, pointing out the window. Sure enough, a plume of black smoke climbed against the horizon, sharp and distinct against the azure blue of the sky. "Where is it coming from?"

"I don't know." The sight made Allen nervous. In a compact city like Hong Kong, the smallest fire could quickly become a major problem. The buildings were so close together that it didn't take much for a fire to spread.

They got their answer soon enough. The road ahead rounded to the left before evening out, and they caught sight of the building. It was a single-story coin laundry. The front window was busted out and flames licked at the outside air. The walls had been spray-painted—tagged—and it didn't take a genius to recognize the Twisted Vipers tag near the wide-open front door.

"Stop the car," Conroy ordered. His voice was so serious, so commanding, that Allen didn't even think twice; he pulled the car up in front of the burning building.

A crowd of people had already gathered on the street. He couldn't be sure, but when Conroy threw open the door and exited, Allen thought he caught the hint of sirens in the distance—though it might have just been his imagination.

A middle-aged woman watched the building decay, sobbing while being restrained by a man about Winston's age, who might have been her son. The air was filled with the stench of burning cleaning supplies and ash.

Conroy reached them before Allen even had the chance to get out of the car. Allen hurried after him.

"What's going on? Is there anyone inside?"

Conroy looked ready to bolt into the building without a second thought if the answer had been yes.

"No," the younger man answered quickly. "Everyone got out."

"What happened?" Allen asked. He shifted his position. From where he stood, the heat of the flames slapped against him physically; sweat had already begun forming across his forehead.

"They wanted money." The boy squeezed the woman's shoulders. His voice shook, volume varying wildly, too loud one moment and then almost inaudible over the sound of the fire and the woman crying the next. "They said we had to pay them, that they own this town now, and we'd pay them if we knew what was good for us."

"Who were they?" Allen asked.

"I don't know. I'd never seen them before. We refused to pay them, and they left. About twenty minutes later, they threw a Molotov cocktail through the window."

"Everything," the woman moaned suddenly. "Everything is gone. Everything is gone. My husband and I poured everything we had into this place. Now look at it. What are we going to do?" She turned and buried her face into the man's shoulder, body wracked with sobs.

Conroy placed his hand on her back. When he spoke, his voice was compassionate, full of emotion and concern—such a stark contrast to the hard-edged man Allen usually saw. "I promise you you'll be taken care of, *siu ze*. The Dragons aren't going to allow you to suffer."

Conroy stepped away to let her be comforted by the younger man. "I need to call Wei," he said to Allen, who nodded. He wasn't going to bother trying to talk Conroy out of it, because it would be a waste of time. Besides, the Dragons were better equipped to handle the Vipers than the police at this point, with Dang at the helm.

By the time Conroy was off the phone, Allen heard the certain approach of sirens drawing closer every minute.

Conroy and Allen returned to the woman and man, and once more Conroy spoke gently. "Wei Tseng and a few of the other Dragons are on their way, *siu ze*. The Dragons are going to look after you."

"*Mh goi, mh goi*," the woman said again and again.

From the sound of the sirens, the fire department was right around the corner—and probably with the police right on their tail.

"We have to get going, Conroy," Allen told him, tapping his shoulder.

"I'm not going anywhere," Conroy said, shaking Allen's hands away. "This is important. If the Vipers really did do this, then Wei's going to need—"

"Wei's going to need us to do what we can to bring this to an end," Allen finished firmly. "If we don't find Trang Nguyen so we can guarantee Hwang stays behind bars, we'll be facing something much worse than this. Imagine every shop at risk, all the time. We have to find her."

Conroy bit his lip, looking back at the burning coin laundry, his face showing just the war between staying and going. Finally, he sighed, deflating visibly, his shoulders slumping. "Fine. Let's go."

They climbed into the car together and pulled away as the fire trucks came into sight. Allen was relieved that they'd managed to get through before the street was blocked.

"We're doing the right thing, Conroy," Allen said comfortingly, though he doubted his words would do much to bolster the man.

"Just because it's the right thing doesn't mean I have to like it."

Thirty-One

THE ADDRESS BAO had given them led to a small apartment building wedged in on either side by larger, newer buildings. It was in good condition, for all that it was old. The walls were weather-worn, and air-conditioning units projected out of some windows, while box fans sat secured in place in others.

Conroy still struggled with the fact that he'd left the burning Laundromat behind. He should have stayed, should have waited for Wei and joined in whatever they would do to find the sons of bitches responsible for the destruction. Instead, he had left with Hong on a manhunt.

He knew Hong was right, that finding the waitress and getting her to safety was the right thing to do, but it felt a lot like running away.

He didn't want to play games. This wasn't the way he was comfortable meeting challenges. He'd take pounding the pavement in search of Twisted Viper punks in the Eastern District any day.

But it was what needed to be done, and he didn't always have to like it.

"Let's go," he said when Hong stopped the car. "And don't even think about telling me to let you do the talking, either."

"Whatever you might think, I'm not dumb," Hong muttered.

Conroy left that one alone.

Hong grabbed the photocopied paper they'd gotten from Bao. "According to this, she's apartment two-three."

"Let's hope we're the first people who got to Bao," Conroy said, pulling the heavy glass door of the building open and then stepping inside. He didn't trust someone like Bao; he'd probably provide the information to anyone who could make it worth his while. If the Twisted Vipers had paid him a visit before Conroy and Hong did, then they no doubt had the same information.

"Here's hoping," Hong agreed, walking behind Conroy.

The entryway smelled strongly of cleaning product, even over the lingering stench of the smoke of the fire stuck in his nostrils, and every surface was spotless. Despite its age, someone tended carefully to the building. Along one wall, directly to their left, was two rows of mailboxes, marked with numbers, the first row two-one through two-five, the second row three-one through three-five.

Conroy watched Hong push up the slot on the mailbox for two-three with one finger.

"No built-up mail," he said, as if that told them anything.

"Maybe she doesn't get a lot," Conroy remarked. "Let's just get up to her place and see if she's home."

"Wait," Hong said suddenly. There was something strange in his voice Conroy couldn't place, and a look had come over him, like he was struggling with something. "Can I ask you a question?"

Conroy looked around. "Now?"

"You were willing and ready to go running into that burning building just now, if it meant you could save someone's life. Did anything cross your mind? Were you afraid?"

Conroy wasn't expecting a question like that, nor the tone of admiration in Hong's voice. For a moment he couldn't find his words to answer the question. Finally, he said, "I don't know; I just knew that if someone was in there, in trouble, then they needed my help. That answer your question?"

"Yeah. I think so."

Conroy didn't like the weird look on Hong's face. "Can we just get to it?"

The stairs were wide enough for them to walk side by side. One edge of the second-floor landing was lined with a wall of screened-in windows, allowing in the noise of the streets. To the other side were four doors—the fifth, the corner apartment, directly across from them as they stood at the beginning of the hall.

It struck Conroy how odd the numbering was, like a train just slightly misaligned on tracks. Instead of the door closest to them being two-one, it was two-five.

He followed Hong as he approached the door, more than okay with Hong taking the lead when there was a chance that another Twisted Viper ambush lay ahead. That was just being smart.

Hong pressed the button on the black box next to the door, and from within the apartment, Conroy heard the answering chime. It rang loud enough that there was no way she didn't hear it, even if passed out drunk.

Each second they waited felt like an eternity ticking by, and she never came to the door, never even pressed the intercom button to ask them what they wanted. The black intercom box that was standard in most apartments also came with a built-in camera, so it was possible she'd looked, seen them, and decided she would feign her absence.

"Maybe you should try again, show your badge to the camera," Conroy suggested. "Try to do *something* useful, at least."

Hong didn't even react to the all-too-obvious barb. He pulled his badge from his pocket and held it up before pressing the button again.

"Trang Nguyen?" he called, loud enough to be heard but not loud enough to disturb the neighbors. "I'm with HKPD. It's all right to open the door, if you're in there."

Conroy snorted at the generic words. If he'd heard that being said, he would not have believed it in the slightest; he didn't think anyone who'd had experience with the Eastern District police would. People learned quickly, especially with important lessons. This neighborhood trusted the police about as much as they trusted some stranger to hold their wallet.

"She must not be home," Hong said at last when they heard nothing from behind the door.

"Or she's smart and doesn't trust the cops," Conroy supplied.

"We're not all bad."

Conroy blinked, surprised at the change the quip brought over him. It wasn't the first time the Dragons—particularly Conroy, Winston, and Wei—made it plain just how they felt about the team Hong'd chosen to join. Why had the remark gotten to him now?

And why did Conroy care? It was Hong's fault; he'd chosen to join the police. He had to have known exactly what the consequences of his decision would be with the Dragons, so the blame belonged to him.

"Let's just ask the neighbors if she's been around or if anything has gone on in the past few days," Conroy said at last, eager to push past the moment—and his sympathy for Hong.

They tried two-two first and found no one home. They went to two-one next, and a balding man on the far side of middle-aged answered. He was wearing exercise clothes and a sweatband, his body drenched with perspiration.

Over the man's shoulder, Conroy caught sight of his apartment. The front area, a very small section of it, was a kitchenette, and beyond it a door that led to the single bedroom.

The man looked suspiciously between them. "Can I help you?"

Hong held up his police credentials. Conroy had to bite his tongue to prevent from saying an *I told you so* when the man looked *more* wary, not less.

"I'm Inspector Hong with the Hong Kong Police Department. I was hoping to ask you a few questions about one of your neighbors."

"My neighbor? Is one of them in trouble? Everyone around here is quiet and sticks to themselves. I can't imagine what they'd do to bring the cops here."

"No one is in any trouble," Hong assured him. "We're looking for the woman who lives in two-three, a Trang Nguyen."

"Trang? I know her. She's a sweet woman. Saves up money to send home to her grandmother in Vietnam."

"Have there been any disturbances here recently? Any noise coming from her apartment or any visitors that you don't recognize?"

The man shook his head. "No, it's been quiet there, as always. She's a great neighbor. Goes to work in the afternoon, comes home in the early morning. Never throws parties. She's had a few guests, mostly fellow Vietnamese people. I met her boyfriend once, a nice guy named Thuy."

"So no strange visitors, nothing?" Conroy pressed. "Nothing weird at all?"

The man seemed to consider the question again. "Well, there was one thing, I guess. Yesterday morning she left here pretty early—I had just come in from a run—and had a suitcase with her."

Conroy's heart began to beat faster. "She didn't say where she was going?"

The man shook his head again. "She didn't stop to chat like she usually does, so I figured she was in a hurry to go. I thought maybe her grandmother in Vietnam was ill and she needed to go home suddenly. It didn't strike me as unusual at the time."

Conroy swore loudly, and the man jumped at the words. "What? What's wrong?"

"You have absolutely no idea where she might have gone?"

"I'm afraid not. Are you sure she's not in any trouble?"

"We're sure," Hong said, his face giving away nothing. "Thank you for your time."

They made their way back down the hall, forgoing the other neighbors. If Trang had left with a suitcase, that could only mean one thing: their chance of locking Hwang up—and maintaining peace on the island—might have just left with her.

Thirty-Two

THE RIDE TO the motel was tense as Conroy's mood grew darker with the miles. Allen observed him cautiously, waiting for the impending explosion. His face was red, his jaw clenched, and his lips pressed thin. He didn't so much sit in the seat as hover on it, mimicking a predator lying in wait.

Allen hoped he could maintain his temper until they got to the motel.

Allen got his wish, but just barely; no sooner had the motel door closed behind Allen than Conroy kicked his bag savagely across the room, scattering shirts, socks, and underwear with it.

"Why can't we ever *catch a fucking break*?"

"We don't know what happened yet." Allen tried to be the voice of reason amidst his own echo of self-doubt. "No need to fly off the handle."

"Don't be stupid," Conroy cried, pacing in a tight path between the bed and the door, his fists clenching and unclenching. "You heard the same thing I did, right? Our one chance to nail Johnny Hwang walked out with a suitcase yesterday. She's gone."

"We don't know that. Sure, she's taken a suitcase, but that doesn't mean we won't be able to find her. I've got connections; if she's on the island, we can find her."

"Did you consider that she might not be on the island?" Conroy countered. "You heard what he said about her grandmother in Vietnam? How do you know she hasn't flown back there? If she has, we've lost her for good."

Allen sat on the edge of the bed, determined to maintain his cool. "If she has, I'll find out. Wei's not the only one with contacts in immigration at the airport. In the meantime, I'll call Ao and get him searching for any possible leads on where she might go."

"The Dragons could help," Conroy suggested. "We've got contacts, too."

"I really don't think that's the best idea."

Conroy literally snarled then, stepping closer to loom over Allen. He didn't want to admit it, but Allen found Conroy's sudden presence, the power radiating off him like the heat from the fire earlier, extremely alluring; even as part of him was concerned Conroy might start talking with his fists, arousal stirred; heat built in his stomach, surprising in its intensity.

"Why? You don't trust us? Think those snakes at your police station can do a better job?"

"No," Allen said carefully. "I meant that Wei's got a lot on his plate right now, especially when you add in the firebombing of the coin laundry. The Dragons' resources are going to be stretched thin enough without sending people out to find our witness. We'll have to handle this ourselves."

Conroy let his breath out with a long huff. "You're right—damn it, you're right. What do we do now?"

"Start making phone calls. I'll hit up Ao and my airport contact and then start tapping my informants. If you've got any people who pass the Dragons information, give them a call, too. The faster someone puts eyes on her the better."

They passed the afternoon making a barrage of calls. In his five years as a cop, Allen had built a very useful network of informants—a network he kept hidden from everyone else, mostly to protect them. They provided him with valuable information, including intel that a dirty cop would not want getting around.

He put the informants to work, hoping one of them would come up with a bite. His contact at the airport was going to call him back when she checked around.

As late afternoon wore into the evening, Allen made a quick run to McDonald's. It wasn't his preference, but it was fast, close, and would at least be filling. He'd just pulled back into the motel parking lot when his friend from the airport called him back. After a quick conversation, he hurried into their room to find Conroy occupying himself with crunches.

"I've got good news and bad news," he said, using his foot to push the door shut behind him.

Conroy did three more crunches before he stopped, looking at him expectantly. "Well?"

"The good news is Trang Nguyen is still in the country, at least for now. Her passport hasn't been scanned to depart."

Conroy climbed to his feet, giving a relieved nod. "Okay. Bad news?"

"The machine was busted so I couldn't get the milkshake."

Conroy laughed, then, a genuine laugh, though Allen could tell he was trying not to. "Just give me the food."

They ate in silence, wrappers spread out on the bed instead of risking the shitty table, which looked like it couldn't handle even the weight of their meal.

"It's my turn for random questions," Conroy said once he'd wolfed down his Big Mac in three bites.

"Okay," Allen said, wiping leftover salt and grease from his hands. He did his best not to show how nervous he was.

"Why did you disappear?"

Allen knew what he meant, but he still said, "When?"

"Don't play dumb, Hong. Five years ago. Why did you just walk out and never come back?"

He'd anticipated the question eventually, but he hadn't expected that day to come so soon. He often mulled over the reasons himself over the years and hadn't been entirely sure at first, but with time, he now understood his motivations quite well.

"The day I did it, the first person I told was Constance. Halfway through telling her, Wei came in, so I ended up telling him, too. His reaction—I don't have to tell you what it was, do I? I'm pretty sure you could guess easily enough—it shocked me. The things he said to me... He accused me of being a traitor, said I was turning my back on everything we'd fought for. He told me if I went through with it, I was no longer welcome near him, near the Dragons."

He took a deep, shaky breath. Thinking about those words, even now, hurt as if pushing his finger into an open wound. The men and women who had become the Dragons were like family to him, after all they'd been through. It wasn't just a friend turning away from him; it was his chosen brother.

"The way he reacted, I figured it was a pretty good indication of what I could expect from you." Allen couldn't bring himself to look at Conroy. His eyes remained glued resolutely to the ketchup stain on his Big Mac wrapper. "Wei's rejection was hard enough. I couldn't handle it if you chose to reject me, too."

"So you made the choice for me," Conroy finished.

"It seemed like the easier option," Allen confessed. "If I already knew the answer, why bother? I knew what the answer would be if you had to choose between me and the Dragons."

"How could you know that if you didn't give me the chance?"

"I wanted to. I did. That same night, I actually went to your place. I didn't get out of the car, though." Allen laughed sadly. "I was too scared. In the end, I figured my way was easier and maybe a little less painful."

"Well," Conroy said, voice filled with something that might have been regret. "We'll never know, will we?"

Allen ached to find words, anything, though he didn't have any idea what. Before he could, though, Conroy loudly crumpled his wrappers, taking the opportunity with it to the trash.

"We need to get some rest," he said, tone suddenly brusque, businesslike. "No use focusing on the past when who the hell knows what tomorrow's going to bring."

Thirty-Three

"I STILL DON'T know why you're going to work when we should be out hunting for Trang," Conroy said, buckling his seat belt. The morning had just dawned and Conroy and Hong were getting underway. Hong planned to drop Conroy off at the coffee shop and go into work.

"There's nothing we can do until we have a lead," Hong said. "Besides, if I don't go to work, then Dang and Internal Affairs are going to get suspicious."

"Fine." Conroy didn't know what had him in such a foul mood; he should have been happy to be free of Hong's presence and back among the Dragons

But after the previous night's discussion, he didn't know what he felt. He'd always imagined that Hong not having the decency to at least tell him to his face had been because he hadn't cared, that it had been easy for him to just walk away. Now he wasn't so sure.

But did that change the fact that, easy or not, Hong *had* walked away? He weighed the conflict in his mind like an uneven barbell.

Get your head out of your ass, Conroy. History existed in stone, and no amount of dwelling would change their past. Hong had made his choice, and Conroy, in turn, had made his.

"I'll send you a message when I finish work and am on my way," Hong said when they reached Coffee by Constance.

Conroy grunted in reply and exited the car as quickly as he could, eager to put distance between himself and Hong.

Maybe he'd been an idiot to give in to his lust and sleep with Hong; ever since then everything had become muddled, confused, and it didn't show any signs of clearing anytime soon.

Despite the early hour, the coffee shop was unlocked, though the "Closed" sign was still showing. The lights inside were off, but Conroy didn't plan on lingering in there. He made his way through to the kitchen. As he approached, he heard Noah.

"So America in Cantonese is *mei gwok*?"

Noah sat in the kitchen with Shelby, a Cantonese workbook open on the counter in front of them. Shelby was helping him with his *hanzi*.

"That's right. But look, you're missing a line in *mei*, here. There should be four, not three."

Noah grumbled before correcting his mistake. They both looked up at Conroy's entry.

"*Dzou son*," Noah said, waving at Conroy.

Noah seemed so confident in his effort to speak Cantonese that Conroy suppressed his chuckle at his mistake. "*Dzou san.*"

Noah frowned. "What did I say?"

"*Dzou son.* Easy mistake."

"Let's keep working on it," Shelby said patiently. She'd taken over Constance's duty teaching Noah Cantonese, since he wanted to learn and was doing a pretty good job of it. Conroy suspected it was part of a scheme by Constance and Wei to keep Noah and Shelby out of the way and out of danger. A pretty smart plan.

"Are they up there?" Conroy asked, pointing upward, and Shelby and Noah nodded. "All right, I'm heading up." Conroy patted Noah on the shoulder as he headed out the back door and upstairs.

Wei, Tony, Chris, and Smile were there, looking at the television in silence. Conroy was not surprised to see the fire at the coin laundry had become a major story.

When Conroy entered, Wei muted the television. "This is getting out of hand."

"Without Hwang to put a leash on them, they're running wild," Tony said grimly. "The leadership is too busy trying to position themselves to take the top to worry about reining them in."

"And it's the people who suffer." Wei leaned forward, elbows on his knees and face troubled. Conroy hadn't seen such distress in a long time. Heavy bags rested beneath his eyes, his hair disheveled and his five-o'clock shadow reaching the point of full-on facial hair, all of it coming together to give him an unkempt, almost crazed look.

"When was the last time you slept, Boss?" Conroy asked.

"That's a good question," he replied with a small shrug. "I get a couple of hours every morning, after coming in."

"You're wearing yourself thin," Tony said, his tone suggesting the words had been repeated numerous times before.

"Well, it comes with the territory. Literally. Listen up, everybody. Since Conroy's here, we can go on and get started."

Wei cleared his throat, and when he spoke again, he didn't sound tired or worried. His voice was that of the leader of the Dragons, calm and in charge and brimming with an inner fire.

"After the fire yesterday, we reached out again to the Twisted Viper redpoles of some of the outlying territories, or those who don't have enough influence to have been part of Hwang's inner circle and so no standing in the power conflict they've got going on. Our goal is to find a way to stabilize things in Hwang's absence, maybe even convince a few of them we can offer better protection than whoever takes the helm there next."

"Sounds like a long shot to me." Steel crossed his arms over his chest.

"Maybe," Wei allowed. "But we did find a few who were willing to at least meet with us and hear us out. Not near enough, but it's a start. You don't build a wall by throwing a pile of bricks together; you do it one brick at a time. Hopefully some of these will be that first brick and lead to others."

"Okay, so when do we go?" Conroy asked. It was no one there's fault, but being in their meeting place, which usually felt so comfortable and homey, reminded him too much of being cramped in that motel. He didn't want to be inside where it was safe; he wanted to be out on the street *doing* something, danger or not. He was a man of action; that was part of what made him a Dragon.

"Listen, Conroy," Wei started before getting up from the couch and crossing the room to him. The look on his face spoke loud and clear, no other words necessary.

"I'm *not* staying here, Wei."

"You're like public enemy number one for the Twisted Vipers right now, Conroy," Tony reminded him. "You're not going to have any friends in that room."

"Yeah, well, neither are you!"

"True, but at this point, they want to kill you a little more than the rest of us," Chris said with his usual casual air. "Though I guess having you along if bullets started flying would be safer, since they'll probably shoot at you, first."

"I don't think that's helping, Chris," Conroy glowered.

"I thought I'd have you stay here and keep an eye on Noah and Shelby," Wei explained. His manner told Conroy he knew good and well that the pity assignment wasn't going to do the trick, but had to try.

"Have you seen your boyfriend in action, Wei? And the way he's been teaching Shelby, I'm pretty sure she could kick most of our asses—except maybe Smile, and you. Or you can leave Steel here to watch them; he's the youngest, and he is screwing Shelby's brother."

Wei didn't look convinced, and Conroy started to get a little desperate.

"You *need* me out there, Wei. I've been right there with you through everything, from the beginning. Are you really going to go into this without me?"

Wei ran a hand down his face as he considered. For a wild second, Conroy feared he'd say no, but instead he nodded with palpable reluctance. "Fine. If we're going into this, I'd definitely rather have you there than here."

Conroy grinned. "Because you know they'll be intimidated by me?"

"No. If you're going to get into trouble, I'd rather it be where I am so I can help get you *out* of it."

Thirty-Four

THEY MET AT a Japanese-style *yakiniku* restaurant, where each table had a built-in grill and the workers brought tins of hot coals for you to cook your meat over. The sign said it wasn't open for lunch, but they'd been able to pay to have it opened since it sat in neutral ground.

The owners weren't present, which wasn't a bad thing. It was probably better for their own safety. There were four men sitting at a single table, facing the door. Four other tables had men at them, their faces wary, most barely concealing hostility, others not even attempting to. They were the muscle of the Twisted Viper redpoles who'd agreed to meet them.

Taking them in, Conroy couldn't help but feel a little outnumbered. Sure, they weren't the biggest, meanest guys the Vipers had to offer, but besides Conroy, Wei had only brought Chris and Tony. Hopefully that wouldn't be a mistake.

The four redpoles stood up when they entered, their postures impassive.

They had obviously decided one of them was the leader, either through a vote or by virtue of him being more powerful, because the others seemed to defer to him.

"Wei Tseng," he said by way of greeting, gesturing toward the fifth chair at their table. "Your men will need to sit elsewhere."

Wei gave them the slightest nod, and Conroy led Tony and Chris to the closest table to where the leaders sat, not taking his eyes off of the other men. The redpoles were Wei's concern; the bodyguards were Conroy's.

It looked like each of the Twisted Viper redpoles had brought along three men, which made the odds twelve to three. Not the best odds, he'd admit, but he'd had worse.

"You really think it was smart to bring *him*?" a second redpole asked, sneering in Conroy's direction.

Conroy gave him a slow, lazy smile in response.

"That's not your concern," Wei said.

"He's a fucking snitch!"

Wei stepped up on him fast, shoulders squared, face hard; he'd slipped into the persona of the leader of the Dragons now that he was in the presence of the Twisted Vipers. Hard, unyielding, and violent if he needed to be.

"I said it's none of your goddamn concern."

Conroy saw the table of bodyguards start to move, but the first speaker held out his hand to stop them.

"Let's get started. Make this fast, Tseng. Last thing we want is Jiang finding out about this gathering. I for one do *not* want to make his shit list. You can call me Ting. This—" He indicated the second speaker. "—is Big Po, and these are Jake Tam and Lazarus."

Wei took his seat. "I wanted to meet with you to discuss what happens next. I'm sure you've seen the chaos going on right now—not just here, but in your territory, as well. With Hwang out of the picture, things are getting out of control, don't you think?"

"Whose fault is that?" Lazarus asked, his voice raspy, and it wasn't hard to see why. A deep scar shadowed his neck; someone had clearly slit his throat, probably deep enough to damage his vocal cords.

Wei met his accusing eyes without blinking, and not for the first time, Conroy swelled with pride in his leader.

"It was Hwang's. He was the one stupid enough to come into *my* territory and gun down a cop in the middle of the fucking street. He left us with a mess to clean up, so that's what we're going to do."

"What is it you want from us, Tseng?" Big Po asked, his tone and body language making it clear he didn't feel particularly inclined to cooperate.

"I want to restore peace," Wei said, earning snickers from the tables of bodyguards. "You think things aren't going to get worse? If Hwang goes to jail, there's going to be civil war in the Vipers—and what do you think will happen to you? The other redpoles, Jiang, they don't care anything about you, do they? You have to know as well as I do that as soon as the opportunity presents itself, someone in a stronger standing is going to sweep in and take your territory in order to better their standing and their chances of reaching the top."

The four redpoles traded looks but didn't deny Wei's words.

"What is your proposal, then?" The question came from Lazarus again. The fourth, Jake Tam, hadn't spoken at all.

"Align yourself with someone stronger."

The four redpoles stared at Wei for a moment, and then they all began to laugh, as if he'd told the world's funniest joke.

Ting had to try several times before he finally managed words through breathless laughter. "You mean you?"

"I do. At least with me you get to keep your positions and your lives. You know as well as I do that whoever replaces Johnny Hwang as the dragonhead is going to do a lot of housecleaning, put people he trusts in redpole positions."

"That's only if Hwang gets replaced." Big Po glared in Conroy's direction.

"Okay, if he doesn't, what do you think is going to happen next? When Hwang gets out of prison, there's going to be a war. There's no stopping that now. If he's free, he will take the Twisted Vipers to war against the Dragons, and that's not going to end well for anyone—but especially not for you."

"You think we're afraid of you Dragons?" Big Po cracked his knuckles. "I say bring on the fight."

"You don't remember the Nine Stars," Lazarus snapped at Big Po. "I do. I saw what these men are capable of. Don't be so eager to fight."

"There's something else you haven't considered," Wei added, clasping his hands together on the table in front of him and leaning forward. "What happens if a fight breaks out? The only thing that has kept the Blue Suns off the island is the fact that they didn't want to go up against both the Twisted Vipers and the Dragons at full strength. We break the peace, and you know they'll swoop in."

"This is a lot to think about, Tseng," Ting said at last. "I don't know what you hoped to accomplish coming here, but I don't think you did. It would be suicide to turn against Johnny Hwang and the Twisted Vipers right now. Jiang would kill us in the slowest way possible."

Wei shrugged and then stood. "I made the effort; that's all I can do. Hopefully the next time we meet, we won't be trying to kill each other."

Conroy, Chris, and Tony stood as well. Conroy was all tension, wondering if perhaps one of these *puk gai* was going to try to pull a fast one on them. None of them moved, though, and they made their way to the door.

"Hey, Wong."

It took Conroy a full beat to detect the speaker, and then he realized Tam had finally spoken. He took a few steps toward Conroy.

"We're letting you go this time, since we agreed to a neutral meeting and the last thing we want to do is piss off Wei Tseng, but next time, we won't. Jiang has put a price on your head. A *very* big price."

Conroy tried to feign disinterest, when in reality his blood went cold. "How much are we talking?"

"Thirty-five thousand US dollars."

Thirty-Five

ALLEN DIDN'T SEE any sign of the Internal Affairs agents when he arrived at work, and no sign of them throughout the morning. He remained stuck behind his desk until Wu and Leong completed their investigation nonetheless.

He did his best to concentrate on the paperwork before him and stay clear of the investigators. It went against his every impulse to not engage Ao and let it be.

Near lunchtime, he received a message from Wei telling him they were going to go have a summit of sorts with some of the lower-level Twisted Viper redpoles, and from that point on, his focus dissipated. Concern for Conroy bubbled up at random times, to the extent that he wanted to do nothing more than take out his phone and call Conroy to make sure he was all right.

He battled the overwhelming distress; it told him the walls against his feelings for Conroy were crumbling—which no doubt started after he couldn't keep control of himself and gave in to his baser instincts.

He would not go down that road again. The bridge home had been burned the day he'd turned his back on Conroy's apartment building instead of going inside. He had to live with that choice, and he'd done so for this long just fine.

Throughout the morning and afternoon, Ao's desk stayed empty. Allen hoped he'd come back in so he could ask him at least a few questions. He wanted very badly to know where things stood. Ao was probably out chasing leads, though—maybe even working on tracking down where Trang Nguyen went.

Use your head, Hong, he told himself. *The police aren't the only angle you can use to get information.* Though they weren't technically supposed to form friendships with anyone in the prosecutor's office, over the years he'd worked with a few prosecutors he'd come to trust, and none more than Prosecutor Yu Chen.

In the last two years, Yu had made a name for himself prosecuting triad-related cases. Allen had no doubt Yu would be the man working the Hwang case—at least if they wanted any hope of a conviction.

Even better, since Internal Affairs had taken him off the case, there was no concern about any misconduct; it would just be a casual conversation.

When he called, it was only to be told Yu had already left for court. Allen would have to hurry if he hoped to catch up with him there, but he wasn't opposed to it. His desk acted as a weight pressing him down, and he wanted to shrug it free. Maybe outside the walls of the precinct he could escape the thoughts of Conroy that never seemed to be far from his mind.

Thankfully there had been no sign of Dang all day; his office remained closed, so Hong didn't have any reservations about leaving on unofficial duty. Besides, anything Dang wouldn't want him to do struck him as a good idea.

The drive was pleasant, as the sun had come out and the day seemed to be warming up above what it usually reached in October. He had the window down, the wind rushing in, and his thoughts were as far from Conroy as he could manage to get them.

Yu's assistant said he'd only left a few minutes before Allen called, so he should be able to get there not long after him—maybe even at the same time, since Yu's office was farther from the courthouse than the precinct.

He pulled into a parking space he technically shouldn't have been occupying, though his police license plate would keep him from getting ticketed, and he was in a hurry.

Jogging from the parking spot in front of the courthouse and up the steps, he barely managed to intercept Yu Chen before he reached the doors. Yu was in his early forties but looked to be far younger, with a handsome face that was dominated by a rather hawkish nose. His too-knowing eyes were wide with surprise.

"Inspector Hong. I didn't expect to run into you here."

"It's good to see you, Prosecutor Chen." Allen stepped closer then, lowering his voice even though there was no one outside. "I have a few questions about the Hwang case. I'm not working the case anymore," he added, seeing the expression of dismay on Yu's face. "This is more for my own curiosity."

"I've got some business in the courthouse." He checked his watch. "I should be done around four. We can get some coffee and I'll tell you what I can."

It was just after two. Patience had become harder for Allen to maintain since Yang's shooting, but he would take the opportunity.

"All right. I'll be here when you get out."

Yu went on into the courthouse. Allen had about two hours to kill, and no real idea how to do it. First he sat there listening to the radio and playing one of those silly phone games where you have to wait for people to send things to you or else spend lots of your hard-earned, real money to progress, but that lost its enjoyment factor quickly.

The free time gave him too much time to think, and his mind kept turning to Conroy and the others. Had their meeting with the Twisted Vipers been as much of a disaster as he feared? Would they have messaged him if something had gone wrong?

As if his fingers had a mind of their own, his phone was out and he was typing a message without consciously processing the movement.

How did the meeting go? Are you okay?

He stopped himself before he hit the "send" button, his thumb hovering over it on the screen. *The last thing Conroy wants is a message from me.* He was letting his confused feelings get the better of him. The blur of emotions led to confusion and doubt. How he felt said nothing for Conroy or Conroy's view toward him.

He deleted the message before he could give in to temptation.

The two hours passed painstakingly slow, but they did pass. When Allen returned, Yu stood outside, clearly waiting for him.

"Hope the wait wasn't too bad," Yu said, motioning for Allen to follow him.

"I'm a cop. I'm used to waiting," Allen said—and even though that wasn't so true today, it was true in general, so it didn't register as a lie.

Yu led him down the sidewalk to a small coffee shop. "We can talk safely here. I trust the staff."

They took a table and ordered from a young man, probably a college student working a part-time job.

"So how is the case against Hwang progressing?"

"I don't know what you're hoping to hear, Allen, but it's not good news."

Allen sighed. "I was afraid you'd say that."

"There's just not a lot to go on. We've no weapon, no confession, and only the word of one witness, who has already been painted as less than credible because of triad involvement."

"The Dragons aren't a triad," Allen protested.

"That's beside the point," Yu said, biting his lip. "Hwang's lawyer has landed a hearing in two days, where he's going to file a motion to dismiss."

Allen's back stiffened in alarm. "Do you think he'll get it?"

"Yes. We just don't have enough to go to trial, Allen. We need more if we want to bring him down."

Allen looked around and then leaned forward. He started to speak but stopped as the young man returned with their coffee. Yu might trust the people in that place, but at that moment, he didn't trust anyone.

Once the server was gone, he said, "There was a second witness. Ao Cheung and I are working on tracking her down right now. If we can find her and get her testimony, will that be enough?"

Yu considered for a moment before answering. "That will depend on her testimony, but yes, it definitely would. It would give us enough evidence to go to trial, and that keeps Hwang behind bars longer. But I can't get the hearing on the motion to dismiss delayed, Allen. Not without letting on why, and the moment Hwang hears it, this witness's life is in danger. You have to find the witness *before* the hearing."

"I understand. We'll double our efforts. I'll get you that witness."

Allen's phone buzzed on the table, making both Allen and Yu jump a little. "It's Ao Cheung. Maybe he's got the answer to our prayers."

Yu took a slow sip of his coffee. "Let's hope so."

Thirty-Six

CONROY AND THE rest of the Dragons were waiting inside Coffee by Constance when Allen pulled up. When he walked through the door, Constance came around from behind the counter and then pulled him into a hug.

"You look worn out," she remarked, pulling back to study his face. "Are you eating?"

"I'm eating fine," he assured her. "Conroy, come on. We've got to get moving."

"In a rush, huh?" Conroy made no move to get up from the table where he sat with Wei and Steel. "Not going to sit down and ask how the meeting with the Vipers went?"

"I don't need to ask. I can tell by Wei's face. Now come on. I've got a lead on Trang Nguyen."

Conroy's cavalier attitude changed immediately. He came to his feet and drained his coffee cup before crossing to join Allen by the door.

"Where are we headed?"

"I'll explain on the way. We don't have a lot of time."

Surprisingly, Conroy didn't argue.

"We've got to find Trang as soon as possible," Allen said once they were on their way. "Hwang's lawyers are trying to get the case dismissed the day after tomorrow, and without Trang, it's going to happen."

"Well, that sucks," Conroy said, which couldn't have been more of an understatement.

"Luckily Ao managed to track down her parents. They live in Causeway Bay. Hopefully she's there, or if she's not, they'll know where she might be."

"Sounds like a good plan."

"It's the best we've had since this whole thing started," Allen said. "Hopefully we get this done, and we can put this trouble to bed."

"That might be harder for some of us." Conroy's voice took on a tone of thinly veiled forced-levity.

"What's wrong? What happened at that meeting?"

"Well, they rejected our peace offer—like I'm sure most of us were expecting."

"Right, so what's with the weird behavior? You're not acting like the normal asshole that you are."

"Turns out Jiang's pretty pissed at me. He's put a bounty on my head."

Allen cringed, though it wasn't entirely unexpected. "How much?"

"Enough to make *me* wish I could collect it. He's guaranteed the Twisted Vipers aren't going to stop coming after me."

"That just means we have to make sure we take Jiang down too," Allen said casually, even though he knew it would not be so simple. Jiang, like Hwang, was a crafty *puk gai*, and he was meticulous in his work, including the cleanup.

The thought of someone trying to kill Conroy sent white-hot fury rushing through Allen. He couldn't concentrate on the road in front of him.

He knew he shouldn't, but he had an unbearable, ridiculous desire to protect Conroy. Conroy didn't *need* protecting; he could take care of himself. But Allen didn't want him to have to.

Dangerous thoughts.

"Hong? Hong?" Conroy's words startled Allen. He hadn't realized he'd zoned out. "You're driving like a lunatic. I don't think you can collect the money, since you're a cop, so no need to have a car accident."

"Sorry. Just eager to get to Trang Nguyen." He hoped that Conroy bought it; Allen was known for his intensity and focus on work, always had been, even before their world changed forever, so he thought it was believable. Better that Conroy never knew what really went through Allen's mind. He'd probably decide he had to kick Allen's ass on principle if he did.

Trang Nguyen's parents lived in an old-fashioned neighborhood, sort of like the one where Wei and Allen and Constance once lived; no apartments, only longstanding houses built before British colonialism. These were smaller, though, meant for the people who worked the ocean for a living. Allen's apartment was probably about the same size, for all these were houses of their own.

Allen pulled in front of the house, double-checking the address.

"This is the place," he said, pointing. "Let's hope she's here."

"The lights are on," Conroy observed. "Must mean *someone's* home."

They climbed from the car and made their way up the walk. As they drew near, Allen caught the distinct sounds of a woman sobbing inside the house.

Allen leaped into motion, covering the distance from the sidewalk to the front door in two massive steps. The front door sat ajar, as if an unintended welcome.

"Conroy, stay—" He stopped himself from finishing his thought. What good would it do to tell him to stay behind him, anyway? All it would accomplish was pissing him off, and he could really do without doing that right now. "Stay alert," he finished weakly.

"We don't have time to worry about being careful." Conroy stepped around Allen and then pushed through the opening, moving into the part of the house where you take off your shoes before going in. Seeing the mess that lay beyond, neither Conroy nor Allen bothered.

The living room was in shambles. In the center of the room, a woman who appeared a few years older than Constance sat, shoulders jumping up and down from the strength of her crying. She sat over the prone form of a man who must have been her husband and Trang Nguyen's father.

Upon their entrance, the woman looked up and started screaming in Vietnamese.

"It's okay, it's okay," Allen said quickly to her in English before switching to Cantonese when she didn't seem to understand the English. "I'm with the police." He dug his badge from his pocket and showed her.

Her screaming quieted then, though her crying didn't abate. She'd moved enough that Allen could get a good look at the man. His face was bloody and bruised, both eyes swollen shut, and his bottom lip busted open. Blood trailed down the side of his face, and strands of his salt-and-pepper hair clumped together in a sick nest of gore.

The shallow movement of the man's chest relieved Allen.

"Is whoever did this still here?" Conroy asked, his voice somehow both sharp and gentle at the same time.

The woman shook her head.

"Do you know who did this?" Allen asked, moving toward her and her husband slowly so as not to frighten her.

"They were looking for my Trang," she said in barely passable Cantonese. "They said we knew where she was and had to tell them. We tried to tell them we didn't know anything, but they didn't believe us. My husband told them to leave, and they—they did this."

Sobs stole her words again for a time. "They told us we'd tell them when we saw Trang or where she went if we know what's good for us. This—" She gestured at the trashed room around them. "—was a warning, for us and her."

"The Twisted Vipers," Conroy said grimly. "How did they know about her in the first place?"

Allen shrugged. "Dang? The police would have access to the same information Ao had. The how isn't what's important, anyway. Now that they're after her, she's in danger."

"Ma'am, if you know where your daughter is, you need to tell us. It's the only thing that might save her life."

"I was telling the truth," Trang's mother cried. "I don't know anything! I don't even know why people would be looking for her! I haven't talked to her in two weeks."

Allen physically felt the impact of the statement, and now that they were one step behind the Twisted Vipers, his stomach twisted unnaturally.

"You don't have any idea where she might go if she was in trouble?" If he sounded desperate, that's because he was. He could all but feel everything slipping from right between his fingers.

"I always thought she'd come here." The questions seemed to ground her, and the tears had finally slowed. "Since she didn't, I don't know."

"What about her boyfriend?" Conroy asked. "Thuy, I think? Know where we can find him?"

"I didn't even know she had a boyfriend. There's nothing else I can do to help you."

"Have you called an ambulance for your husband? The police?"

"No police," the woman said, caressing her husband's head. "We'll be fine."

"It will only take a moment." Allen began to reach for his phone. "I can have the Anti-Gang Task Force here soon. They'd be interested in—"

"No cops," she shouted, though it wasn't anger that tinged her voice but fear. "Do you think I'm stupid? Do you know what they would do to us if we went to the police?"

"We can keep you safe," Allen protested.

"No, you can't. You can't even keep my daughter safe. Just go. Leave us. We don't need your help."

Allen itched to push the issue, at least the ambulance, but Conroy grabbed his arm before he could. Conroy shook his head firmly and led him from the house.

"We can't just leave," Allen said once they were outside, pulling his arm free of Conroy's grip. "They need help."

"Some people don't want help. You can't force it on them, Hong." Conroy must have seen Allen's distress because he added, "We'll call Wei, then, and at least get some Dragons over here to keep an eye on them. Come on, there's nothing more we can do here."

Thirty-Seven

CONROY AND HONG fell into a funk. Conroy had grown accustomed to watching a door inch open only to be brutally shut in his face. This was just another lead that had fallen flat.

The next move was a mystery. It could only be a matter of time before they ran out of opportunities. Maybe they were just outplayed on this one.

"Are you hungry?" Hong asked suddenly, his voice sounding loud and cutting through the silence that had settled over them in the car.

Conroy wondered if the stress of the situation had finally gotten to him. "Hungry? With all that's going on, that's what you're concerned about?"

"A man's got to eat. Since we don't know what to do next, might as well get some food in us."

"I could eat." It was an understatement; his mind had been so far from food he hadn't had anything to eat since the McDonald's the night before.

"Okay, I know I place we can go to."

Conroy nodded, not really caring where they ate. There were more important things to think about, like how they were going to find Trang Nguyen now.

He was so wrapped up in his thoughts he didn't realize a full ten minutes had passed until Hong announced, "We're here."

Conroy looked around, surprised. They were in the parking lot of a small, single building across the street from a gas station. The building was ancient—older than either man in the car—an ugly square structure that might have been constructed from the cheapest metal available.

The sign over the door was newer, though, a gaudy red thing with gold lettering. It looked more like shops Conroy saw in American dramas where the characters had to venture into "exotic" Chinatown. The entire thing was offensive.

"*This* is where you want to eat?" Conroy turned a skeptical gaze on Hong. The sign had changed, as it had come under new management, and the gas station across the street was new, but Conroy would know the place anywhere. You didn't forget a place you spent two years of your life.

"It's close and it has pretty good food," Hong said defensively.

"It was a crappy place when I worked here six years ago, and it's probably a crappy place now."

"Just come on. I'm hungry."

Conroy followed Hong reluctantly, though he did seriously consider staying in the car and letting Hong eat. The growl of hunger from his stomach cast the final vote.

A shiver traveled down his spine as he stepped into the humid dining room. It was a strange sensation, returning to a place you once worked after half a decade. The smell of boiling noodles, seared meats, and various spices hadn't changed. It was the same one he'd tried to scrub away for hours after a shift, though he was never quite successful.

The aroma wasn't the only familiar thing about the restaurant. The new owners hadn't changed the furniture or decor; everything was as it was the last time he had been there—well, maybe cleaner.

"Allen!" a heavyset man called, bald head gleaming with sweat in the heat of the restaurant. He held his arms out in a welcoming gesture. "I was wondering where you were. It's been, what, two weeks?"

Conroy could hardly believe it. The staff knew his name?

"Things have been busy," Hong said while shaking the man's hand warmly.

The man nodded darkly. "That I've seen. Come on in. Let's get some food in your belly." He led them to a two-top. "I know you don't, but does your friend here need a menu?"

"I think two of my usual would be fine," Hong said and then looked quickly to Conroy. "If that's okay."

Conroy shrugged. "You know I can eat pretty much anything."

"I'll get working on that, then. You two enjoy."

The man lumbered off to the back, calling their order out to the cook.

"How often do you come here that you have a usual?" Conroy asked.

Hong shrugged. "A couple times a month."

"The food that good, then?" Conroy would be surprised if it was, given the look of the place, though great food could be found in the most unexpected of spots.

"I guess it's average."

Conroy didn't understand. "So the place doesn't even have food that's all that great, and you eat here repeatedly anyway? Why?"

An idea dawned on him. There was no way in hell that Hong frequented the restaurant because it's where Conroy used to work.

But more than that—it was where they met. He remembered Wei bringing Hong there with Constance to discuss the formation of the fight against the Nine Stars.

It felt ridiculous and not at the same time. Hong *did* keep the photo from their trip to Disneyland. Most people didn't hold on to obvious mementos of failed relationships—or, if they did, it was put away in some box of bittersweet memories, not openly displayed in their apartment years after the relationship ended.

Hong shifted uncomfortably. "It's familiar. I don't mind the food, and Jao is a good man."

Conroy didn't push, though he wanted to. He glanced at the single television jammed into the corner of the bar—it looked like the exact television from a decade before—and saw a picture of Johnny Hwang in the corner next to a news anchor.

The TV was either muted or the volume so low that Conroy couldn't hear the report, but the captioning along the bottom said it all: *Alleged Twisted Viper leader's lawyers move to dismiss charges.*

The anchor was soon replaced by video footage shot earlier that day of Hwang's lawyer, a man who looked like he'd been striving to match every stereotypical description of an evil lawyer there was.

"I can't believe there's a chance that motherfucker might walk free." Conroy scowled at the television. "How does a man like that live with himself?"

"The same way Henry Dang does, no doubt," Hong replied, barely sparing a glance for the television. "They sold their souls for money a long time ago. Whatever shred of conscience they've got left probably isn't enough to move them."

"I'll never understand men like that."

"Good men rarely do."

Conroy quirked an eyebrow at him, and Hong frowned a little.

"What?"

"You think I'm a good man?"

"Of course I do." Hong's tone made it clear he thought Conroy had asked an absurd question. "If you weren't, you'd be a Twisted Viper, not a Dragon."

"Considering how much shit your boss talks about—"

"I am nothing like Henry Dang!" An edge had come into Hong's voice, and Conroy regretted the comment. "I've never agreed with his assessment of the Dragons. Come on, I fought next to you, for crying out loud. I doubt anyone could find a better group of people in Hong Kong."

The words moved Conroy, more than he thought they could. The day Hong turned his back on him—on them—he'd written him off, turning his hurt to a cold, hard anger that fit right in with Wei's. It wasn't an anger born of hatred, not for either man, but one of wounded pride and betrayal.

That Hong could still speak highly of them after the way he'd been treated by the Dragons said a lot about him.

"I know you're not like him," Conroy said softly. "That wasn't how I meant it. I think..." He didn't know what to say, so he fell silent. He never had been a man of words—no, that was Wei. Wei was the diplomat, Conroy the fighter. But this, this felt like a fight of a different kind, a fight he could not win.

When he spoke again, his throat felt tight. "The Dragons—we—haven't been very welcoming to you—"

"You don't say?" Hong's mouth turned up just a bit, taking the bite from his words, but Conroy felt them nonetheless.

"What I mean is...we're dicks to you. But you still come when we need you. I don't get you or why."

Hong answered without pause. "I knew the consequences when I joined the police. I knew Wei wouldn't be able to support my choice. And despite what Wei might have convinced himself, it wasn't about turning my back on the Dragons, either."

"You don't owe me an explanation." Conroy wasn't sure he wanted one, if he was honest with himself. That door in his life needed to remain shut.

"You're the one person I *do* owe an explanation to," Hong admitted. "Now that I've explained myself to Winston, anyway. I joined the police because I thought it was the best way to keep the Dragons safe—from police corruption, but also from having to go through that hell again. I still remember waking up in the middle of the night to hear that another building had been burned, or more innocent people killed, sometimes even one of our own. I remember the docks."

Conroy shuddered involuntarily. The docks. That had been one of the worst nights of his life and one of the darkest points in their war with the Nine Stars. They'd gotten the phone call early in the morning from a concerned citizen saying something was going down on the docks. Wei had sent a group to handle it. When they didn't report in, Wei, Constance, Conroy, and Hong had gone to investigate. They'd found the Dragons Wei'd sent—fathers, sons, lovers, friends, *family*—butchered, bodies hacked apart. Blood had coated every visible surface, and sometimes Conroy could still smell that place in his nightmares.

"Me, too."

"Winston and Steel and the other young Dragons, they didn't really go through it like we did. I wanted to spare them. And make sure you wouldn't be in danger anymore. All of you, the Dragons," he added in the tone of a man afraid he'd said too much.

Before the conversation could take a more awkward turn, their food arrived, two big bowls of *wun tun mien*—wonton noodles. They were Hong's favorite.

The food gave both men an excuse to disengage, retreat into their thoughts. After a few minutes of eating, Conroy was surprised to realize he found the silence almost comfortable.

He wouldn't have believed it possible only a week ago, but he was actually becoming accustomed to Hong's presence. This security detail or whatever Hong called it no longer felt like an unbearable inconvenience.

Their silence lasted through the rest of the meal, right up until they both finally pushed their empty bowls away. While it wasn't the best bowl of noodles he'd ever eaten—and certainly not enough to warrant coming there several times a month—it had filled his hollow stomach.

The two tossed money on the table and started for the door.

"Once we get back to the motel, we really need to start coming up with a plan," Conroy said as Hong waved goodbye to the friendly man who'd greeted them earlier. "We can't rely on Trang Nguyen falling into our laps."

"I know, I know." Hong sounded like a kid whose mother told him he needed to finish his homework.

Just as they started through the door, Conroy caught sight of a black car idling in the parking lot—not in an actual parking space, just in the middle of the lot—facing the road.

Afterward Conroy wouldn't be able to say what it was that made him act, only that instinct kicked in. He was experienced with danger, and he'd come to trust those reflexes that kicked in; ignoring them could get you killed. He grabbed Hong and threw him to the ground, barely dropping down himself before the bullets began to fly.

Thirty-Eight

HENRY DANG WAS not a man who liked expending favors he'd collected throughout the years unless he absolutely had to. Tonight he had no choice, unfortunately, so he'd expended a good bit of the capital he'd made for himself in arranging a secret meeting with Johnny Hwang outside visiting hours in a room that wouldn't be recorded.

He waited, working to mask his anxiety. He forced himself to sit calmly at one of the tables arranged for visitors.

He remained seated when the guards brought Hwang in and pushed him roughly into the chair across from him. Hwang looked infuriatingly unperturbed by the late summons, which only reinforced Dang's desire to put him in his place before things got wildly out of hand.

"What's with the late-night visit, Dang?" Hwang asked, the barest hint of amusement in his voice—amusement at Dang's expense, no less.

"You know why you're here, I'm sure," Dang replied tersely. He didn't want to give Hwang any more chances to play games with him. "What the hell were you thinking? I've got Twisted Vipers firebombing shops and shooting up restaurants—trying to kill a police officer, no less! Do you realize how complicated you're making things? An innocent man was killed in your most recent stunt."

Hwang's eyes went cold. "Don't blame me for this, mess. You were given the chance to put an end to this and you couldn't, so now I am."

"I had it taken care of!" Dang hissed, leaning forward. "I had Allen Hong discredited; no one would believe any evidence he brought against you, and without it you would have been free in a matter of days! After tonight, though, you've lended credence to his claims and have made it that much harder to handle this properly."

Hwang stood; the guards didn't try to stop him. "This is your bed, Dang. Your idea of 'properly' is no longer on the table. I'm done with the status quo. I will watch the Eastern District—hell, the entire island—burn if it means bringing down Wei Tseng and the Dragons."

The man was crazy, Dang realized. He didn't want power, he wanted revenge, and he'd destroy everything Dang had worked so hard for—everything he'd sold his proverbial soul for—in the process of getting it.

"What's wrong, Dang? This not what you bargained for? Sometimes you should read the fine print. We're done here. Next time you come see me, it better be to tell me that Wei Tseng is dead or that I'm going free."

Dang could do nothing but sit there helplessly as Hwang left the room. Watching the Twisted Viper dragonhead leave, he felt like he was watching the future he'd worked so hard for crumble to dust around him.

But no, he could salvage this. There had to be some way that he could turn that situation to his advantage; there always was. If it existed, he'd figure it out. He was not about to give up so easily.

He left the prison, all the while thinking of a way to turn the situation around. A scapegoat, that's what he needed. If he could make that work, then there was still a chance to salvage everything.

And he had the perfect person in mind.

Thirty-Nine

MORNING HAD NEARLY come while they were still at the restaurant talking to police. Neither Conroy nor Hong had been hurt, but the friendly man—Jao, Hong said his name was—had been hit, probably while trying to see what the commotion had been. He'd died before they could get him loaded into the ambulance.

Hong took the death hard; he'd been quiet, except for when he absolutely had to answer a question. He didn't say a word on the way back to the motel and let Conroy drive.

For the entire trip, Conroy tried to think of the right words, but all combinations fell flat. If the Twisted Vipers hadn't been after Conroy, Jao would still be alive. Words couldn't fix that.

He put people at risk just by going out to a restaurant. He hadn't taken the threat the Twisted Vipers posed seriously enough, and this, it seemed, was his punishment. Why was it the universe saw fit to use other people as tools of its will? It should have been Conroy who took that bullet, not Jao.

But it wasn't his fault, not really, and he knew that. Blame rested with the Twisted Viper who pulled the trigger. First Yang, then the coin laundry, now the restaurant and Jao...

Conroy tightened his fists on the steering wheel. The Twisted Vipers were going to pay. They had to.

By the time they trudged into the motel room, it was nearly five in the morning. The sky was rapidly brightening from violent mauve to gunmetal gray. Thankfully the curtains, while ugly and worn, blocked all but the barest sliver of light.

Hong moved like a zombie, sitting down on the bed and staring blankly. Conroy remained quiet; he figured Hong would talk when ready, and pushing him wouldn't accomplish anything.

"I should have been the one to go notify Jao's wife, not the police officer." Hong shook his head. "She shouldn't have to hear something like this from someone she doesn't know."

"Maybe it's better if you don't," Conroy said gently. He remembered what it was like to make notifications to the families of fallen Dragons. He'd accompanied Wei on almost every one, and it never got easier.

"If I hadn't taken you to that restaurant, this wouldn't have happened." Hong words mirrored Conroy's earlier thoughts. "It was stupid of me. I'm not going to make that mistake again. You're staying right here until this matter is handled."

"Like hell I am!" Conroy moved around the bed to look Hong in the eye.

"It's the best way to protect you and the people around you."

"No, the best way to do that is to make sure a psychopath like Hwang doesn't get back on the streets. We have to find Trang Nguyen. That's the only thing that matters right now."

"No, it isn't," Hong argued, but Conroy could tell he wasn't going to fight him on it. "Every second you're on the street is a chance for the Twisted Vipers to strike."

"If you think I'm going to stay cooped up here and let this shit spiral out of control around me just to save my own skin, you don't know me very well, Hong!"

Hong shrugged. "No, I knew you wouldn't go for it." Hong checked his watch. "Fuck me, it's already five. I guess I can sleep for a few hours before going to work. Don't even want to think about the mess I'll be walking into."

"Yeah, I'm beat." Conroy collapsed onto the bed. He'd known he was tired, but he hadn't realized until he let his body relax quite how exhausted he was. He lifted his head as Hong got off the bed. "What are you doing?"

"Going to sleep," Hong replied, noticeably confused.

Conroy sighed and then, against his better judgment, said, "After the night you've had, I think you deserve to sleep in a bed. I doubt it's much more comfortable than the floor, but hey, it's better than nothing."

Hong stood, regarding him suspiciously, like he didn't trust the invitation. In response, Conroy looked at him expectantly, and Hong gave in.

Conroy shifted over, slipping the blanket down enough to slip under it, and Hong followed suit.

"Just one thing, Hong," he said once they were both settled.

"What's that?"

"Stay on your own side."

Forty

IT SEEMED LIKE Allen's head had just touched the pillow when his alarm startled him awake. He lay there after silencing his alarm, staring up at the ceiling. Conroy slept beside him, his even breathing nearly soothing Allen back to sleep; he had to force his eyes to stay open.

He hadn't begun to recover from the events from the night before, either physically or emotionally. Jao's death weighed heavily on him.

He could remember when Jao had bought the restaurant. He'd continued to go there after joining the police, thinking of it as one of the few places he could still feel close to Conroy, especially in the early days after entering the police academy, when the pang of loss was fresh.

Jao had welcomed him as an honored customer right away, and eventually as a good friend. He'd met Jao's wife, and occasionally gone to their house for dinner. Their friendship had begun four years ago, and last night, it had ended with Jao dead.

But life went on, and the only comfort Allen could provide was to ensure those responsible—those bastards in the Twisted Vipers—paid for it. That required leaving bed and starting now. If he couldn't work the Hwang case, they could at least let him bust the sonofabitch who had tried to shoot him.

He left the motel as quietly as he could, taking one last look at the sleeping Dragon. He remembered the previous night, the closeness of a distant enemy named death. Conroy'd thrown Allen to the ground and shielded him.

Instinct or not, Allen owed Conroy his life.

And he hadn't said thank you.

Then again, saying thank you would make things awkward between them, just when Allen could feel things beginning to thaw. He'd try to leave that in the past, if that's how Conroy wanted it.

He all but sped to get to work, eager to hear what progress, if any, had been made in the last few hours. He didn't have high hopes, but there was always a chance something would turn up, especially if they were sloppy. It looked like sloppy had become the Twisted Vipers' MO, so he might get lucky and have some news for Jao's wife—his widow, now.

He took the steps leading up to the precinct door two at a time, trying to remember the name of the officer in charge last night. Who was it? He couldn't recall the face clearly; he hadn't been paying attention to much of anything, could barely think about the questions they'd thrown his way.

His eagerness was short-lived, though. Wu, Leong and Dang, the three people he wanted to see least, greeted him inside the entryway. Wu and Leong's faces were unreadable, but Dang met Allen with a smug smirk.

"Inspector Hong, we were waiting for you," he said, his superior tone combined with his nasally voice setting Allen's teeth on edge.

"We'd like you to follow us," Wu said before turning on his heel and marching away, Dang behind him. Leong waited until Allen fell in behind Dang before taking up the rear.

When Allen saw their destination was Dang's office, the blood in his veins cooled to ice. He felt a heavy, hard lump of dread settle in the pit of his stomach.

Once Leong pulled the door closed, Dang rounded on Allen. "Did you really think you could keep your shady dealings secret, Inspector Hong? Did you think you were so clever that we would never ferret you out?"

"*My* shady dealings?" Allen repeated. He wondered if he'd stepped into an alternate reality when he'd entered the precinct that morning.

"Yes, your shady dealings! And now an innocent man is dead as a result! We can no longer ignore this, I'm afraid."

Was Dang actually attempting to pass the blame for Jao's death onto him? "Wait just a damn minute." he said, not bothering to conceal his temper, not in the face of allegations like these from the likes of Dang. He was no idiot; Allen saw exactly what Dang was doing—using every trick he could think of to discredit Allen so the heat would be taken off Hwang and the Vipers. "What happened last night was a case of the Twisted Vipers trying to silence a witness against Johnny Hwang, something they've tried repeatedly to do. For you to turn this back around on me—"

"From where I stand," Dang interrupted coldly, "last night was the result of violence between two triads. The fact that you happened to be involved cannot be a coincidence. First you fabricate evidence against

Johnny Hwang, and then you happen to be in the company of a known triad member at the time of the shooting? It's plain that you are abusing your position in the Hong Kong Police Department to increase the power and prestige of a triad. I imagine you've been in their service this entire time, yes? You disgust me."

His years of being dirty, of playing the dutiful superintendent, had given Dang impressive acting skills. Those skills allowed him years in the pocket of the triads without getting caught. He was a dangerous snake.

Wu spoke after watching the exchange between the two men. "This is a serious matter, Inspector, one that will require more intensive investigating. We're going to have to suspend you without pay until we can conclude an investigation into your conduct, including investigating every case you've worked on since you first joined the department."

Vicious, hateful triumph burned in Dang's eyes as Leong said, "We're going to need your badge and gun."

Disbelief radiated through Allen; he'd gone completely numb. His hands worked as if they were independent entities, removing his badge from his belt and then the comforting, constant presence of his gun, as well, placing them down with a soft, hollow thud on Dang's desk.

"We need you to be prepared to make yourself available for questioning at all times," Wu told him in a detached way that seemed standard for Internal Affairs officers. It appeared they'd been trained to school their emotions while watching a fellow officer burn.

"Of course, there is something you could do for us that would go a long way in this investigation," Dang said, walking around behind his desk. He steepled his fingers, looking ridiculously like a villain in one of those bad James Bond movies like *Moonraker*. "Given that you're in the Dragons' pocket, you could provide us with all the information you have. Their organization, their numbers, illicit activities you might know about—whatever could benefit the Anti-Gang Task Force's investigation into them."

So that was Dang's game. He was going to dangle his badge in front of him, effectively forcing him to choose between the job and the Dragons.

Allen had weighed the option before. The day he turned in his paperwork for the police academy, he'd made the very choice Dang was offering.

No, he reminded himself fiercely, it wasn't the same. He'd chosen the job in order to protect his friends and family. If he took this offer now, he might be securing his job, but he would be betraying the Dragons.

He held Dang's eyes for a long moment, hoping Dang could see the promise in his eyes: *I'm coming for you.*

At last, he turned to Wu. "You have my number."

Dang most likely expected him to be feeling despair or regret or even fear, but the man didn't know him very well. Allen felt none of those things as he strode purposefully out of the Eastern District Precinct of the Hong Kong Police Department.

Fury raged within him. Dang had made a mistake attacking him directly, and soon he'd make sure the *puk gai* knew it.

Forty-One

WHEN CONROY WOKE, Hong was gone, though his side of the bed was still warm, so he couldn't have been gone for too long.

Though he chafed at the thought, he decided it would be best to just stay inside the motel as long as he could. Wei and the other Dragons had apparently come to the same conclusion, because his phone remained silent.

It made sense, even if it was annoying. Wei posed a big enough target for the Twisted Vipers without adding Conroy and his bounty to the mix. No matter what happened, he wouldn't put others at risk unnecessarily, not after the restaurant.

So he did something he hadn't done since he was a teenager: he sat in the motel and watched television. It didn't take long for him to come to the conclusion that daytime television was not the best the medium had to offer.

He contemplated giving up on the TV altogether and turning his attention to his phone, where he could at least watch porn when he heard heavy footfalls outside. Initially, he thought some poor bastard in the neighboring room was cheating and about to catch hell from his or her spurned lover. The sound kept coming, though, growing louder. The sound of a key being shoved roughly into the door identified the source of the noise as Hong.

The timing combined with the volume of his footsteps told Conroy all he needed, but Hong's livid expression added another dimension.

"That good of a morning, huh?"

Hong growled in response, slamming the door shut.

Conroy sat up and then watched Hong carefully. It had been years since he'd been around a pissed-off Hong, but he remembered the power of the Hong temper—Constance had it in spades. He needed to be careful that it didn't get turned on him.

"You want to tell me what happened, or are you just going to keep making animal grunts all day and hope I guess it?"

"It's Dang," Hong spat.

"I could have guessed that much."

Conroy listened as Hong explained.

"They suspended you? Are you kidding me?"

"You should have seen the look on Dang's face when they did, too. He's got Internal Affairs buying into his bullshit now. But that's not even the worst of it."

Given Hong had just told him he'd lost his badge and gun and was now having every single piece of his life as a police officer combed over, Conroy had a hard time imagining anything worse.

"Dang all but said this whole thing could go away if I told him everything I know about the Dragons. He tried to make me choose the badge or you—the Dragons." Hong's hands tightened into fists.

Sympathy overcame Conroy. He should have been gloating that Hong's choice to join the police was coming back to bite him in the ass, but he couldn't.

"That must have been a hard decision."

He didn't mean the words to be antagonistic, but Hong took them that way, judging by how he wheeled on Conroy, eyes flashing.

"What? You think I'm not above throwing you and everyone else in the Dragons—including my own nephew—under the bus if it means getting to keep my job?"

Conroy winced. "That's not what I meant."

"Then what *did* you mean?"

"I meant that I understand how hard you've worked to get where you are. It must suck to be getting that ultimatum from a piece of shit *jing jang* like Dang."

"Yeah, it does." Hong collapsed on the bed, his shoulders buckling forward like a puppet whose strings had been cut. "Five goddamn years and it all gets taken away."

Conroy didn't want to ask, but had to. "Were you tempted? Even a little?"

For a moment, fire returned to Hong's eyes. "No. Sorry to shatter whatever bad image of me you've got, but no. I would never make any kind of a deal with Dang, or anyone else for that matter, even if it meant saving my career. I joined HKPD to protect the district from people like that, not to become one of them."

"I never thought you joined them for any other reason," Conroy admitted. The confession had been his deepest secret for years. He honestly didn't think he'd ever tell, especially not Hong himself. He couldn't take it back once the words had left, and he found he didn't want to.

"You sure do call me traitor enough, right along with Wei," Hong said bitterly.

"Not because you betrayed the Dragons, Hong. Because you betrayed me."

Hong's head jerked up so fast it was almost comical. His eyes caught and held Conroy's, searching. They were surprisingly candid, revealing a vulnerability Conroy doubted any other, even Constance, had ever seen.

Hong opened his mouth to speak, but whatever he wanted to say—a denial, perhaps—didn't come, no doubt because he couldn't disclaim what Conroy said.

Once he started, Conroy found he couldn't stop. "You turned your back on me, walked away without a look back, like it was the easiest thing in the world. Like I meant nothing."

"It wasn't easy for me," Hong said, voice catching on the last word. "I struggled with my choice for so long *because* you meant something to me."

Conroy shrugged. "You can say that all you want—and I might even believe you, but it doesn't change how I feel, or the fact that you left."

"I did it because—"

"I know why you did it." Nervous energy took hold of Conroy. "You've always been about protecting people. In another city, or in a perfect world, that would mean doing exactly what you did. Not going to say it wasn't idealistic—but that's something I've always admired in you. You're naive as fuck, and you see the world for how it should be, not how it is. That's why I'll never understand why you didn't think I would understand. You didn't even give me a chance."

"I don't remember how long I stood outside of your apartment that night." Hong's voice was far away, like he'd traveled back in time. "I probably looked like a stalker, staring at your place, all while this battle took place in my head.

"In the end, I made the choice I thought best. Wei had already made up his mind about me and my decision, and I didn't want to make you choose between the Dragons or me. We both know who you'd choose."

The words were stated as a simple fact, but they stung Conroy anyway. He'd spent so long accusing Hong of walking out on him that he didn't consider what would have happened if he'd come to his door and told him. He didn't have to think about it long, either; Hong was right. It was a foregone conclusion. He would've chosen the Dragons, would've turned away from Hong as quickly as he felt Hong did to him.

"I wish I could say it was entirely altruistic," Hong went on, completely unaware of the deep well of shame he'd unintentionally tapped inside Conroy. "But it was selfish, too. As much as I didn't want to force you to make that decision, I didn't want to have to experience it. Knowing your answer hurt, so I couldn't imagine what it would have felt like to actually hear it, to see you when you said it. I was too much of a coward to face you."

Conroy remained silent. These words were five years too late. But if that was the case, what was the strange cloud of feelings that were beginning to swirl through him, like leaves picked up by the beginnings of a strong autumn wind?

It didn't matter, in the end; he couldn't voice those treacherous feelings. Conroy gazed down in pity at Hong, who himself stared intently at the spot on the floor between his feet. They remained there, suspended in that moment, scarabs caught in amber.

When it felt like time would stretch out forever, Hong's phone rang, loud and echoing in the room. Conroy cleared his throat and turned away, letting Hong keep his dignity as he answered the phone.

"What's up, Ao? What?" Hong came to his feet quickly, startling Conroy. "You did? Hold on, hold on." Hong scrambled to the pitiful excuse for a writing desk and took up a pen. "Okay, I'm ready. Go ahead."

He scribbled something down, muttered a hurried thanks, and hung the phone up. "Well, Conroy, our luck might be about to turn. Ao thinks he's found Trang Nguyen."

Forty-Two

ACCORDING TO HONG, one of Ao's informants had offered a lead. An area near North Point had been inhabited by groups of individuals in Hong Kong illegally, mainly Southeast Asians. They were insular and didn't trust many people. Informants with knowledge of the community were rare.

"I guess Dang actually did you a favor taking your badge," Conroy told Hong as they reached streets too narrow for more than one car to pass at a time. "These people would run at the first sign of a cop."

"Great," Hong muttered darkly. "You found the silver lining."

Eventually they had to set off on foot. The streets had become a warren of slim alleys between old, boarded-up buildings and warehouses. During the days of the Nine Stars, this area had been home to a plethora of flophouses, from old-fashioned opium dens to the much more modern crack house. The Dragons had cleared the neighborhood of drugs, and occasionally patrols were sent in to make sure it stayed that way, though Conroy himself had never been there.

It was early enough in the day that most of the people who lived in the area were at work. The ones who weren't peered out at them from behind windows or in huddled groups in front of the rundown buildings.

The distrust sat clear in their eyes. These were people who lived in constant fear, when any unknown person could turn out to be an immigration officer or a prelude to a raid.

It had been a long time since Conroy felt so much dislike directed toward him. With each step they took, the weight of it seemed to increase.

"Ao said his person would meet us around here."

"How can you tell in this maze?" Conroy asked. There were no street signs, no addresses written that he could see, no clear markers of any kind to indicate where they were. He didn't think anyone who didn't live there would be able to navigate with ease—a safety precaution in case the residents' worst fears came to pass and the law swept in.

"Ao gave me some pretty detailed landmarks." Despite the words, Hong sounded less than confident.

He turned out to be right, though; as they stood there, a man stepped out of one of the many side alleys. He was an old man, dark-skinned from a life of toiling in the sun, though now his back was bent, his knuckles swollen. His hair was paper-white, still thick despite age. His eyes looked sharp, and he moved with a surprising spryness.

"You Hong?" His voice was strong and deep, pitched low. He spoke Cantonese like a man not born to it but who'd picked it up; no matter how fluent someone became, you could just tell.

"Yes. And you're—"

"We have a mutual friend," the old man interrupted. His eyes moved to Conroy. "He's not one of them, but I was told to trust your judgment. Follow me."

He motioned over his shoulder, and Conroy and Hong fell into step behind him. The alleys around them seemed clear, but Conroy could still feel eyes on him.

"I do my best to keep an eye on all of the people living in this area," the old man said as he guided them. "Someone has to do it. I help our friend, and he makes sure your kind don't come in here. I don't usually make exceptions to that, either, but I was told this is a special circumstance."

"A—our mutual friend said that you found the girl we've been looking for?"

"Can't say for sure, but maybe. Girl turned up in the middle of the night, begging to be taken to see one of our locals—Vietnamese guy by the name of Thuy. She looked scared."

Hong looked over to Conroy, his eyes clearly saying what his mouth didn't: they'd found her. The old neighbor had mentioned a boyfriend named Thuy, so this had to be him. Conroy wasn't a religious man—hard to be growing up on the streets and in a city like Hong Kong, where there were so many meshing cultures as well as pressure from Mainland China to be religion-free—but he was about ready to give thanks to every god worshiped on the island. They'd found Trang Nguyen, which meant they had found their best shot at putting the Twisted Vipers out of commission forever.

"Thuy lives here," the old man said, stopping in front of a thin but tall building that had been a storage facility for the nearby docks in its previous life. "There's about seventeen of them in total, all Vietnamese, all fishermen or their families. They're not going to like talking to you." He paused for a moment. "They'll feign inability to speak, but a good bit of them can speak English, and a few of them Cantonese—even some Mandarin. Good luck."

"Thank you," Hong said, making as if he wanted to shake the man's hand, but as quickly as he appeared from the alley, he was gone. If he heard Hong, he didn't acknowledge him.

"They do it because they get paid," Conroy said dismissively. He was wary of informants by nature.

"Some of them do it to protect others," Hong corrected. "You heard what he said about doing what he does to keep the police out of here. Can you imagine the panic that would set in if a full-scale investigation went down here?"

"Yeah, yeah. I get your point," Conroy said, wanting to head off any lecture so they could get inside, find Trang, and start to think about getting back to normal life. He wanted to ask Hong if any of the inspectors had informants close to the Dragons, but he doubted he'd get an answer, and even if he did, he wasn't sure he'd believe it.

"We should have brought Tony with us," Conroy said as Hong knocked on the door.

"Why?"

"Because he speaks like six languages. Pretty sure one of them is Vietnamese."

Hong shook his head. "He speaks seven. Cantonese, Mandarin, English, Japanese, Korean, Tagalog, and Thai."

Conroy did a double take, gaping at Hong.

"What?"

"It's just...I don't know what all he speaks, and you can list them without even thinking about it?"

"I spent a lot of time with Tony back in the day. He also tried to teach me every single one of those languages, but I just didn't have the head for it. Hell, maybe he should teach Noah."

Conroy chuckled. "I just might suggest that."

The conversation opened when a young woman pulled the door cautiously open. She had a baby in her arms. Her clothes were wrinkled but clean and smelled of flower-scented detergent even from a distance, which made Conroy guess she washed them by hand.

She spoke to them in Vietnamese, and though the words were unfamiliar, the tone of fear was recognizable enough. She might have been unable to hide the fear in her voice, but her eyes were wary and cold, the eyes of someone who would do anything to protect her family.

Conroy decided he liked her.

"We're looking for Thuy," Hong said.

Conroy hoped that wasn't a super-common Vietnamese name. The woman merely stood there, staring at them without blinking.

"We're not with the police," Conroy added. "Well, we're not," he said when Hong gave him a look. The woman didn't look inclined to trust them, and Conroy couldn't blame her,.

He looked around, and seeing no one watching them, turned his back to the woman, lifting his shirt to expose the dragon tattoo on his back. When he was certain she'd had a chance to take it in, he dropped his shirt back down and turned back to her.

"We're not here to start anything. We just need to talk to someone. This guy, Thuy, and his girlfriend, Trang Nguyen."

The woman studied them, her face giving nothing of what she was thinking.

"Come on in," she said at last in near-perfect Cantonese.

"Sometimes the ink opens way more doors than the shield," Conroy said with the smallest of smirks before stepping inside the building.

The moment the door closed, they were consumed in near-darkness, the only light coming from two dingy bulbs along the ceiling. The air was heavy with sweat, an unavoidable price for the number of people living in such small spaces.

They followed the woman past doorways where beaded curtains and other cloth had been hung to provide the sense of privacy. A staircase led upstairs, creaking protests under the weight of every step.

On the second floor, voices floated out from behind the curtains. A baby cried somewhere, the mother's soothing noises calming it.

They didn't linger; Conroy and Hong were led up to the third floor and one of the curtained areas. She stuck her head through the curtain and said something to whoever was on the other side. She turned back to them, and a tall Vietnamese man came through the curtain, followed by a young woman.

Conroy recognized her immediately. It was the waitress from Indulgence, all right. The way her eyes widened when she saw Conroy told him she recognized him as well.

"Trini said you were looking for us," Thuy said brusquely, crossing his arms over his chest. His bearing made his lack of interest in them clear. Trang looked frightened.

"Well, for Trang, actually," Hong said, turning his attention to her and bypassing Thuy entirely. "I want to ask you a few questions."

"I know what you want to ask," she said, fidgeting with her thumbnails. "Yes, I was there the night that man got shot."

"And you saw who shot him, right?" Conroy pressed.

"Yes," she admitted. "I saw the man who did it. I know who he is. That's why I haven't said anything. Do you think I want to bring trouble like that down on me?"

"If you don't say anything, he gets off," Hong protested. "I understand that you're afraid, but he's going to do this again, because there doesn't seem to be anyone willing to stop him. You can be that person, Trang. You can be the one who puts Johnny Hwang behind bars. Think about all the good it could do!"

"What she should be thinking about is her family," Thuy interrupted, scowling fiercely. "We know what happened to her parents. You people are asking her to put herself and her family at risk."

"We can protect your family," Hong said quickly.

Trang gave him a pitying look. "Do you really believe that? You didn't do such a great job yesterday, did you?"

Hong flinched as if he'd been struck. "That wasn't our fault! We didn't know who you were, who they were. I wish we could have gotten there in time to help them, but this is different. We know who they are and where, so we can keep them safe from Hwang and the Twisted Vipers."

Conroy could see that despite his best efforts, Hong fell short of convincing her.

"Listen, I know you don't trust the police. I don't either. I'm not going to tell you that you don't have plenty of good reasons not to, either, because we both know you do." Conroy took a beat, looking toward Hong briefly. "But this man? You can trust him. He's a damn good man, and he's fought hard and sacrificed for this city. If he says he's going to keep you safe, he will."

Trang seemed to consider it, and neither Hong nor Conroy rushed her. The decision wouldn't be easy, and she needed to make it on her own.

"Fine," she said, though the word was nearly drowned in a sigh.

Thuy immediately began to argue with her in fast-paced Vietnamese. Conroy didn't need to understand the language to know he wasn't happy. They argued back and forth for a time before Thuy threw up his hands in defeat and Trang turned back to them.

"I'll help put this man away," she said solemnly.

"You won't regret this." Hong sounded relieved. He took out his phone and dialed someone, stepping away from them to make the call.

Trang watched him, an unsettled look on her face.

"Don't worry," Conroy told her reassuringly. "You're going to be safe."

She nodded, though she didn't look hopeful.

Forty-Three

ALLEN AND CONROY remained with Trang until Yu arrived to take her into protection. As Yu was leaving with her, Allen pulled him aside. "She needs to be watched, Yu. I mean it. Everything in this case against Hong is riding on her."

"Don't worry. I'll make sure there are eyes on her clear up until she is ready to speak at the hearing tomorrow."

"Good man." Allen nodded his farewell to Yu as he climbed into his car.

Thuy watched them from the doorway, his face dark and worried. Allen had seen that look on plenty of faces before; it promised retribution if anything should go wrong.

Locating Trang Nguyen had lifted a weight from Allen's body, his lungs finally expanding to full capacity. The complications in their lives would soon be over, and he could clear his name and return to his job.

After all that he'd gone through trying to operate within a system corrupted by its leaders, he wasn't sure he wanted to. If he didn't, Dang would win. He wouldn't let Dang drive him away from the police. He'd worked too hard.

He was about to take down Johnny Hwang, and Dang would be next; he'd make sure of it. The best way to do that was to get back inside.

The somber air that had permeated the motel room the last time they were there was gone. The whole room felt free, though it was certainly still a dump.

"I'm glad this might be the last time I see this room," Conroy declared, following Allen inside.

"Considering the state of your apartment, you might want to stay here a bit longer until you get it fixed up."

"No way. I'd rather sleep in a dingy in Victoria Harbor than stay here longer than I have to." Conroy relaxed, arms propped on his thighs. "At least we convinced Trang to testify against Hwang."

"*You* convinced her," Allen corrected. "She wouldn't have agreed if you hadn't convinced her she could trust me. And we wouldn't have gotten in there at all if you weren't a Dragon. This time you're the hero."

Conroy chuckled. "As usual. Okay, Hong, let me ask you a question."

"Okay." Allen steeled himself.

"Do you regret joining the police?"

"I've thought about that a lot myself, especially recently," Allen admitted. "But no, I don't. I do regret the way I handled the situation with you, though. I should've given you a chance. Maybe—maybe we could have figured something out." He shrugged. "I have a question, too."

He fell silent, then, the question stuck in his throat.

"What?" Conroy pressed, and Allen knew Conroy wasn't just going to let it pass.

"Did you mean all of those things that you said to Trang about me being a good man?"

"I did," Conroy said without hesitation. "I've never thought you weren't, Hong. I might not have liked your choices, but I still thought you were a good man."

Surprised, Allen turned and met Conroy's eyes. Intensity danced there, a heat that stoked a fire deep inside Allen. Everything suddenly slowed, and Allen leaned forward, not breaking eye contact. Then Conroy was leaning in, and Allen's eyes closed as their lips made contact.

The first kiss was tentative, testing the waters after having not been in them for a long while, but it didn't last; the fire in Allen's stomach wouldn't allow it. Their tongues dueled, arms coming around each other.

Conroy pressed Allen back until he was flat on the bed. He could feel Conroy's erection against his thigh, and it spurred his passion further. Allen reached up and pulled Conroy's body until he was flush against him, Conroy's mass a comforting presence.

The barriers of clothing between them became unbearable, and Allen rolled Conroy off before tugging his own shirt up over his head and then throwing it to the side. He reached out and caressed the obvious bulge of Conroy's cock as Conroy followed suit.

Allen, impatient, started on Conroy's pants, freeing his thick cock in record time. He took it into his mouth with a satisfied moan, and Conroy let out an encouraging hiss of pleasure. Allen gripped Conroy's cock by the base and held tightly while he worked his tongue along the underside of Conroy's shaft, tracing the veins that lined it.

Conroy wiggled his hips and legs, working his pants and underwear down until he could kick them off, and all through that Allen didn't take his mouth off of Conroy's cock.

He would have happily kept sucking, but Conroy pulled him up and pushed him onto his back once more before claiming his lips in a scorching kiss that lingered long after Conroy's mouth moved farther south.

Hot lips trailed down Allen's neck and then across his chest, not stopping until they reached a nipple. While his lips, teeth, and tongue assailed one, sending jolts of pleasure through Allen, Conroy's finger and thumb tweaked the other nipple, twisting just on the side of too rough, creating a jumble of pleasure/pain that confused Allen's brain and left him incapable of thought.

The entire universe faded, leaving only lips and fingers and heat. He let out a disappointed moan when Conroy stopped his ministrations, but anticipation soon overclouded disappointment as Conroy's target became clear.

A shiver ran up Allen's spine as Conroy's hand closed around his cock, aiming it toward the ceiling. When Conroy's mouth closed around it, Allen found heaven.

He propped himself up on his elbows to watch Conroy, his mouth working its way up and down his shaft. It was an incredible sight, one he never expected he'd see again. He'd fantasized over the years about sex with Conroy, especially around the time things had ended between them, but the reality of it all was so much better than his fantasies or memories could possibly be.

Allen arched his back, attempting to get more of his cock into the warm wetness of Conroy's mouth. Conroy allowed it, easing farther down the shaft until his nose was nearly pressed against Allen's groin.

"Fuck, that's amazing," Allen said when his brain could finally string words together. "Don't stop. Please don't stop."

Conroy grinned at Allen as best he could with his lips spread over thick flesh. He added his fist, his strong fingers wrapping over the spit-slicked skin. Allen shuddered every time Conroy's palm met the sensitive head of his cock, the sensation a lightning bolt.

"I forgot how fucking hot you look like this," Conroy said, his voice husky. "Just lying there, flushed, body responding to me like this. Seeing you let go drives me fucking wild."

He stroked his own cock as if to demonstrate.

Conroy's lips trailed down to Allen's balls and then lower, his hands levering Allen's thighs into the air. Allen reached down and held his them back, hands gripping behind his knees to spread his legs wider for Conroy.

"You still like having your hole eaten as much as you used to?" Conroy didn't wait for an answer; he dove in, his tongue lapping rapidly at the puckered ring, and Allen saw stars.

"I take that as a yes," Conroy said. At first Allen couldn't understand why he'd said that and then, when Conroy's lips returned to his hole, he realized he was letting out breathy gasps with each slip of Conroy's tongue.

"I want you inside me," Allen pleaded, uncaring of desperate he sounded. The only thing he wanted right then was Conroy's cock inside him.

"You don't have to ask me twice." Conroy straightened. He rummaged around until he found another condom and wasted no time in rolling it down his cock. "There's not a lot of lube left."

"Then use spit," Allen said impatiently. "Lay back. I'll help."

Conroy shrugged and obeyed, settling in the middle of the bed. Allen spat a liberal amount onto his hand and applied it to Conroy's cock before squirting what remained of the gel lube along with it, spreading it all with a few strokes.

He rubbed his hole with slicked-up fingers, pressing his middle finger inside in hopes of easing Conroy's entry. He kneeled over Conroy and reached back, holding Conroy's cock steady, lowering himself down on it slowly.

The first few seconds of penetration were accompanied by a familiar burn, but he gritted his teeth and breathed through it, moving carefully until he adjusted to Conroy's presence.

Allen didn't take his eyes off Conroy's face as he took him in inch by inch. Conroy's head was thrown back, his eyes closed, and he bit his lower lip in a way Allen found incredibly sexy.

Once Allen was fully seated on Conroy's cock, he placed his hands on Conroy's chest for leverage and began to rock his hips, moving around until Conroy's cock struck a place deep inside him that caused his cock to jump. Too much too soon and he'd be blowing his load in record time; he already felt the beginnings of orgasm and didn't want to hurry it on.

Allen caressed Conroy's chest as he rode his cock, thumbs moving in small circles around his nipples.

"You know exactly how to drive me wild," Conroy said, opening his eyes. He slid one hand down to grip Allen's ass firmly, squeezing it possessively. The other hand went behind Allen's neck, tugging him down roughly until their mouths met.

Conroy took over then, each upward thrust of his hips drawing a moan from Allen, muffled by Conroy's mouth.

"Feels so good being inside you again," Conroy murmured against Allen's lips as he slid his hand down to join the other on Allen's ass, spurring him on.

"God, yes," Allen agreed, shoving himself back onto Conroy to meet each thrust. He shifted slightly—whimpering in pleasure as the change brought Conroy's cock across his prostate and sent proverbial stars into his vision—so he could free his hand to touch himself, his cock desperate for contact.

Part of him regretted it the moment his hand made contact; he knew he was at the point where if he started stroking he wasn't going to stop until he accomplished his goal, and the way things were going, it wouldn't take long.

Every thrust pushed him closer to the cliff, until he attempted to say "I'm coming!" but managed nothing more than a guttural growl and unloaded across Conroy's chest and abdomen.

"I want to come on your stomach," Conroy said, and Allen nodded, still panting and unable to manage words. He rose off Conroy's cock and let himself fall over onto his back, body semi-limp.

Conroy stripped the condom from his cock, tossing it over his shoulder, and then took his cock in hand, stroking it furiously. Allen didn't think he lasted even a minute before his come sprayed out, warm and sticky where it struck Allen's stomach.

Conroy collapsed facedown on the bed, head turned toward Allen. His eyes were closed, his face content. Sated, Allen stared up at the patchy, peeling ceiling of the motel room. Though still dancing with a post-orgasmic high, Allen couldn't fend off the aching doubt that when the haze faded, everything would change.

But that was a question for a different moment, he decided, closing his eyes and feeling more relaxed than he had in a long while. Next to him, the sound of Conroy's steady breathing helped lull him into sleep.

Forty-Four

THE ROOM WAS dark when Conroy awoke, and he lost all sense of time and his surroundings. Someone lay next to him, not quite touching but close enough he could feel their warmth.

He lay there still, blinking until his eyes adjusted to the lack of light in the motel room. The red glow of the clock numbers was blurry to his still-sleep-weakened eyes, but he was pretty sure they read eight twenty-seven, though it could have been twenty-nine.

Time and place came back to him. He moved slowly from the bed, doing his best not to disturb Hong. Vivid memories of a few hours ago swirled through his head, making him want to slide back into bed and right back into Hong.

That was a stupid impulse, though, and he kept it under control like a massive dog on a leash. If he gave those thoughts even the slightest slack, they'd have him doing something he might damn well regret.

He'd lived so long holding on to the hatred of Hong, and now that they'd been forced into close quarters, it began to thaw, giving way to confusion and uncertainty, and he didn't like it one bit.

He dressed slowly, clutching his belt buckle in his hand so it wouldn't knock against anything. He was well aware as he slipped out of the motel room, taking what felt like a full minute to shut the door, that he was in a very real sense running away from the room, what had happened in it, and the man in that bed.

The one good thing about the crappy motel was a conveniently located dive bar down the road. He made a quick phone call as he reached it—luckily it wasn't yet midnight, though it was creeping up on that time—and thirty minutes later, he had company.

Tony greeted Conroy with a raised eyebrow, no doubt curious as to why he was there, but he didn't say much as Conroy waved over a waitress and ordered a beer for Tony.

"This is an interesting place," Tony remarked, looking around. It was your typical dive bar—dirty floors, cheap beer and cheap *shaojiu*, the patrons quiet, hunched over, sulking into their beer. It lacked laughter and noise, though it did have background music, a mix of Hong Kong pop and popular Korean girl bands.

Conroy shrugged. "It's got good *shaojiu*. Well, it's got *shaojiu* anyway. There was something I wanted to talk to you about."

With Tony next to him, he struggled to find his voice. Part of it was not knowing how Tony would react, but part of it was also him not wanting to say it aloud, because that would make it true and that would make his life more complicated than it already was, and given everything going on, the last thing anyone needed was more complications.

"It's about Hong, I'm guessing?" Tony asked.

"I'm that easy to read, huh?"

Tony shrugged. "Considering how much time you've been spending with him, that was the only answer that made sense. What's going on?"

"Well, like you said, we've been spending a lot of time together. At first it sucked because all this time I've held on to so much anger. Every time I looked at him, all I could see or think about was him up and disappearing years ago. Now, I start thinking about when we were together, and it's bringing back a lot of really confusing feelings."

"Makes sense," Tony said, pausing to take a sip of his beer. "You never had a chance to address those feelings or have closure."

Conroy nodded, drumming his fingers on the sides of his glass. "I guess that makes sense."

"What is scaring you so much about this?" Tony asked.

Conroy didn't want to answer—it was too personal—but he needed advice, and Tony couldn't give any good advice without knowing everything, so he bit the bullet and told him, keeping his eyes on his beer the whole time.

"We might have fooled around. Twice, actually. The first time was just, you know, fucking. This second time, though... I didn't even plan to do it; we were talking, and I wanted to kiss him, so I did. Whatever it was, it wasn't just fucking that time."

"Even more reason for you to really settle in and ask yourself about your feelings. Try to leave the past out of it; don't think about what you did before, or what anyone else thinks. Ask yourself what *you* are feeling."

"I get what you're saying, but it's not just my feelings that matter. What about Hong? I have no idea what any of this is to him. Well, I think I do, but I'm not sure. He's got this picture, from—you know, before—and he still has it out in his apartment. That means something, right?"

Aware that he was babbling, Conroy silenced himself with beer.

"You can't worry about how he feels until you figure out how you feel."

Conroy didn't know how to respond, so he nodded. The two men sat in silence for the time it took them to finish their beers.

When he'd drained his glass and set it back on the table, Tony spoke again. "Not that I'm not happy to do this, but what made you call me out here? I'm surprised you didn't call Wei, since the two of you are best friends."

"Honestly? Wei's got too much on his mind right now, with everything escalating with the Twisted Vipers."

"Is that all?" Tony pressed.

"No, it's not. I don't think Wei is the best man to talk about this. He and Hong have history of their own; it doesn't seem right to bring him into this, too."

"Sound reasoning." Tony patted Conroy's arm, a brotherly gesture. "You want to get another beer?"

Conroy was tempted to take him up on the offer, to lose himself in the sweet embrace of drunkenness, at least for a few hours.

"Sorry, but I'm pretty sure Hong would blow a gasket if he knew I was out here at all, let alone getting drunk."

Tony chuckled. "You're probably right. Want me to give you a ride back to wherever it is Hong has you laying low?"

"It's not too far. Besides, the walk will do me some good, I think."

Tony reached for his wallet, but Conroy stopped him. "No, I've got this. I dragged your ass all the way out here, I'm sure as hell not about to let you pay for your own beer, too."

Conroy dug some bills out of his wallet, more than enough to cover the cost of two beers, and handed them to Tony. "Keep the change. Consider it your listener's fee." Conroy stretched, one hand braced against his side. "That damn motel bed isn't doing shit for my back. Hopefully this is the last night I have to spend there. Tomorrow we're putting that sonofabitch Johnny Hwang behind bars for good."

Forty-Five

ALLEN AWOKE TO an empty motel room. He fumbled around until he found his phone. Twenty past one.

The first thought that crossed Allen's mind was that Conroy was off hooking up. Maybe he found someone on Unzipped and gave Allen the slip to have some fun.

That option seemed unlikely, given the intensity with which he'd come only a few hours earlier. Then again, recovery time could be pretty miraculous, given the right circumstances and the right person.

Maybe he'd been called out by Wei on Dragon business. It was a pretty shitty thing to do, leaving him there completely unaware why they went off and did god knew what.

Maybe it was a way to remind him they were in two separate worlds, and Allen wasn't welcome in theirs. The Dragons had certainly made that clear over the years. He was an idiot if he thought now would be any different.

But he did, at least a little. The sex that night, it had been different, he was sure of it. The first time, that had been animalistic—no foreplay, no kissing, just two men trying to scratch an itch. The second time, though, there had been a true, fiery passion between them. It wasn't just his imagination. Sex without emotion behind it didn't feel like that.

This time he'd been spending with Conroy had brought back things he hadn't thought about—hadn't *let* himself think about—for a long time. Now that those oh-so-carefully constructed walls were down, he wasn't sure he would be able to put them back up.

He went to the bathroom, and when he returned to bed, he had to fight not to call Conroy. He wasn't Conroy's boyfriend. Even if they *were* a couple, he wouldn't do something like that. That was not something that Conroy would appreciate it.

Hell, Allen wouldn't have, either.

He grabbed his clothes, intending to go hunt for Conroy. He was in danger out there, and if he was alone, it was just compounded. Even here in Dragon territory, safety no longer existed for Conroy. It wouldn't until Jiang and every last Twisted Viper was taken out.

Luckily, he didn't need to go out; he heard the footsteps coming toward the room and knew they belonged to Conroy, somehow. He kicked the jeans he'd half pulled on back off and lay down on the bed. He thought if Conroy came in and knew he was awake, he'd want to talk or else Allen himself would be compelled to say something.

The longer he could put off that conversation, the better.

He pretended to be asleep as Conroy came back in, safe and in one piece. He didn't open his eyes as Conroy went to the bathroom. He couldn't be sure, but Allen thought Conroy might have stopped at his side of the bed and looked down at him.

It didn't take him long to fall into a restless state, constantly hovering somewhere between asleep and awake. He stirred a few times, waking up at something, though what it might have been he forgot the moment he stirred.

He dreamed, but he could only remember brief snatches of them, and that they were each unsettling, and Constance had starred in at least one.

When he came awake at half past seven in the morning, he almost thought it was another dream that woke him, until Conroy growled out, "Answer your damn phone."

His mind still a fog, he answered his phone without reading who was calling.

"Hello?"

"Allen, get up. We've got a problem."

"What?" Allen was still half-asleep and struggled to process the words.

"Get it together, man! This is serious!" The urgency in the speaker's voice was like a bucket of cold water thrown over him; Allen awakened completely. It was Yu.

"What's the problem?"

"Trang Nguyen was supposed to be at my office at seven sharp so we could prep for her testimony before the judge at the eight o'clock hearing, but she never showed. I went to the place we had her put up and she's gone. Just—gone."

After that was a bit of a blur for Allen; he roused Conroy and dressed and then they were out the door and in the car. They drove to a quiet neighborhood of post-colonial houses.

Yu stood in front of one of those houses along with three other men in suits, all looking incredibly anxious.

"How the hell did you lose her?" Allen cried as soon as he jumped out of the car. "All you had to do was keep an eye on her for one night!"

"I know, Allen. I know." Yu's voice made it clear he'd beat himself up already, but Allen didn't care.

"How the hell did your office lose her, then?"

Yu's shoulders squared back, and he raised his chin in indignation. "Hey, it wasn't *my* people that lost her, Allen. It was yours!"

"Wait. What do you mean it was mine?"

"She was under police watch overnight." Yu's voice became nervous. "You...you didn't know?"

No, he hadn't known, but he was starting to understand now. "Who ordered the protective detail?"

"Superintendent Dang," Yu replied. "I told him my office could handle it, but he said he didn't want to take any risks with such a high-value witness."

"This is why we should have taken her to the Dragons," Conroy spat. "Can't trust anyone else around this place."

"Maybe she ran away because she was afraid," Yu suggested.

"And none of the police see her leave?" Conroy snorted. "Not likely. Hong, you saw her face, you saw the argument she had with that boyfriend of hers. You think she'd agree to this and then change her mind?"

It wouldn't be the first time a witness had done something like that. Witnesses ran away all the time, usually because they feared the repercussions and lost their nerve. She'd already run away once, slipping into hiding to escape what she feared might happen if Hwang's men found out about her.

"No," he said at last, and he meant it. "I don't think Trang Nguyen left this place of her own free will. Conroy, call Wei. Let him know what happened, have him send someone to get you, or get Yu here to give you a ride to the coffee shop. The Twisted Vipers have Trang, and we've got to find out where they'd keep her."

Allen turned on his heel and marched back toward his car, rage burning through him.

"Where are you going?" Conroy called after him.

He didn't stop and didn't look back when he answered. "To pay a visit to our friendly superintendent."

Forty-Six

ALLEN KNEW ALL eyes were on him as he stormed into the police station and past the reception desk. Ao was making his way across the bullpen when he spotted Allen and hurried over to him.

"What are you doing here?" Ao took in Allen's furious state. "Don't be stupid. Turn around and go. You don't want to do this."

"Like hell I don't."

Allen stepped around Ao and marched right up to Dang's office. The door was shut, but he didn't let that stop him. He flung the door open to find Henry Dang in the middle of a phone call, and he had no doubt what it was in regard to.

Dang hadn't expected to see Allen; that much was clear from the expression on his face. He hung up the phone without a word, eyeing Allen like he was a dangerous animal—and as far as Dang was concerned, Allen was.

"You shouldn't be here, Inspector Hong," Dang said in his unctuously oily voice after Allen slammed the door shut behind him. "You're suspended, remember?"

"Where the hell is she, Dang?"

Dang raised his eyebrows in his best approximation of an innocence. "Where is who, Inspector?"

Allen took a menacing step toward Dang's desk. "Do I look like I'm here to play games with you? How can you stomach sitting behind that desk, pretending to uphold the law when you've been in Johnny Hwang's pocket for who knows how long? You're a fraud, Dang. You might have everyone fooled right now, but how long do you think that's going to last? Really, I'm curious."

"Need I remind you I'm not the one currently under investigation for being a dirty cop, Hong?" Dang grinned, more like a rabid animal baring its teeth than a real smile. "Ah, yes, and here are the results of your corruption."

Dang gestured over Allen's shoulder. Allen turned and saw a television, where a news conference took place in front of the courthouse. Johnny Hwang stood next to his lawyer. The headline underneath read "Charges against accused triad leader Johnny Hwang dismissed by judge." The television was muted, but Allen thought that was a good thing; he didn't want to hear whatever nonsense Hwang's lawyer was spewing into the microphone.

When Allen turned back to Hong, he had this disgustingly pleased look on his face. The *puk gai* didn't even try to hide it.

"Pretty happy to see your pal Hwang back on the streets, huh, Dang?"

"Me? Why no, of course not! Remember that this is *your* doing, not mine."

Allen marched up to the desk, planting his fists on it and leaning over until they were eye to eye, their noses almost touching. "I'm going to find her, and when I do, we're going to put Hwang right back behind bars where he belongs, and there will be absolutely nothing you can do to stop it."

Dang leaned back in his chair, unperturbed. "You know, Hong, my boy, men like you should be very careful with the threats they make and the avenues of investigation they pursue."

"Men like me, huh?"

"Men with something to lose." There, with just the two of them present, Dang let the facade drop. He glared cold disdain at Allen, studying him as if he were something unpleasant that had somehow slipped inside and needed to be chased out. "You're not only putting yourself at risk, you know that, right? Haven't you got a family? Sure, one of them has already run off to join those *gau* the Dragons, and that sister of yours has thrown her lot in with them as well, but you have a niece, don't you?"

While the words might have been an innocent question, the intonation made the threat clear.

The urge to punch Dang in his smug face nearly overwhelmed him; only the suspicion that Dang *wanted* him to act out kept him from going through with it. It would have felt incredible, but it would also land him behind bars, which meant he wouldn't be able to track down Trang again.

He wouldn't let Dang win.

"You sit here, looking like you think you've won. Get real comfortable, Dang, and enjoy it, because it's not going to last. I'm going to devote however long it takes—the rest of my life, even—to exposing you for the dirty piece of shit you are."

"Keep up that attitude and your life might not be as long as you think," Dang said snidely.

Allen shook his head in disgust and started for the door.

"Leaving so soon? Pity."

Allen waited until the door was open, and when he spoke, his voice boomed loud enough for everyone to hear.

"Don't worry, I'll be back real soon, and then you'll be the one leaving—in handcuffs."

Forty-Seven

NEARLY TWO IN the afternoon, and there had been not a single sign of Trang Nguyen. Hong and his lawyer friend were out looking with their people, and Wei had called the Dragons together as soon as Conroy contacted him.

Now they were all gathered together—almost all; Tony was off doing something for Wei—in Wei's apartment. Constance was there with Shelby, though Noah sat with her away from the business chatter.

"I still don't know what we're doing in your place, Wei," Walker Teng said, complaining simply to complain.

"You think Hwang don't know about the coffee shop?" Conroy rolled his eyes. He wished Walker would use his head more and his mouth less. Of all the Dragons, he was by far the most annoying.

"I'm willing to bet he knows about this place, too," Walker returned.

"Yeah, but he'll have a harder time throwing a Molotov through this window than the coffee shop."

"Let's just get started," Wei said. He didn't speak loudly, but everyone turned to him.

"What about Tony?" Chris Ma asked.

"We'll catch him up when he gets here. Now, I know you all know why we're here. Johnny Hwang was released this morning, because the second witness Conroy and Hong secured disappeared."

"Convenient, that," Chris said sarcastically.

"I don't think any of us are surprised that Dang found a way to smooth things out for Hwang," Steel said.

"Hong probably told him about the girl," Walker added.

"He didn't," Conroy snapped, surprising himself with the intensity with which he'd come to Hong's defense. "He couldn't have. I was with him the whole time after we found her." *Mostly*, he added silently, glad Tony was late so he couldn't contradict that statement—not that he thought he would. "Hong's not the enemy here."

"He's a cop!" Walker spread his hands open as if that single statement said it all. For Walker, for a lot of the Dragons, it did. There was a time when it did for Conroy, as well, but not anymore.

"The world is never black and white," Constance said, an unreadable expression in her eyes as she looked at him.

"None of that is important right now," Wei reminded them. "There's nothing we can do about it now. Hwang is out. What we have to do is figure out what to do next."

"Do we have a lot of options?" It was Smile Kang who spoke. The fact that he was actively engaging in the discussion underscored the level of danger surrounding their situation.

"Smile's right," Constance said, though she sounded like she wished he wasn't. "We don't have any choice, really. We know that Hwang's going to be coming for us. We have to get ready for war."

Conroy's stomach clenched at those words. Some of the younger Dragons, like Kevin, who hadn't gone through it before, looked almost excited at the prospect. Conroy could see on their faces that Wei, Constance, Chris, and Smile shared his feelings of cold dread at the prospect. He'd prayed they would never have to go through this again, and yet here they were.

"There are some arrangements that need to be made, and quickly," Wei said, his voice all business. "We need to get even more men on the street right away. Double, triple the numbers. We need to increase recruitment."

"I'm going to arrange an overseas holiday for Shelby," Constance said, the barest of tremors noticeable. "Send her to Japan, maybe."

"Noah speaks Japanese," said Wei. "He can go with her."

"Mom, no!" Shelby said at the same time Noah said, "Wei, no!"

"We can't handle this if we're constantly worried about you," Constance explained. "This is the best way to keep you safe."

"I can help!" Noah protested.

"This isn't your fight," Wei said firmly.

"It's your fight, which makes it my fight."

"This isn't up for discussion!"

Conroy winced. It was Wei's "I'm the boss, do what I say" voice, and while that might work on the Dragons, he didn't think it would go over well with a boyfriend.

Sure enough, Noah squared his shoulders, hands on his hips. "I'm a grown man, Wei. You can't tell me what to do like I'm some child. You can't make me go anywhere I don't want to."

"I'll have someone physically drag you all the way to Tokyo, if I have to!"

Noah rolled his eyes. "I feel sorry for whoever you give *that* task to."

Conroy did his best to hide the smile that had come unbidden to his face. Noah had fire inside of him, and he had the self-defense know-how to make things very difficult for anyone who tried to make him do something he didn't want to do, short of pulling a gun on him.

But Conroy wouldn't put anything past Wei, not where keeping Noah safe was concerned.

"I see I came in at a good time," Tony said from near the doorway.

"We'll talk about this later," Wei said to Noah in a low voice.

"Oh, you bet your ass we will."

Wei actually chuckled deep in his chest, squeezing Noah's shoulder before walking past him to speak to Tony. "What have you learned?"

"It's already started. Twisted Viper territory is in an uproar. It sounds like Hwang has started culling people whose loyalty he doubts. According to what I could gather, some of his redpoles questioned the wisdom of a street war with the Dragons, and he shot them in the head, right in the meeting. In front of everyone."

Chris whistled. "Sounds like prison fucked with Hwang's head. He's gone crazy."

"Yeah, and that's not necessarily a good thing for us," Wei mused.

"Maybe we can make it a good thing, though," Winston said. He had a look on his face, like he expected to be told to be quiet or stay out of Dragons' business. Conroy wondered when he'd fully adjust to the fact that he was now one of them and grow into his role.

"What do you mean, Noisy?" Conroy prompted, using the nickname Winston had earned in the Dark Streets races just to annoy him.

"What I mean, *K-Pop*," Winston said, making fun of the fact that the Dragons often said Conroy looked like a Korean music idol, "is that with Hwang going around putting bullets in his own people, maybe this is the time to get that alliance we were after before."

"Noisy makes a very good point," Conroy agreed. "They might be more open to our offer now that Hwang's gone all 'Off with their heads' or 'Bullets in their heads' or whatever."

"It's definitely worth trying," Wei said. "I don't know if they'd even take a meeting with us, though."

"I'll see what I can set up," Tony said while digging his phone from his pocket and then stepping out of the apartment.

"Okay, this isn't going to be the same as last time," Wei said. "We're going in there ready for something to go down. There's a fifty-fifty chance they'll try to put bullets in us just to save their own heads from Hwang."

"You know shit's really hit the fan when we're following one of Noisy's ideas," Conroy said, walking over to Winston and throwing an arm around his shoulder.

"Are you ever going to stop calling me Noisy, Conroy?"

"Sure I will. As soon as I come up with something more amusing to call you."

Forty-Eight

CONROY WAS SURPRISED how quickly a meeting was arranged. Within thirty minutes of Tony's phone call, they were on their way to a rendezvous point with the Twisted Vipers, firmly in Dragons territory. That they'd been willing to concede the meeting place spoke of their desperation better than anything else could have.

This time the Dragons entourage included Conroy, Steel, Winston, Chris, Kevin, and Walker. Mimi had wanted to join them, but Constance was firmly against it, saying she needed more time to recover from the gunshot if she wanted to be of any use to them in the future.

Wei had chosen an auto shop, the same place where not so long ago, he'd met with Leo Tong. It felt like a lifetime ago, considering everything that had happened since. Thinking about that moment, Conroy wondered if *that* had been the start of it all—the spiral that led to this inevitable moment. Maybe it was fate that this meeting was happening in the same place, a chance to stop the events Leo Tong had put in motion.

"Be ready," Wei warned them. They stood inside the shop, the roll-down door open, arranged in a half circle, with Wei at its center. A few minutes later, two cars arrived, both of them large and foreign. The first car was a Hummer, the second a Ford Expedition. Five men exited the Hummer—the bodyguards. Six more men left the Expedition, two more bodyguards and the four redpoles they'd met before: Jake Tam, Ting, Big Po, and Lazarus.

"The muscle stays back," Wei called as the Vipers approached. "You four can come closer, but they don't."

Jake Tam snorted. "What, so you can pull us into a trap?"

"If I wanted you in a trap, you'd already be in one," Wei said, sounding bored of the whole situation. "You can turn me down if you want to, but then you'll be getting right back into those too-big cars and going back to a dragonhead who seems to be losing his grip."

The men traded dark looks, but signaled their bodyguards to stay back. "I see you aren't extending us the same courtesy." Ting sniffed as he took in Conroy and the others.

"Let's just get on with this," Wei said impatiently. "I don't want to be around you any longer than I absolutely have to. You guys know why we're here. We've come with the same offer we brought before. Maybe this time you'll be less inclined to dismiss us."

"What, you want us to become *Dragons*?" Lazarus said the last word as if it physically pained him.

"Doesn't sound like you've got a better option on the other side," Tony said, arms crossed over his chest. "From what I hear, it's only a matter of time before Hwang puts a bullet in your heads, too."

"What are the details of this offer, exactly, Tseng?" Big Po asked.

"That's easy enough: you agree to abide by every rule I've set for Dragons territory—no profiting off prostitution, no drugs, no trafficking."

Ting stared at Wei like he'd grown a second head. "You want us to give up our most profitable businesses?" To his fellow Twisted Vipers, he added, "I told you this *puk gai* is crazy!"

Conroy stepped forward, grabbing Ting by the front of his shirt, bringing his fist hard into his gut, and doubling him over. The bodyguards behind the redpoles made as if to move on them, but Big Po held up a hand to stay them off. At least one of them had some semblance of intelligence, it seemed. He pulled Ting back up straight, staring him in the eyes. "Watch your fucking mouth, you hear me?"

"I think he gets it, Conroy," Wei said, and Conroy released him, stepping back into place.

"What if we don't agree to this deal?" Lazarus asked.

"We'll find someone who will," Wei said with a shrug. "Given what Hwang has turned into, that shouldn't be too difficult."

"And if we do agree, we stay in charge."

Wei shook his head. "Not a chance. You can stay near the top of the food chain in your own areas, but you'll answer to one of my men and to me."

"This doesn't sound like a very favorable deal for us," Jake Tam sneered. "What do we get out of this?"

"You get the protection of the Dragons," Tony answered. "I'd say your life is favorable, yes?"

Ting shook his head indignantly. "The other Twisted Vipers—"

"The Twisted Vipers are finished," Wei snapped. "You can cling to that idea or you can just accept it."

"The other Twisted Vipers," Ting repeated with a scowl, "will resist. They're not going to want to give up their money."

"They won't have a choice. Sure, there will be some holdouts, but once we take down Hwang, none of them will have the balls to challenge us. This is going to happen, whether you like it or not. The only question you have to answer is this: do you want to be part of this? We'll have no problem finding someone willing to cooperate if you don't."

The four Twisted Viper redpoles traded looks, but they didn't seem entirely convinced, so Conroy decided to give them a little push.

"Look, you know as well as I do that Hwang is bad for business now. Publicly killing cops? Cutting down his own people? Planning a war on the Dragons? How is any of that going to bring you money? There's too much police attention on you; the Anti-Gang Task Force is going to tear the Vipers apart piece by piece."

"He's right," Big Po said to the others. "The police are going to be shadowing everything we do as long as we have Hwang. He's drawn too much attention to us. He was warned about taking action against Yang, and he did it anyway. He doesn't care about the organization." He cast an appraising eye toward Wei. "I believe that it might just be time to accept Mr. Tseng's offer."

"The offer doesn't come free," Conroy told them, not bothering to suppress his smugness. This felt like a true victory, small as it was. It was in that moment that the Dragons would truly begin the work of putting an end to the Twisted Vipers—and not soon enough, in his book; they'd been a scourge on Hong Kong for far too long.

"What, our money isn't enough?" Jake Tam hissed.

"Consider the money the cost of doing business. The deal, however, has a different price."

"What is it you're asking for?" Lazarus asked, face giving away nothing.

"Information," Conroy said. "We know that Hwang took a woman—a Vietnamese woman—who was going to testify against him. We need to know about her, whether she's alive and if so, where did Hwang take her?"

"I've heard about the poor girl," Big Po admitted. "Last I heard, she was alive. Someone managed to convince Johnny that if she turned up dead it would look bad, considering everything that has recently gone down. He's got her put away somewhere."

She was alive. Relief flooded through Conroy. He hadn't dared hope they would be so lucky, but whatever gods existed out there in the universe seemed to be favoring them.

"Where is he keeping her?"

"We want full protection," Lazarus said before Big Po could answer. "We want your word, Wei Tseng. We want you to guarantee our safety, should your plan fail."

Wei stepped toward Lazarus, slowly extending his hand. "You have my word that the Dragons will do everything in their power to make sure Hwang can't come after you for this."

Lazarus stared at Wei's hand, clearly weighing the choices put before him. He didn't have much of a choice, and Conroy knew they knew it. A quick look at the other three redpoles—they all nodded their approval, Ting more than a little reluctantly—and Lazarus reached out and shook Wei's hand.

"You have a deal, Mr. Tseng."

Hopefully we're not making a deal with the devil.

"Now, how do we take out Hwang? A well-timed hit could—"

"No. I'm not going to resort to violence if I don't have to. The only way to maintain the legitimacy of the Dragons is if we take Hwang down the legal way. That's why we need the woman he's taken."

"So hurry up and tell us where Hwang took her," Conroy urged. He itched to get out there and find her, and to get away from the Twisted Vipers. He didn't trust them, not for anything; they might be siding with Wei now, but that was because it was their heads on the line. Conroy had no doubt they'd double-cross Wei the moment the opportunity presented itself.

"Well, we don't know exactly," Big Po said delicately.

"But we know a place he might be using," Lazarus added before the angry explosion could come from Conroy. "We can't promise you she's there, but there's a good chance."

Conroy rolled his eyes. "You talk too damn much. Just give us an address."

Forty-Nine

ALLEN SLUMPED DOWN behind the wheel of his car, defeated. He'd exhausted just about every avenue he could think for finding Trang Nguyen. It was pushing three o'clock, and every hour that ticked by made the situation that much graver.

According to his sources, Hwang was unraveling more by the minute. His instability had turned toward his own people as he culled out the upper ranks, but that wouldn't last. It was only a matter of time before he targeted the Eastern District and the Dragons, and—like the Nine Stars before—he wouldn't care who got caught in the crossfire.

A lot of innocent people were going to die if Hwang wasn't stopped, and Trang was their one last chance, short of killing the man, which would plunge them into a war anyway. They needed to find her.

He grimly mulled over the possibility that she'd been killed, played it on repeat in his mind. If they'd killed her, then there was no hope. He was convinced she was alive, though he didn't have any evidence to support the theory other than his own wild hope.

Still, if she was alive, he'd yet to find any sign of her. Given the chaos of the Twisted Vipers, few informants were willing to talk, lest they draw down Hwang's ire on their own heads.

He tried his hardest to come up with something, anything, that might give them a leg up, tell them where they held her, but could come up with nothing. After his confrontation with Dang at the police station, he didn't dare contact Ao for fear of turning Dang's attention to his partner. As things stood, Ao was in the clear; he wouldn't even suffer guilt by association. Allen intended to keep it that way.

Allen contemplated a third trip to the community they'd found her in when his phone rang. It was Conroy, and seeing his name on the screen sent a flood of relief through him, and he breathed a little easier. It was a strange sensation, to say the least, considering they'd been engaged in their personal Cold War less than a week before.

There would be time to marvel at the strange turns life could take later, though.

"Hong, we've got a lead," Conroy said when Allen answered. "Hwang might have taken her to a place in the old neighborhood. We've got it on pretty good authority that Hwang occasionally takes people there who he wants out of the way."

"Is she alive?" Allen asked, bracing himself for the answer.

"She was last these *puk gai* had heard. Doesn't mean she will be for long. Wei wants to move on it tonight. We're meeting at Wei's old family home to plan it out. Wei said head on over as soon as you can."

Allen had no trouble getting to the home Wei's family had once lived in; he'd been there plenty of times since it had been used as their base of operations during their fight with the Nine Stars. It was an old pre-colonial neighborhood, much like the one Trang Nguyen's parents lived in, only much larger, with bigger houses. The neighborhood was slowly emptying out as its residents either died or moved away. Now most of the homes were unoccupied, sitting like lonely shells on the beach.

The air felt heavier there, weighed down by memories. It was not a place Wei liked to revisit, so it must have simply been a matter of convenience that led him to use it.

The front of the house was dark, giving no sign that there was anyone there, and no cars were parked on the street. That didn't surprise Allen; they'd come up with that concept during the street war, so their meeting place wouldn't be easy to figure out. They all parked in completely different areas and walked to Wei's home.

An alley ran back between the side of the house and a fence that separated the property from the neighbor's. Allen went down it. The backyard was already dark, the sun having dropped below the city line. Night seemed to come faster as the year progressed into winter.

Wei sat alone outside on the steps leading up to the porch, smoking a cigarette and looking deep in thought. He gave Allen a neutral nod when he saw him.

Allen walked up the steps and stopped, standing beside Wei. "This all feels kind of familiar, doesn't it?"

Wei grunted. "Yeah. I didn't think we'd be back here like this."

"Me either." Allen sat next to Wei. Wei offered him a cigarette, but he refused. "But I guess we both should have seen this coming. We were being naive to think that the peace would last. How could it, with men like Johnny Hwang in the world?"

Wei was silent. Allen didn't know if Wei was considering his words or if he was lost in his thoughts, but he didn't mind either way. He used the silence to gather his courage.

Wei finished his cigarette and put the cigarette out on the step before standing up.

"Let's get inside and get this started."

Allen stood and together they went inside. The room they entered was a kitchen, open and airy; all of the windows meant that they didn't need to rely on any artificial light, just the dusk for the time being. All of the furniture that had been there while Wei's family lived there remained, since Wei had never bothered getting rid of it. He still owned the house, and probably always would. Allen doubted he'd bring himself to sell it.

Most of the higher Dragons were already inside: Walker, Conroy, Steel, Winston, Chris, Kevin, and Tony. Smile was noticeably absent. There were also four men Allen didn't know, but their tattoos made it clear that they were Twisted Vipers.

Allen hadn't had much faith in the plan, but he'd been proven wrong.

Allen crossed the kitchen to stand next to Conroy without really thinking about it. He regretted it once he began, but there wasn't much he could do about it; he couldn't simply turn on his heel and walk back to where he'd come from. He passed Conroy's position and went to stand in the corner where the kitchen countertop met the refrigerator. He hoped the choice hadn't looked as clunky and unplanned as it felt.

"We don't have a lot of time to talk about this," Wei said without preamble. "Our objective here is to take Trang Nguyen to safety. She's our best shot at getting Hwang behind bars."

"I still say we should kill the *ga tsan* and be done with it," Walker protested.

"We kill him and we give the Twisted Vipers reason to unite," Tony explained. From his impatient tone Allen assumed this wasn't the first time this discussion had been had.

"He's right," one of the Twisted Vipers spoke up, drawing glares and scowls from the Dragons. He pretended not to notice them, though, and went on. "There's no love lost between most of the Vipers and Hwang—especially after the shit he's pulled here—but the Dragons killing him? It would be an insult to the Vipers, and something they'd have to answer with force. The only way a war is avoided is if Hwang is alive and behind bars."

"The discussion on that is closed," Wei added, his tone brooking no argument. "Right now, we're—"

Footsteps on the porch outside silenced Wei. Everyone in the room tensed; Allen saw Chris deftly draw a switchblade from his front pocket and flick it open with a quiet *snip*. The tension in the room skyrocketed for a moment, only to be brought back down when the door opened and Smile Kang stepped inside.

"Yo, Smile," Conroy called. "What took you so long?"

"Did you want it done fast or right?" Smile asked, speaking more words in that one sentence than Allen had heard from him over the last five years combined. To Wei, he said, "Their information was right, at least. The house is definitely occupied. I didn't try to get close enough to see if Trang Nguyen is actually inside, but someone is. It's also well defended. I counted at least nine men outside. Could be that same amount inside. Maybe more, maybe less; no way to know without getting closer."

"You did good." Wei nodded approvingly. "Now we need to figure out how we do this."

"We distract them," Allen said, straightening. "It's basic when running this sort of operation in the cops."

"You keep interesting company, Wei Tseng," one of the Twisted Vipers said, not bothering to hide his disgust.

"Shut the fuck up if you want to keep your teeth," Conroy growled. For a microsecond, Allen thought Conroy might have been lashing out at the disdain directed Allen's way, but his logical right-brain voice overrode that. It wasn't about Allen; it was the fact that the speaker was a Twisted Viper.

"Go on, Hong," Wei said, sending his own warning glare to the Twisted Viper, who held up his hands as if to say *Understood*.

"We run a distraction to concentrate their attention where we want it while a few people can slip past."

"What sort of distraction could we pull that wouldn't result in a gun fight?" Winston asked. He was seated on the edge of the counter directly across from Allen.

"That's easy. Me."

Conroy wheeled on him so quickly Allen imagined he could hear his bones creak. "What the hell are you talking about?"

"With all the shit I've given Hwang with this arrest and investigation, he's going to want to deal with me personally."

"What's to stop him from shooting you in your idiot head the moment he sees you?" The vehemence in Conroy's voice confused Allen, sending signals he couldn't decode. After their last round of sex, Allen wondered if maybe the feelings Conroy had for him hadn't vanished entirely.

"I'm a cop. If I show up, he's going to want to know who else knows about the place, how many others are coming, and when they might get there."

"This is a really fucking bad idea."

"No, it's the best plan we have, and Wei knows it."

"It's the only plan we've tried! Give us some time!"

"We haven't got time," Allen argued. "The longer we wait, the more likely it is that Trang Nguyen dies. If we ride in guns blazing, then y— people I care about might get hurt, or worse. This is the best plan we have for keeping everyone safe."

Allen turned to Wei. "Am I right?"

Wei nodded slowly. "Hong is right. We'll handle this the right way. We get in, we get out, and nobody gets hurt."

"Except maybe some Twisted Viper fuckers," Winston added, cracking his knuckles with too much enthusiasm for Allen's taste.

Allen's heart tore slightly as he watched his nephew get excited about going into a situation that might well end in bloodshed. Allen knew Winston's father wouldn't have wanted that life for him. Neither did Allen.

They worked on logistics for nearly thirty minutes, finally deciding that Conroy and Kevin would have the best chances of getting in close— Kevin because he was agile and small, and Conroy because he was most equipped to take out the Viper grunts without killing them.

"So we all know what we're doing," Wei said when they were finished. It was by no means a perfect plan—Conroy continued to voice his protests over it, as did Walker—but it was the best they would get. "Let's get in there and get her out. Tonight, the Twisted Vipers come to an end."

The Dragons in the room let out whooping cheers, and Allen couldn't help but join in. He'd worked just as hard as Wei and the Dragons to bring the Vipers down, in his own way, and all of that was about to come to fruition.

Allen left first so he could get to his car and be ready when it was time to go.

"Yo, Hong!"

Allen stopped, surprised to hear Conroy calling out behind him. He turned around hesitantly, uncertain what he'd find on Conroy's face when he did. What he found was mostly fury.

"What the fuck are you thinking with this plan?"

"I'm thinking I should be doing my job to protect the people of the Eastern District. I thought you'd get that."

"You shouldn't be the one to go in there like this."

Allen pursed his lips. "Why? Because I'm a cop? You don't trust me to see this through? You think I'm going to turn on you?"

"No, because I think you're going to get hurt, and I don't want to see you die!" The words came out of Conroy like an explosion and left Allen mentally reeling. Conroy appeared just as surprised by the outburst. "Listen, Allen, I want to give you the choice you thought I would five years ago. Who would you choose, right now, in this moment? The Dragons or the police?"

Allen's heart hammered rapidly in his chest, a sound that conjured the image of ancient drums beaten to spur men on to war. But this—this was war of a different kind, and a battle he was in no way certain of his chances.

"You don't get it, Conroy. The choice that I was afraid of was never about the Dragons. It was *you.*"

Conroy started to speak and cleared his throat when the words didn't come. "Well? The same question, then. Who would you choose, me or the police?"

"I didn't...I didn't realize that you were still an option I could choose."

Conroy shrugged, and for the first time, Allen realized that Conroy was just as confused as he was.

"Maybe the option could be put back on the table. If it was—"

Allen decided to take a risk. He stretched out, grasping Conroy's hand in his own, and was bolstered when Conroy didn't pull away.

"If I could travel back in time to when I made that choice with the knowledge I have now? I'd choose you, Conroy Wong."

They stood there like that as the sky overhead deepened into the bruised purple of early evening. There was so much left unsaid between them. Allen could see it all hovering around them, like spirits haunting them. But there would be time to deal with those ghosts later.

And, just maybe, when they put those ghosts to bed, they could start dealing with the future.

"I've got to go," Allen said at last, dropping Conroy's hand.

Conroy nodded. When he spoke again, his confusion was once again masked behind the constant and effortless swagger he exuded.

"I know this will be hard for you, but don't do anything too stupid."

Allen smiled. "You be careful, too."

Fifty

T WENTY MINUTES LATER, Conroy and Kevin slowly made their way through the yards of empty properties, weaving an indirect path toward the house Smile had told them about.

It was one of the larger homes in the area, occupying twice the amount of land as Wei's family home. There were several lights on, and Conroy counted four cars parked in the driveway. The entire property was surrounded by a wall a little shorter than Conroy.

Conroy and Kevin had no problem getting to the wall. Once there, they kept to its shadow, crouched down and out of sight. Conroy had been hesitant to have Kevin with him, but now he couldn't see why. Kevin might have been a loudmouth and a goof, but he also knew when it was time to get serious, like now. His face was set in concentration and he moved with purpose, his feet making barely a sound on the ground as he walked.

Once they rounded the corner of the gate and slipped fully out of sight of the main road, Conroy raised his head, watchful for any Twisted Viper that might be nearby. A quick scan of the back of the house revealed a sliding door thrown open and dim light pouring out. Three men stood near the door, looking bored, like they'd rather be anywhere else. In contrast, a bright glow illuminated the yard from the side of the house farthest from their current position.

Satisfied, Conroy returned to a squat.

"How does it look?" Kevin asked, voice pitched low enough that no one but Conroy would be able to hear it over the persistent chattering of crickets and katydids.

"Three men back here," Conroy replied. "I'd prefer better odds for a blitz attack. We'll have to wait until the plan gets put into action."

Kevin pulled his cell phone. "Well, that should be any minute now."

Conroy and Kevin stared down at Kevin's phone, awaiting the notification that everything was a go. The minutes ticked by—first one minute, then two minutes—and finally the message from Wei appeared. All it said was *Now*.

Conroy tensed, cocking his head and straining his ears to hear it. Yes—there it was. A loud, blaring siren, and soon after, the sound of Hong's car approaching. He couldn't see the front of the house, but he could hear Hong's tires squealing as he came down the street and to a stop. He was definitely making a flashy entrance.

Conroy risked another look over the wall. The three men were making for the front of the house. So far so good.

Conroy nodded to Kevin and held his hands together to boost the shorter man over the wall before effortlessly hauling himself over.

Conroy felt incredibly exposed there; if someone came around the corner or happened to look out the window, he had nowhere to take cover, and they would be caught. Both Conroy and Kevin had switchblades on them, but they would be useless if they were shot before they could even draw them.

They made for the side of the house the brighter light was coming from as quickly as they could. Conroy didn't dare breathe until they were safely shielded by the house.

The light came from a window about halfway along the side of the house. Conroy and Kevin settled low on the ground beneath the window. Conroy itched to look into the window, but he didn't dare. The glass was thin, so it wasn't too difficult to hear what was going on inside.

"Will someone tell me what the fuck is going on out there?" The irritated voice no doubt belonged to Johnny Hwang; Conroy would recognize it anywhere.

"Looks like you've got a visitor, Mr. Hwang." Conroy recognized the voice of Hwang's second, Jiang, as well. It was hard to forget the voice of the man who had threatened his life.

Conroy clenched his hands into fists. He owed Jiang for his little visit, not to mention the bounty he'd placed on Conroy's head.

"Well, I won't try to hide my surprise at seeing you here, Inspector Hong," Hwang drawled. "Or should I say *former* Inspector Hong?"

Conroy tensed, knowing Hong had entered the room. He decided it was worth the effort and raised his head to look inside.

Hwang's back was to him, with Jiang standing off to the side, also not looking his way. In the corner of the room, Conroy could just barely see a set of legs, bound at the ankle by rope—Trang Nguyen. So they'd found her.

In the other corner Conroy saw Inspector Leung. Of course Dang had one of his puppets there. Conroy guessed Leung was the person who'd abducted Trang from wherever the prosecutor friend of Hong's had her.

"I told you I was going to bring you down, Johnny," Hong said calmly, like he hadn't just walked into a room full of dangerous men who wanted him dead.

Upon hearing Hong's voice Conroy decided to risk a better look. "No matter what you do, no matter where you go, I'll find you. You might as well consider me your new shadow.

"And you!" He gave Leung a look one usually reserved for a cockroach or something equally disgusting. "Is this what you thought you'd be doing? Abducting innocent women on Dang's orders? You're pathetic."

"Let's cut the sermon short, shall we?" Hwang asked impatiently. "I'm curious to know how you found me and who else knows about this place."

"A lot of people," Hong said, sounding pleased with himself. "Backup should be here any minute."

"The police aren't coming," Leung sneered. "I would have gotten a call if they were."

"You think so? We know you're dirty, Leung, just like we know Dang is dirty. He's out of the loop. The Anti-Gang Task Force is on its way. I think you're going to have a hard time getting out of this one, Johnny, even with Dang in your pocket. This time you're caught red-handed. Sure, kidnapping and holding someone hostage isn't a murder charge, but there's no way in hell a jury doesn't believe Trang after this."

"If this task force of yours *is* coming—which I'm not sure I believe— all they'll find here is your dead body. Maybe we'll leave some drugs or money, make it look like a dirty cop engaged in another illegal deal gone bad. Jiang?"

Jiang reached behind him and pulled out the gun he had tucked into his waistband. Conroy didn't know what made him look toward the window at that moment—maybe he was looking for a cue from Hwang— but he did. Conroy ducked down behind it, but he knew he'd been spotted. Jiang yelled out.

"Let's go," Conroy hissed to Kevin. "We've got to get back to Wei and the others."

They ran. Conroy hoped they got over the wall before someone with a gun got out there.

As he reached the corner, one of the Twisted Vipers came around the corner. Conroy wasted little time; he barreled forward, his shoulder catching him in the solar plexus and knocking the wind out of him. He didn't stop as he ran. He heard a groan of pain and figured that Kevin had stepped on the Viper on his way over.

Conroy chanced a glance over his shoulder at the sound of the sliding door opening. Jiang was there, backed by two more Twisted Vipers, but Conroy and Kevin were at the wall. Conroy bounded over it with little effort, Kevin just behind him. A sickening gunshot split into the air, breaking the quiet façade of a peaceful neighborhood. He stayed hunched over and hurried to the safety of the neighboring property.

Once he thought he was out of immediate danger of gunfire, he looked back toward the house.

Good luck, Hong.

Fifty-One

ALLEN HEARD THE gunshot and prayed that Conroy was all right. He didn't have time to think about it, though. Trang Nguyen's life was on the line. He couldn't worry about Conroy while she was still in danger.

Allen took advantage of the uproar and slammed his fist into Leung's jaw, knocking him to the ground. He stumbled across the room to where Trang Nguyen was tied and gagged on a wooden dining room chair.

"You're going to be okay," he assured her.

"I think you're speaking too soon," Johnny Hwang said, drawing his own gun. "So you have a few friends with you. They won't do much good out there while you're in here alone."

"You've always been a cocky sonofabitch, Johnny. I don't need anyone to help me take you on." Allen spread his legs shoulder-length apart, inserting his body between Hwang and Trang.

Hwang laughed snidely. "Now who is being cocky? I've got a gun, Hong, if you haven't noticed. I'm going to kill you and this stupid bitch, and then I'm going to do what I've wanted to do for a long time. I'm going to crush Wei Tseng and the Dragons beneath my feet. This entire island will be mine."

Allen threw himself at Hwang suddenly, taking advantage of his narcissistic babble. He didn't fall, unfortunately, but he was caught off balance. Hwang tried to bring the butt of the gun down on Allen, but Allen caught his wrist and pushed him back. The two of them stumbled into the wall. Allen used his grip on Hwang's wrist to slam his hand into the wall once, twice, three times, and the gun dropped from his hand.

Leung stirred and made a lunge for the weapon, but Allen kicked it with his heel, sending the metal skittering across the floor. He then kicked out, Leung rolling so the blow was deflected by his shoulder.

There was one chance for Allen to get the upper hand. He released Hwang and made for the gun. Allen almost had the gun when Trang, eyes wide and fearful, tried to say something through her gag. Before

Allen could turn, a foot caught him in the small of his back, sending him staggering forward. He collided with Trang, nearly sending her tumbling out of her chair.

By the time he turned around, Hwang had the gun drawn and pointed at him again.

"Nice try, but it looks like I still come out on top. I don't think you've been having a very good week, have you, Inspector?"

A door banged open somewhere. Footsteps approached their location. The victorious smile on Hwang's face faded somewhat when Wei strode into the room, followed by Tony and Conroy. It returned when the Twisted Viper redpoles Allen saw at Wei's house brought up the rear. Each of them had a gun raised. Jiang brought up the rear, a shit-eating grin on his face.

"Wei Tseng! I see you've done me the favor of coming to me, spared me having to track you down. This simplifies things for me quite a bit."

Jiang crossed the room to where Trang was tied up. He stood behind her, one hand patting her shoulder—she flinched each time its weight came down—the other holding his gun. He used the barrel of it to brush strands of loose hair back from Trang's forehead.

Hwang surveyed the room like a kid at Christmas. "Now I get to take care of every last loose thread that's been plaguing me, and all in one easy evening. I'm a man of honor, so do you have any last words, Wei?"

Wei stared the Twisted Viper dragonhead down stoically. "Just two. You lose."

"*I* lose? Do you see what's going on here, Wei? You're surrounded by *my* people, and..." Hwang's smile faltered. "What did they offer you?" he asked at last.

The four Twisted Vipers stepped forward, around Wei, Conroy, and Tony. One pointed his gun at Leung, another at Jiang, while the other two kept theirs trained on Hwang. "Stability and our lives. Your vendetta has destroyed the Twisted Vipers, Hwang, and you just can't see it. Your lust for revenge brought hell down on us. There's no recovering from the damage you've done. We decided to abandon ship while we still could. Drop the gun."

"Are you going to kill me, Big Po? Put a bullet in my head?"

"Give me one good reason I shouldn't."

Allen saw something in Hwang's eyes that he'd never had before: fear. He couldn't have ever imagined it would come to this, his own people there for his blood.

"You've killed a lot of my friends, Hwang," the Twisted Viper went on menacingly. "What did Crow do? He begged you to not take any risks, to wait until the heat was off, and you put a bullet in his brain."

"That death was too good for him," Hwang snarled, eyes wide like a cornered animal. "He was a traitor, just like you!"

"*Diu lei!*" Big Po cocked the gun, raising it until it was aimed right at his forehead.

Hwang's eyes flew to Wei. "You must be loving this, Tseng. Finally going to be rid of me. I know it's what you've always wanted."

Wei shook his head. "This was your doing, Johnny, not mine."

"I can give you something you want, Wei," Hwang said quickly. "You keep your men from killing me, and I'll give it to you. Send me to prison—I won't be there long, no matter what sort of case you might have. I'll take that. Let me live, and I'll give you something no one else can."

"You're not going to try to make a *deal* with this *puk gai*, are you, Johnny?" Jiang protested.

Big Po didn't hesitate. He turned, aimed, and fired. The shot echoed painfully in the cavernous space, and Trang screamed against her gag. Jiang's neck snapped back and then he was on the ground, bits of blood and brain matter decorating the wall.

"Jesus fucking Christ!" Leung cried, pressing himself back against the wall as if trying slip through it.

Allen saw Wei grimace. That hadn't been part of the plan, he had no doubt.

Big Po must have caught Wei's expression as well, because he said, "He had it coming a thousand times over. No one will mourn his death."

"Tell me about Dang," Wei said at last, turning his attention back to Hwang.

"I needed insurance in case he ever decided to go back on our arrangement, or throw me under the bus," Hwang explained. "I have recordings of almost every conversation I've ever had with him, more than enough dirt to land him in jail right beside me." Hwang flashed a dark smile at that.

"Where are these recordings?"

"They're all stored in a cloud drive. My phone has access to them all." Hwang reached slowly into his pocket, pulled out his phone, tossing it to Wei.

Wei turned to Tony. "Get the police here. There's a lot of Vipers who scattered when we showed up. I want them tracked down. Conroy, get Trang out of here."

Big Po acted suddenly, the motion a blur, just like when he shot Jiang. This time he cracked Hwang over the head with the gun, knocking him unconscious. "What? I was tired of listening to him."

The imminent danger passed, and Allen went over to Trang to free the gag. She immediately began to sob, head hung low and hair shielding her face from view.

"You're okay," Allen assured her, working on the bindings on her wrists.

Conroy joined him, drawing his switchblade and cutting her ankles free. Allen glanced at him as he worked on her wrists and saw the beginning of a nasty bruise under his left eye.

"You all right?"

"Huh?" Conroy grunted. "Oh, the eye? Yeah, I'm fine. *Ga tsan* got me with his elbow as he tried to run away. His face might have hit the ground a few times once I got him down." Conroy grinned.

"Well, I'm glad you're okay."

"You too." There was an awkward pause before Trang's wrists came free. "Okay, let's get her out of here."

Fifty-Two

ONCE THEY HAD Trang Nguyen safe and sound at her parents' home, Conroy rode along with Wei and Hong to the Eastern District precinct. Anticipation bubbled in his stomach. This visit had been a long time coming. He could hardly believe they'd accomplished so much.

The Twisted Vipers were finished, Hwang was on his way to jail for good this time, and Jiang, perhaps the biggest threat after Hwang, was dead. Conroy couldn't say he blamed Big Po for doing what he did. He knew Wei didn't approve of the action, but the man was a threat to them, and he would have been as long as he was still breathing. Conroy wouldn't have pulled the trigger himself, but he wasn't sad to see the bastard dead.

As the precinct came into sight, Allen started to say something. "Try to—"

"Let me guess." Conroy smirked at him from the passenger seat. "Let you do the talking?"

Hong arched an eyebrow at him. "Actually, I was going to say try to rub it in as much as you possibly can."

"You two have gotten awfully friendly," Wei observed from the back. Conroy could hear in his voice that Wei knew exactly what had transpired between the two of them, but didn't care.

"Well," Hong said with a shrug, "you put two people in close quarters for long enough and it's bound to happen. That or they kill each other."

"That one still might happen," Conroy added with the smallest smile.

Conroy could only imagine how strange the three of them looked, marching into the precinct with purpose. Inspector Cheung met them near the door, and Hong gave him a nod, which Cheung returned before heading off somewhere.

They found Henry Dang pacing in his office, moving as if a caged rat going stir-crazy, which is exactly what he was. When they entered, Dang froze, beady eyes focused on Wei. Various emotions played over his face too fast to track, but Conroy had to think he knew he was done for.

When he spoke, though, it was in the same superior, smug tone he always had. Conroy wondered if he'd come out of his mother with that arrogance or if he'd developed it later in life.

"If it isn't Wei Tseng and his pet cop."

"That's interesting, coming from Johnny Hwang's personal rat," Hong quipped.

"Those are serious allegations," Dang said. The only indication of nerves came from the way the index finger of his right hand had begun tapping against the side of his leg, an unconscious tic.

"Yes, they are." Wei pulled Hwang's cell phone from his pocket. After a few silent beats, the recording reverberated through the room.

"*I've told you before, Dang, I want this investigation finished,*" Hwang's cold voice said, echoing loudly. Conroy had no doubt the people in the bullpen could hear it as well.

"*I'm trying,*" Dang's voice replied, the barest hint of exasperation under it. "*Yang is too straight and narrow to be easily swayed. I've had to try more subtle methods.*"

"*I don't care what you have to do. Pay him, threaten his family, blackmail him—it doesn't matter. Just get him off my ass, or I'll do it myself.*"

Wei ended the recording as those damning words hung in the air. Dang's face was slack, and he looked like a brisk wind would blow him right over.

"Did you catch that, Inspectors?" Cheung's voice asked behind them.

Conroy turned to see two men in suits standing behind them. He assumed they were the Internal Affairs guys who had taken Hong's badge. He immediately disliked them.

"We got enough of it," the taller of the two said. They squeezed past Hong, Conroy, and Wei. "Henry Dang, you're under arrest." He approached Dang, who seemed to be stunned into silence. Conroy couldn't have imagined how satisfying hearing the click of metal on metal was as the handcuffs locked into place.

As the man led Dang out of the office, Wei caught Dang's arm, holding it until Dang finally met his gaze.

"I just want to savor this look on your face right now. You're going to have a long time to think about every little mistake you made leading to this point. I hope it was worth it. I'm sure there's a lot of people in prison who are looking forward to the chance to have a close conversation with you."

"You're trash and you always will be," Dang managed to choke out before being dragged from the office. There were actual cheers and applause from the officers in the bullpen.

The second Internal Affairs inspector reached inside his suit pocket and pulled out a badge, which he handed to Hong. "I think this is yours." He didn't wait for a response from Allen before he followed his partner out the door.

Wei and Conroy shared a look, and Wei nodded.

"Let's go log this phone into evidence or whatever," Wei said to Cheung, guiding him away from Dang's office with a hand on his shoulder.

Hong stood there, looking down at the badge in his hand.

"Looks like your name is cleared," Conroy said, uncertainly. There was a lot he wanted to say, but he wasn't sure where to begin. "You're back on the force."

Hong made a noise deep in his chest that Conroy couldn't interpret before walking to Dang's desk and placing the badge on it.

Conroy blinked, unsure what it was he was seeing. "What are you doing?"

"One important thing I've learned through this mess is that the police precinct is no longer where I can do the most good."

"I don't believe that," Conroy said, stepping up next to him and picking up the badge. "Look what you did. You took down one of the most corrupt figures in the police department. A lot of lives are going to be saved and a lot of criminals are going to be punished because you fought to get Dang out of here."

"But I didn't do that as a police officer," Hong said. "I did that with the help of you and Wei and the Dragons. Besides..." He went quiet.

"Besides what?" Conroy prompted.

"Besides, I've been thinking about the choices I've made in my life, and—"

"Listen, I know we've got a lot we need to talk about, like where exactly it is we're going from here, but there is one thing I know. I never want to make you feel like you have to choose between having me in your life and something else. I went a long time without having you in my life, and I tried to convince myself I was fine with that, but this time that we've spent together made me realize I never got over my feelings for you, just buried them under a whole lot of misplaced anger."

"I don't know about misplaced," Hong said sheepishly, daring to meet Conroy's eyes. "I hurt you, and I know it. I never should have just walked away from you like that. It was stupid, and it's the biggest regret in my life. I don't know if I can ever make it up to you."

Conroy shrugged. "I'm sure we'll come to some kind of agreement. What do you say we talk about it over dinner?"

Hong's smile sparked a warmth in Conroy's chest, and he held the badge out to Hong.

"I think this is yours."

Hong hesitated briefly before he reached out and took it, attaching it to his belt. "That's better. Now let's get out of here; this place smells like Dang."

Epilogue

THE DOOR TO the intake shower opened, voices from the hallway outside echoing around the tiled room. There were ten slightly partitioned showers, nothing more than a few inches of ceramic wall to divide the spaces. The floor sloped down, leading to a central drain in the middle.

One of the guards came in first, followed by the prisoner, Johnny Hwang. The second guard remained at the door.

"Hurry up," the guard who came into the shower with Hwang said. "I could get in serious trouble for this. Just take your shower fast. You got five minutes, tops." With that, the guard stepped out, like he was eager not to be in there.

Hwang went to the nearest shower, in no hurry despite the guard's urgings. He sure as fuck wasn't about to shower with the other *puk gai* in this place. He may have fallen some, he had to admit, but he hadn't sunk that low.

He removed the prison jumpsuit he'd been given, making sure to place it out of the way so it wouldn't get wet. Naked, he turned the water on, running it until the place was steaming. He'd always enjoyed a hot shower, and he wasn't about to let the minor setback of being here take that from him.

He didn't hear the figure approaching him, didn't know they were there until he turned around to find a man standing barely a foot away.

"Woah—who the fuck are you?"

The man wore a prison jumpsuit like Hwang's, but it looked different, discolored, older. His age was hard to determine, but he'd guess somewhere near forty. He wore glasses with a metal frame, the sort that inmates weren't typically allowed. Something in his features struck Hwang as different, maybe Japanese or Korean. The man simply stood there, surveying Hwang silently.

"Listen, *puk gai*, you need to step the fuck off me."

The man shifted his weight, and Hwang noticed too late the small blade of the penknife in his hand. Before Hwang could even move to defend himself, his assailant closed the small distance between them, driving the blade into his stomach. The action was expertly aimed, puncturing Hwang's kidney.

The man pulled it out before stabbing him again, repeating the movements like a conducting an orchestra. Hwang lost count after the tenth stab.

Finally, it was over and the man laid Hwang down almost gently on the shower.

As his vision grew dark, all he could see was the tile floor, the water rushing past his body to the drain—colored red with his blood, and his assailant's feet.

Hwang's breathing grew ragged as the blood loss pushed him further toward the edge of unconsciousness. Before the darkness claimed him, he heard his assailant speak. He didn't understand the words being spoken, but he recognized the language as Korean.

Hwang struggled to make sense of the words, though it seemed clear they weren't aimed at him. There was a pause before they resumed, but no audible answer.

There was another, longer moment of silence where Hwang closed his eyes, praying for the end to take him so he could be free of the burning pain that stabbed at him as surely as the penknife had.

A shadow fell over him, and Hwang forced his eyes open to find his assailant crouched over him, looking dispassionately into his face. Hwang knew with a fierce certainty that the man was there to watch him die. He knew that as surely as he knew that very soon, they would both get their wishes.

Dramatis Personae

This is a glossary of the characters that you will find reappearing throughout the world of *Hong Kong Nights*. *denotes viewpoint character for this novel.

The Dragons

Wei Tseng—30 years old, the leader of the Dragons.
Conroy Wong—28 years old, second in command of the Dragons.*
Tony Lau—53 years old, friend and advisor to Wei.
Chris Ma—29 years old.
Jesse Zhang—27 years old.
Kevin Shen—22 years old.
Smile Kang—33 years old.
Steel—24 years old, real name Jian, Winston's boyfriend.
Walker Teng—29 years old.
Winston Chang—20 years old, brother of Shelby Chang, son of Constance Chang, Steel's boyfriend.
Mimi—31 years old, a racer in the Dark Streets who befriended Winston, newest Dragon.

The Cops

Allen Hong—32 years old, an inspector, brother of Constance Chang, former friend of Wei.*
Ao Cheung—34 years old, an inspector, partner of Allen Hong.
Henry Dang—47 years old, Superintendent of the Eastern District, corrupt.
Inspector Leung—34 years old, one of Dang's.
Yu Chen—44 years old, prosecutor.

The Twisted Vipers

Johnny Hwang—38 years old, leader of the Twisted Vipers.
Jiang—30 years old, Hwang's second in command.
Leo Tong—rogue redpole, moved on Dragon territory (deceased).
Ting—a redpole of low standing.
Big Po—a redpole of low standing.
Jake Tam—a redpole of low standing.
Lazarus—a redpole of low standing.

Others

Constance Chang—41 years old, sister of Allen Hong, mother of Winston and Shelby Chang, owner of Coffee by Constance.
Shelby Chang—17 years old, sister of Winston Chang, daughter of Constance Chang.
Noah Potter—27 years old, American, lover of Wei.
Songmin Choi—26 years old, friend half Korean, half Hong Konger, friend of Noah Potter.
Trang Nguyen—26 years old, Vietnamese, employee at the karaoke bar Indulgence.

Glossary of Cantonese Words and Phrases

This is a list of the Cantonese phrases used throughout the book. It is by no means comprehensive, nor do I include tonal markings for ease of reading in the book itself. There are a lot of online resources for studying Cantonese if you are interested.

Da fei gei—Jerk off (literally translates as shooting airplanes)
Daih dai—Little brother
Dim Sum—Dim sum
Diu—Fuck (exclamation)
Diu lei—Fuck you!
Diu lei lo mo chau hai—Fuck your mother's stinky vagina*
Dzu pa—Ugly girl (literally translates as porkchop)
Fai di laa—Hurry up!
Fo Wo—Hot Pot
Ga tsan—Asshole
Gau—Dog
Gong dzau tin ha mou dik, dzou dzau mou lan wai lik—All talk, no action.
Gwei—White, foreign. (literally means ghost)
Gweilo—White guy, foreigner
Gwei mui—White girl
Ham sap lou—Horny bastard
Hanzi—Chinese characters
Hou sei la lei—Drop dead, go to hell
Jai—Son
Jin jang—Low-life (pariah)
Joutau—Good night
Lan—Dick (body part)
Mah ma—Mom
Mei gwok—America
Mh goi—Thank you (for a service)
Ong lan gau—Dumb fuck

puk gai—asshole, bastard
Sau seng—Shut up
Sei—Damn (adjective)
sei bat po—Damn bitch
Sei gei lou—Fag (derogatory, obviously)
sei yan tau—Jerk
Shaojiu—Chinese sorghum-based alcohol
Sik si la lei—Go to hell
Siu ze—Lady, a polite address for a woman you don't know
Yan you—Slug
Yau mo gau lan chou—You fucking kidding me?
Zhou—Clumsy

*This is pretty much the worst insult you could possibly say to someone; it *will* get you attacked if you use it with a Cantonese-speaking person or on the streets of Hong Kong; this isn't even something you could say to your friends, jokingly.

About the Author

J. C. Long is an American expat living in Japan, though he's also lived stints in Seoul, South Korea—no, he's not an army brat; he's an English teacher. He is also quite passionate about Welsh corgis and is convinced that anyone who does not like them is evil incarnate. His dramatic streak comes from his lifelong involvement in theatre. After living in several countries aside from the United States, J. C. is convinced that love is love, no matter where you are, and he is determined to write stories that demonstrate exactly that. J. C. Long's favorite things in the world are pictures of corgis, writing, and Korean food (not in that order…okay, in that order). J. C. spends his time when not writing by thinking about writing, coming up with new characters, attending Big Bang concerts, and wishing he was writing. The best way to get him to write faster is to motivate him with corgi pictures. Yes, that is a veiled hint.

Email: jclongauthor@gmail.com

Facebook: www.facebook.com/authorjclong

Twitter: www.twitter.com/j_c_long_author

Website: www.jclongauthor.wixsite.com/home

Other books by this author

On Andross Station (coming in 2018)

Unzipped Shorts
New Year's Eve Unzipped
Unzipping 7D

Hong Kong Nights Series
A Matter of Duty
A Matter of Courage

Gabe Maxfield Mysteries
Mai Tais and Murder
Hula Dancers and Hauntings
Palm Trees and Paparazzi (coming in 2018)

Also Available from NineStar Press

Connect with NineStar Press

www.ninestarpress.com

www.facebook.com/ninestarpress

www.facebook.com/groups/NineStarNiche

www.twitter.com/ninestarpress

www.tumblr.com/blog/ninestarpress

9 781948 608152